THE CURSE OF
BURR OAK FARM

THE CURSE OF BURR OAK FARM

WILLIAM MITCHELL ROSS

To order additional copies of this book, contact:
Xlibris
844-714-8691
www.Xlibris.com
Orders@Xlibris.com
827198

Books by William Mitchell Ross
in "Monroe Mystery Series"

Deceived by Self
All Passion Denied
Love's Obsession
Echoes Screaming in the Night
A Greedy Vengeance
Murder for Malice
Who killed Fritz Zuber?
Swirling Shadows of Guilt
The Curse of Burr Oak Farm

ACKNOWLEDGMENTS

My special thanks to professional photographer Marissa Weiher, Madison, Wisconsin, for the cover photo; Lucien Knuteson Photography, Seattle, Washington, for the author photo; my wife Marilyn, whose continuing support, patience and understanding that I have imaginary friends is very much appreciated; and the Monroe readers who take great pleasure and amusement in trying to identify my fictional characters who, I insist, have never been issued birth certificates.

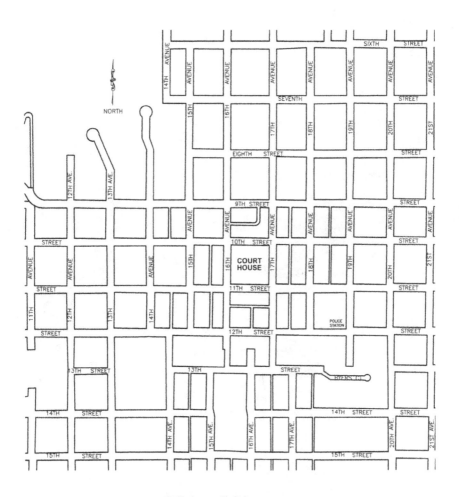

City of Monroe

DOWNTOWN AREA

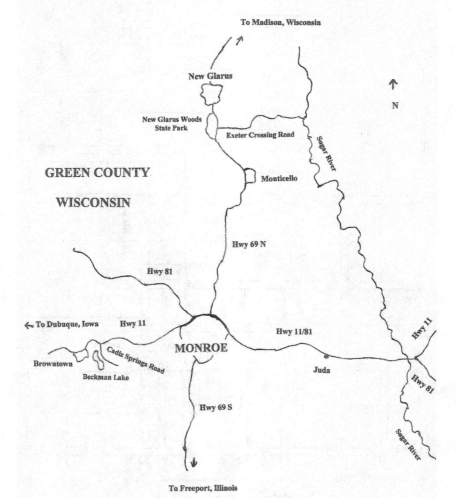

In May 1802, Sean McNutt was born in County Cork, along the rugged southwest coastline of Ireland. He was the youngest of nine children born to Conor and Amelia McNutt. The family was poor and rented a small farm to scrape out a meager day-to-day living. The owner of his parents' farm was an absentee landlord living in the United Kingdom. Sean's elder brothers helped on the farm and were agricultural laborers, finding work anywhere they could, at poverty wages, to help support the family. Being a good Catholic family, religion played a big part in their lives and helped them survive in miserable economic times. Their meals consisted mostly of bacon and cabbage with potatoes, groats, black pudding, Irish soda bread, and Irish stew, when meat was available.

Sean's widowed grandfather, Jack McNutt, lived with the family. He was a crippled, worn-down old man who barely managed to get by each day with chronic pain after many years of backbreaking physical labor. His one talent, his passion in life, was music. He had a gift for playing the fiddle and the tin whistle. Sean would spend hours watching his grandfather perform in front of the fireplace as burning peat kept them warm during damp cold winters. He had his grandfather's gift for music, and Jack taught his young prodigy how to play. At an early age, Sean showed remarkable skill at imitating bird songs with his tin whistle. He had a natural ear for music. Sean learned to play his grandfather's fiddle, but his true love was the whistle. He memorized popular Celtic tunes as "Come Back, Paddy Reilly," "When He Who Adores Thee,"

"She Is Far From the Land," and "Forget Not the Field." He kept his family and friends entertained, following in the grandfather's footsteps. He even resembled his grandfather in appearance with oval-shaped blue eyes, thick eyebrows, a slim straight nose, and a square jawline. He was short, stout, and strong with a bewitching smile.

When Sean turned sixteen, he left his family farm and traveled to the cathedral city of Exeter in Devon, England, to work in the copper mines. His mother cried salty tears and tightly hugged her youngest child as he left the nest to start his own life experiences. A cousin, a year older than Sean, had written to him about job opportunities in the mines that offered livable wages. The work was hard, but the pay was good. In the Fox and Hound pub at night, he earned extra money playing the fiddle and his tin whistle for the patrons. Like a dutiful son, he sent one half of his wages home to his family and saved the rest. On his twenty-seventh birthday, a mate showed him a flyer from the United States. Lead had been discovered in the Wisconsin Territories, and experienced miners were needed. Jobs were readily available to anyone with mining experience. What got his attention was that the brochure listed the settlement of Exeter, located along the Sugar River. The name of the settlement immediately resonated with him. Was the name a coincidence or fate? The idea of going to America fired his imagination with a sense of awe and adventure. He immediately wrote to his parents and told them of his plan. They readily agreed and wished him well in a new land across the ocean. Sean had saved enough money to book his passage, so he left Liverpool and sailed for New York. From there, he took a train to Chicago and left—on foot—for the Diggings, arriving in Exeter in late July 1829.

The settlement was crude with log huts and the rough living. The territory was wild and unsettled, except for the miners and the Native Americans. The work was familiar, and he soon fit in well with other European immigrants mining the lead ore. One of the characters he met was a man called Devil John from Kentucky. He was a hard-working, hard-drinking miner. He hated Easterners and called them "damn Yankees" after a snoot full of whiskey. The amazing thing about him was that he could drink all night and do stupid things until he passed out drunk, and then he'd be up bright and early the next morning for work like nothing had happened. Sean had never seen anything like this before.

A smelting blast furnace processed the lead ore into bars, which were loaded onto pack mules and oxen heading East. The Native American Indians from the Winnebago Tribe assisted in the mining. Sean found these peaceful people fascinating. He quickly picked up their language and made friends with them, often acting as an interpreter. They enjoyed listening to his tin whistle playing at night after a long day's work.

Then tragedy struck. One of the support timbers for the mine gave way, trapping Sean beneath it. His leg was fractured in two places. The doctor was able to set his leg, but the wound got infected and became toxic to his body. Subsequently, Sean's high fever and dehydration were life-threatening. He was destined for a slow painful death according to the local doctor. Nothing else could be done for him. One of the Indians asked permission to take Sean to his small village to try to save his life. Sean agreed, having no other choice. One of the elders, a medicine man, took Sean under his care, using only herbal plants and mineral remedies to save his life. The next week went by in a blur for Sean, going in and out of consciousness. He was given a bitter-tasting potion daily to drink, which made him sweat profusely. On the eighth day, his fever broke, and he was nursed back to health by an Indian squaw. The whole mining community was awestruck. The idea that savages could save a man's life, bringing him back from the brink of death, was incomprehensible to them. It had to be a fluke or a miracle.

The damage to Sean's leg was more severe than first anticipated. It didn't heal properly, causing a noticeable limp. Sean's life as a miner was over. However, he was readily accepted into the tribal village and became one of them, learning the Indian way of life. The village was located about a half mile from the Sugar River Diggings. At the village, a natural surface spring provided pure drinking water for the Indians before meandering its way to the Sugar River. A stand of trees—oak, burr oak, hackberry, maple, and cherry—surrounded the village, as well as prairie grasses. Sean was taught how to hunt, fish, and grow crops in a peaceful society centered on hard work and getting along.

With a culture that had been in existence for ten thousand years, the Indians couldn't understand the white man's ways, which included greed and killing one another. Sean discovered a deep level of respect and contentment as he become more and more immersed in a culture of disciplined behavior, outlook, values, morals, and goals. The sounds of cool nights with soft breezes and rustling tree branches, crickets, and bull frogs lulled him into many a peaceful night's sleep under full moons and the lunar shadows blanketing the earth.

In April 1830, word circulated around the Sugar River Diggings that the U.S. Congress had passed the Indian Removal Act, signed by Pres. Andrew Jackson, that designated the land west of the Mississippi River as Indian Territory and ordered the U.S. Army to forcibly relocate all the Indians from their ancestral homelands and vacate the land east of the Mississippi. The removable was a systematic genocide that was opposed by the Native American Indians. Through military might and brute force, the Indians east of the Mississippi River were rounded up, killed, or frog-marched west. A platoon of soldiers from Fort Crawford, a U.S. Army outpost located in Prairie du Chien, was dispatched to remove the Indians from the Sugar River Diggings area. The remote fort was built with logs and encircled by spiked pickets buried 3 feet deep in the ground for protection against Indian attacks. The fort housed approximately sixty military personnel. The gaggle of soldiers on horseback that arrived at the Diggings was led by a Lt. Joseph Brisbois. He was a young, surly, short man with an arrogant attitude and no conscience. His commissioned appointment to Fort Crawford was through family connections in Washington DC.

When the soldiers arrived at the Sugar River Diggings, they were told of a small Indian village and Sean McNutt. They rode the short distance to the village and demanded to see McNutt. Sean presented himself dressed in Indian attire. A group of twelve villagers stood behind him as he addressed the lieutenant, who remained seated on his horse. He laughed when he saw McNutt. There were two older men, four women, and six children looking on at the proceedings.

"You must be McNutt?" Brisbois barked.

"Who wants to know?"

The soldiers giggled from their fidgeting horses at McNutt's response.

"I am Army Lieutenant Brisbois," he flatly stated in a monotone, condescending voice. "My orders from the U.S. government are to remove all Indians from this land and relocate them west of the Mississippi River."

"On whose authority?" McNutt asked, challenging him.

The lieutenant's face reddened. "Like I said, the U.S. government. This is no longer Indian land. It will soon become government land."

"You can't do that," McNutt replied. His face flushed beet red. "You can't force these people from their land like some tyrannical despot. They have every right to be here, as you do. Obviously, the U.S. government doesn't respect or value indigenous sovereignty."

Brisbois laughed. "Savages with rights? Who are you kidding? These weak, ignorant, uncivilized people? The white settlers are terrified of these savages, and they must be removed."

"Those same white settlers who get drunk, steal from one other, and kill each other while blaming the Indians?"

"So what of it? This land needs to be settled to relieve the growing pressure of immigrants on the East Coast. My orders are to make that happen. Who gives a shit about the Indians anyway?"

"I do!" McNutt exploded in a loud voice.

Brisbois was taken aback by the outburst. "Look, McNutt, if you don't let me do my job, I will have to kill you and these savages. No one cares about you or them."

A moment of silence passed as McNutt glared up at Brisbois who was pompously sitting on his horse. The look in the lieutenant's eye, the tilt of his head, his smug expression, and his hand resting on his gun told the whole story. Sean could tell a lot about the man delivering the horrific message of death. It was the devil himself.

"I think we both know the outcome here today," McNutt said in a loud clear voice.

Brisbois straightened up in his saddle, staring down at McNutt with contempt.

McNutt waved his right arm, pointing at the Indians behind him. "These innocents—tired old men, women, and children—are going about their daily lives when, suddenly, you come into our village with all your sanctimonious bullshit to murder them in the name of God and country. These are honorable people who look upon death as a victory going on a journey to a land that you will never see. Your detestable behavior today will rush them into the secret house of death and rock them to sleep. They will go on this journey with a clear conscience. When you bury my bones in this hallowed ground with these noble people, remember that this will be my greatest gift to humankind. I pity you, knowing that the disease eating away at your soul is self-inflicted and beyond remorse. Go ahead and kill us, and let the devil's work be done!"

Brisbois drew his pistol from his holster, angrily pointed it a McNutt with a screeching, loud, harsh, piercing cry, screaming, "You bastard!" He fired twice into McNutt's chest, felling him to the cold, damp earth. He instantly died.

The children started screaming and tried to run away. The troops opened fire and mowed them down like fish in a barrel, as well as the men and women. The carnage was complete in less than a minute. They were all slaughtered without mercy. Brisbois ordered his men to dig shallow graves, 30 inches deep, and bury the bodies. He mocked the dead by saying that the worms were about to have a feast buffet on their flesh. After the burials were completed, he rode back to the Diggings with his men and told the miners gathered there that the Indians attacked them, and they had to defend themselves. He said it didn't matter, though, because what happened here today will quickly get lost and disappear into the mist of history. The miners stared at him in disbelief at his lies. Brisbois informed them that his official report would justify his actions. For weeks, the miners were haunted by the screams of the little children being murdered. The agony of bullets smashing into their little bodies was horrifying. The miners ventured out to the fresh gravesites and hung their heads. In the early morning or at dusk, some of them reported seeing ghostlike figures floating across the sacred ground. At night they swore that they could hear a tin whistle playing in the dark. The massacre at the Sugar River Diggings became folklore legend that was passed down from generation to generation. One miner predicted that the ghostly figures of the dead will continue to walk the land for all eternity.

After the Black Hawk War ended in 1832, government surveyors descended on the Wisconsin Territory to survey the forced abandonment of Indian land for government purposes and sell it to the pioneer settlers for $1.25 per acre. It was now known as government land. It took two years for the surveys to be completed. Boundaries of a newly-formed county were established in 1837. William Boyls, the newly-elected territorial representative to the Wisconsin Territorial Legislature from Cadiz Springs, was given the task of naming the new county. A number of folks suggested the name Green County, given the lush green foliage found there. Boyls wasn't so sure. He thought the county needed a more proper, distinguished name, along the lines of Madison, Monroe, or Lafayette— names with a historical significance. He thought that Greene County, named after a Revolutionary War hero, Maj. Gen. Nathanael Greene, would be better. The early documents of Greene County reflect his decision, but later the "e" was dropped to the more familiar Green County. The village of Exeter was located in the northeast quadrant of the county, 13 miles from Monroe, the county seat.

In 1839, Thomas Somers, age thirty-five, from Ohio, came to Green County looking for land to purchase and begin farming. The lead mining enterprises in the territory were slowly dying out, and the land was being cleared for wheat farming, given that food shortages on the East Coast were driving up prices. The lead miners who didn't move on after gold was discovered in California in 1848 became farmers. Somers was a man of some wealth and bought 160 acres of land close to Exeter. It was, in fact, the same land where the Sugar River massacre had taken place. The locals told him about the site being haunted, but he dismissed it as silly superstition. The land had everything he was looking for: a natural spring for good pure drinking water, a stand of trees to build a home, a barn and outbuildings, and the rich prairie soil needed to grow wheat and oats. He left his wife and four children in Ohio and spent the next two years clearing the land and building his future home. He hired the help he needed and brought his family to their new home in 1841.

Mrs. Somers was especially taken with the beauty of a burr oak tree standing 100 feet tall on the edge of the grove on the east side of the new house in an oak savanna. The savanna was surrounded by rolling hills of prairie grass reminiscent of thousands of years of nature's beauty and wonderment. The tree had an ancient texture of gray gnarly bark with branches that looked like arthritic boney fingers; 5-8-inch-long lobed leaves hung from a canopy of leaves like Christmas tree ornaments. The tree reminded her of her homestead in Ohio. As she gazed up at the tree, a flood of childhood memories overwhelmed her. The bark was dark gray with distinctive vertical ridges. The distinctive leaves were a comforting familiar sight. In the spring, greenish-yellow flowers measuring 1-2 inches in length appeared with a large acorn cap wrapped around the nut. Wild animals like bears, deer, and porcupines fed off the leaves, twigs, and bark. She had her husband attach a rope swing to a lower branch for the children to enjoy. She named her new home Burr Oak Farm. All went well for the young family. They planted and harvested three cuttings of wheat per year, bringing in a tidy income. A big vegetable garden and livestock kept them well fed during the cold winters. As their children grew older, they were a big help on the farm, requiring less paid labor. Life was good.

The cholera outbreak of 1848 killed 10 percent of the residents in Green County, including the four children of Thomas Somers. The children were buried in a pioneer cemetery behind the house. The heartbreaking distress and sadness of the loss of their children was devastating to the couple. They barely managed to hold on to their sanity. Thomas had a brother in Columbus, Ohio, Steven Somers, who suggested that he send one of his eight children, Louisa, to help Mrs. Somers. Louisa protested the move but wasn't given a choice. She was a clever, self-taught girl studying medicine in the hopes of one day becoming a nurse. She was sixteen and exceptionally beautiful. Disease, illness, and death were dark clouds hanging over the pioneer settlers in the early days. Funerals were commonplace and well attended by the community. Within a year after Louisa's arrival, both Thomas and his wife became unwell. The local doctor was flummoxed as to a cause. Did it somehow have to do with the cholera epidemic? He prescribed neutralizing powders, but they didn't help. The couple was slowly going downhill and didn't respond to his treatment. In January 1850, they both died. The village was in shock. Louisa was eighteen years old and was suddenly cast into the role of managing a farm that she inherited. All the neighbors pitched in to help her. What she needed was a husband. But who? She had many suitors whom she rejected. One young man named Robert White, from Monroe, courted her. The fact that he was ten years older than Louisa didn't seem to be an issue for the couple. He was financially well-off, inheriting family money, and seemed the perfect solution to her problem. They were married in the spring. The following winter was brutally cold, fierce, and bitter, and he caught pneumonia. He died on New Year's Day. The doctor who attended to him wasn't sure of the exact cause of death but signed the death certificate stating pneumonia as the cause.

After his death, the townspeople spun out theories of superstition and the supernatural and started to ruminate on the history of the farm—the Sugar River massacre, the deaths of the four children, the deaths of their parents, and now the death of Robert White. Was the farm cursed? Was Louisa safe living there? Louisa ignored their concerns. She said that she had never seen a ghost or heard a tin whistle playing at night. She reasoned that death was just a part of pioneer life and she had to accept it for what it was. The following year, 1851, she married a farmer from New Glarus, John Wescott, whose former wife had died in childbirth. Like her first husband, he was older than her and had no children. He sold his farm after his marriage to Louisa and moved to Burr Oak Farm. He was a good manager, and the farm prospered. They talked about starting a family. In the summer of 1853, Wescott became ill. A non-life-threatening virus had been going around the county, but he didn't get any better, so he went to see a doctor in Monroe. Dr. Adams couldn't diagnose his condition with any certainty. He prescribed some remedies and told Wescott that whatever he had would pass and he would get better. Two weeks later, Dr. Adams was called to the farm. Wescott was dying. Louisa left him and the doctor alone in his bedroom on his death bed. She was sobbing and said she couldn't bear it. After she left the room, Wescott whispered to Dr. Adams that he was convinced that his wife had poisoned him. The doctor was shocked. Could this be true? She seemed to be such a kind and caring creature. After Wescott died, Dr. Adams couldn't shake the bedside accusation of murder from his mind. Just to be certain, he contacted a doctor friend in Madison who agreed to an autopsy. Wescott's body was sent to Madison, where the cause of death was confirmed as arsenic poisoning. The county sheriff went to the farm. He found Mrs. Louisa Wescott dead in the barn, hanging from a rope attached to a support beam—an apparent suicide.

The news quickly spread throughout Green County and the surrounding area that Louisa was a murderess. Folks from all over came to drive past the farm and the enormous burr oak tree to see it for themselves. Speculation ran wild. Were evil spirits haunting the farm, entered the soul of Louisa, took over her mind, and turned her into a killer? The sightings of ghostlike figures from the pioneer cemetery near the house and barn were greatly exaggerated. Local kids would dare one another to go to the house at night and look in the windows. One of them reported seeing a ghost of a woman in a white dress, swinging back and forth on the children's swing from the burr oak tree near the house. The horrific deaths at the farm site caused a heightened degree of anxiety and stress for the village residents in Exeter. They all agreed on one thing: The land was cursed. And that was that.

The ownership of the farm and land deed reverted to Steven Somers, the brother of the late Thomas Somers, who was still living and farming in Ohio. After all the tragedies at the farm, no one was interested in living there. Steven rented out the land. The house and the outbuildings fell into a state of disrepair and abandonment and deteriorated. Locals would occasionally pass by the house, looking for ghosts and the sound of a tin whistle, keeping the myth alive. Some said they saw ghosts; others were skeptical. But the legend of the cursed farm continued to live in the minds, imagination, beliefs, and absolute certainty of the local people. Over the succeeding decades, the village essentially disappeared with only a few remaining buildings and a post office, becoming a rural residential area. However, the macabre legend of the Burr Oak Farm remained a constant theme over time, attracting many curious visitors to the farm site. The farm was located on Exeter Crossing Road, a couple of miles east of State Highway 69, before the turnoff for the New Glarus Woods State Park to the west.

In 1947, 108 years after Thomas Somers bought the land, the farm went up for sale. The descendants of Steven Somers decided to sell what remained of the farm and the land. The curse surrounding the property continued. The local dark humor maintained that anyone who would live at the farm would meet his maker with an early mysterious death. That fear kept many buyers away. But a WWII veteran, Fred Bennett, from Monroe, borrowed money from his parents to buy the 160 acres, including the old broken-down, rodent-infested relic of a house. The house faced north, off Exeter Crossing Road. Not interested in farming, Bennett rented out the land and razed the house. In its stead, he built a new two-story white house with a pillared front porch. He delighted his neighbors with tall tales of seeing ghosts at dusk and listening to the tunes of a tin whistle putting him to sleep at night. But there was a much darker side to Bennett.

Bennett married his high school sweetheart in November 1942 while home on leave from the army, before going to Europe to fight against the Nazis in Italy. They were both nineteen years old and were married in the First Christian Church of Monroe. They planned for a honeymoon getaway after the war was over. When Bennett returned from the fighting, he was a changed man, no longer the affable young man whom people knew and loved. He never spoke of his war experiences, but his behavior exhibited all the typical characteristics of shell shock. He frequented local bars and drank himself into a stupor. His wife was worried and fearful for him and herself when he acted out. During one of his drunken episodes, he attacked his wife and broke her arm. Bennett couldn't hold down a full-time job, so his wife worked at the First National Bank in Monroe as a teller to make ends meet. They got by financially using farmland rental income, her job at the bank, and the occasional work that Bennett found during his better days. Being a veteran, local people hired him for odd jobs, blaming his horrific war experiences for his erratic behavior. He ignored his parents' pleas to stop drinking and didn't make a single payment against the loan from them. Whatever was going on inside his head, it didn't square with reality. Some people speculated that the disease he suffered from was eating away at his strength, his will, and his very soul.

As the years slowly passed, his behavior became more bizarre. He became fixated on the myth surrounding the farm. All his talk of ghosts and tin whistles morphed into an elaborate Halloween hoax. A week before Halloween, he would stage his front porch with the scariest, spookiest Halloween décor he could think of: life-size ghosts and ghouls, black cats and scary witches, skeletons that swayed in the breeze, and a figure of a woman stuffed with straw hanging from a rope from the burr oak tree as a reminder of the macabre past. To make all this spooky presentation even more scary, Bennett rigged up eerie orange lights that lit up his display at night. People came from miles away to slowly drive past his creation. Sometimes he would dress up as a ghoul and leap from the front porch and race toward a car full of kids. Their screams sent him into spasms of laughter. At midnight, he would turn off the orange lights and retire for the night, satisfied that he had terrified the countryside. While all this was going on, his wife sometimes stayed with her mother in Monroe. To keep the myth alive, he rigged up a dusk-to-dawn light in the pioneer cemetery on the hill behind the house. The faint orange light could be seen from the road to entertain the curious onlookers. Bennet called it a ghost light to scare people. He told anyone who asked about the light that death would find you if you visited the graveyard at night.

On Halloween night in 1952, a Friday night, the macabre display went on as usual. By now, the stream of cars driving past the farm was so great that it required the presence of the sheriff's department to keep the traffic moving. At midnight, the orange lights didn't switch off. Making his midnight rounds, a deputy sheriff on patrol turned up the driveway at 2:00 a.m. to investigate. He entered the house and found the murdered bloody body of Bennett's wife in the kitchen. She had been bludgeoned to death, nearly decapitated, by an axe lying next the body. No sign of Bennett. The deputy raced outside and vomited on the lawn. He immediately radioed in the incident and waited for backup. When the other officers arrived, they searched the grounds, looking for Bennett, fearing the worst. One of the officers shined his flashlight on the hanging figure dangling from the burr oak tree. He instantly froze and was paralyzed in horror. The other officers quickly joined him. The final investigative report concluded that Bennett had murdered his wife and then hanged himself in plain view for all the hundreds of visitors that passed the farm that night to see, not realizing that they were viewing a real corpse.

The response to the murder was immediate, and the hysteria reached a fever pitch. All the drama surrounding the creepy, terrifying, and haunted farm was again on full display. Some locals were so scared that they wanted to burn the place down. Others saw the devil's work and wanted to bring in a priest to perform an exorcism on the farm to drive the evil spirits away. After six months, the emotional fever broke, and people got back to their normal routine lives. After the funeral of his son, Mr. Bennett lamented that there was no logic, no reason, no explanation for the prolonged nightmare that his son endured. A nightmare in which fear and isolation walked hand in hand through the shadows of his troubled mind that couldn't be explained, only observed. The great promise of a son with high expectations sadly ended on a low-hanging branch of a burr oak tree. Mr. Bennett burned the fiendish rope.

Nine months after the funeral, Mr. Bennett put the farmhouse up for sale. A man from Madison bought it and rented it out to a retired couple who guffawed at all the superstitious nonsense. Yes, bad things had happened there, but they were all explainable. They found it somewhat amusing watching cars that drove slowly past the house. They lived there in peace until 1964, when they went to the Parkview Nursing Home in Monroe. The 5-acre homestead was once again put on the market for sale.

Mr. and Mrs. Paul Leonard from Monroe bought it. Leonard owned and operated a pharmacy located on the north side of the historic square. In spite of its history, they fell in love with the pure beauty and charm of the homestead and bought it at a reduced price. Some of the local folks told them the macabre tall tales about the place, but they never saw or heard any evidence of hauntings of any kind and lived there in peace and harmony. They enjoyed the homestead for six years until the sudden untimely death of Mrs. Leonard in 1970, who died in a terrible car accident. Paul Leonard was devastated by her loss. Two years later, he married a younger woman out of loneliness and a broken heart. His new wife resembled his deceased wife in her physical appearance: her slight build, her pale blue eyes, her smile, and the way she wore her hair. His new wife, Stacy, a music teacher at Monroe High School, moved into the house after a short honeymoon to the Wisconsin Dells.

CHAPTER 1

heryl Kubly-Schultz, the choir director at the First Christian Church in Monroe, was getting ready to drive to New Glarus to have coffee with the choral director of the Swiss United Church of Christ at her home for a scheduled meeting at 10:30 a.m. Cheryl was twenty-nine years old, married, medium height, slim, had shoulder-length blond hair and blue eyes. She wore black rimmed glasses. It was Saturday, May 18, 1974. The ticking antique clock on her fireplace mantel rang out eight times. She had plenty of time before she left for her meeting in New Glarus, so she poured herself a second cup of coffee and sat down at the light green Formica table in her kitchen. The short drive north from Monroe, along State Highway 69 to New Glarus, would take about twenty minutes. Looking out her partially-opened kitchen window, the morning sun was shining brilliantly against a clear blue sky. She could hear the bird songs through the open window. The temperature outside was currently sixty-eight degrees Fahrenheit according to the outside thermometer. A high of seventy-five was forecasted for the day. *A perfect spring day*, she thought. Cheryl and her friend in New Glarus had talked on the telephone several times about an early summer concert to be sung in Swiss German with the combined two choirs. They needed to set a date in early June and to agree on the music. The two concerts—one in Monroe, the other in New Glarus—would be the spring finale for both choirs until the fall. Cheryl had picked out a few pieces of music that a Swiss member of the choir had given to her. The songs included "Guggisberlied,"

"Warum syt Dir so Truuvig," "Louenesee," and "Landler." Some of the choir members were in the Monroe Swiss Singers, so learning the music would prove less challenging for them.

"The Songbird of Monroe" was what Cheryl Kubly was called during her high school years. She was a special talent with an exceptional singing voice spanning four octaves. Her voice made her the darling of Monroe. She sung in many venues, including high school musicals, churches, weddings, and funerals. Occasionally, she teamed up with other singers for special occasions. She majored in music and accounting at the University of Wisconsin in Madison. After graduating college, she left Monroe for New York to audition for Broadway musicals. She shared the same Broadway dream that thousands of other talented performers had and flocked to New York from all over the United States. After arriving in New York, she answered an advertisement in the newspaper to share an apartment in Greenwich Village. It was a small two-bedroom walk up on the fourth floor of a building without an elevator. The apartment had a piano, which surprised her. She played it frequently to keep her piano skills sharp. It was a rent-controlled apartment, making it affordable for the tenants. She soon learned that sharing a small apartment was referred to as "living backstage." Her two roommates were also young aspiring women performers hoping to make their fortunes on Broadway. Cheryl slept on a couch in the living room. Her two new friends were a gold mine of information for the upstart singer. Cheryl quickly learned that she needed acting classes and choreography lessons, as well as a fantastic singing voice, to make the audition cuts.

To support herself, she got a job at a dinner club, waiting tables and singing popular songs with other staff to entertain the New York patrons for big tips. It was incredibly expensive to live in New York, but somehow she managed. She worked very hard to improve her chances for a part in a Broadway musical. As part of the audition casting calls, Cheryl had a headshot taken by one of her roommates who also helped her with a bio-resume. She went to audition after audition, hoping for a callback. The routine became very familiar and tedious. Not exactly the instant success she was looking for. She wore clothing that closely fitted the part she was auditioning for; used her newfound acting and choreography skills; gave the piano player a heads up with the music she was singing, usually thirty-two bars, and in what key. She also planned to improvise if the director asked her to perform a sketch in different way, which was a ploy used by a director to learn if she could take theatrical direction. The competition was extremely fierce, with only about twenty-five out of one thousand receiving callbacks. Nevertheless, she soldiered on, waiting for a break. It was hard to keep her spirits up with so much rejection, and sometimes she thought about chucking the whole dream and going back to Monroe.

Then suddenly, success! She received a callback and was cast in a minor role in an off-Broadway musical. She was ecstatic. Was the dream still alive after all? The rehearsals were brutal, but she enjoyed every minute of them. The kinship she felt with the other performers was more like family than actors in a musical play. They nailed it opening night. The musical performance couldn't have been any better. But the reality of filling seats night after night was disappointing. The cast sang and danced their hearts out, but the musical didn't catch fire with the print critics or the public. After six weeks, the musical closed. All the hard work and sore feet went down the drain. Cheryl took the closing very hard and went into a funk. Her dream seemed more and more like a nightmare. Her stage friends tried to comfort her and told her that she had talent and not to quit. But she had to face the fact that she wasn't going to be the next best thing to hit Broadway. She sadly packed her bags, left New York, and returned to Monroe. Her dream was shattered and lay in the smoldering ruins of a once-promising career. On the bus trip back, she cried and cried until she had no more tears to shed.

When Cheryl arrived in Monroe, she was warmly welcomed by the community, and she continued singing. She applied for and got a job at an accounting firm located in the 1200 block of 17th Street, preparing taxes and doing financial bookkeeping for local businesses. She enjoyed the job. At a Turner Hall dance, she met and dated a newly-minted lawyer from the University of Wisconsin, Brian Schultz. He was hired by the Newcomer, Pahnke, and Fouts law firm located on the east side of the historic square. It turned out that he was a distant relative of hers, sharing a second-great-grandmother. Their families and the locals had a good time teasing them. "A Kubly dating a distant cousin, well, I do declare! Whoever heard of such a thing?" It was all in good fun, and the happy couple didn't mind. Brian was two years older than Cheryl. They knew each other in high school but never dated, just good friends. Brian was as surprised and delighted that he and Cheryl connected romantically at the dance. They later called it the "magic of Turner Hall." The wedding reception was held in the grand ball room at Turner Hall, a fitting reminder where their love began. After the wedding, they bought a house in the 1700 block of 16th Street. Both their families generously helped with the down payment.

Cheryl sang in the choir at the First Christian Church, performing many solos. The choir director, who was sixty-five years old, developed health issues, retired, and moved to Florida. Pastor Carl Peterson asked Cheryl to take his place, and she readily agreed. She found the job challenging and rewarding. She felt she was blessed having so many talented people with good singing voices in the choir. The choir received high praise from the congregants after special performances and Sunday services.

Earlier that morning, Brian had left the house at four thirty to help milk cows on his family's dairy farm south of town. His father had the flu, and the hired man was in Stoughton, Wisconsin, attending a funeral. With Brian out of the house early, Cheryl had plenty of time to sort through reams of music, looking for ideas for the upcoming concert. In addition to the Swiss German songs she had already received, she was looking for something that was lively and upbeat to begin the special music performances for the summer. Sitting on a table next to her front door was a music folder that Stacy Leonard had forgotten to take with her after Wednesday night's choir practice. Stacy was an alto with a strong pure voice. She could read music and performed at a high level. Standing behind her on the choral risers was the tenor section. A man named Herbert Milz also had an excellent singing voice that complemented Stacy. The two of them would sing duets to the delight of the Sunday morning worshippers.

Being the choir director, Cheryl had the unique opportunity of getting to know the individual choir members on a personal, intimate basis while giving them special attention to help them improve their performances. She was also privy to some of their secrets that they sometimes shared and confided in her. At times she felt more like a licensed counselor than a choir director. Brian just shook his head when Cheryl told him some of the drama taking place in people's lives. He advised her not to get involved and stay neutral, for nothing good would come out of taking sides in marital disputes or other personal problems. Cheryl agreed with him, and she became a very good listener with a nonjudgmental ear; offering empathy, not advice. Two of the people who shared their troubled marriages with her were Stacy Leonard and Herbert Milz. There was an eight-year gap in their ages, but Cheryl closely observed them getting more familiar with each other as time went on. It all started after Herbert returned from his Florida vacation in March. The innocent touching and the knowing smiles started to alarm her. Their behavior at the Wednesday night rehearsals was taking too much of her attention away from the music. Did other choir members see what was right in front of them? If they did, no one mentioned it, at least not to her. Once again, she went to Brian for advice. She didn't want this behavior to disrupt a choir that was at the apex, the high point, of their musical performances.

Stacy's complaint was that she married a widower, Paul Leonard, twelve years older than herself. He plied her with expensive gifts and lavish compliments while dating. Being a pharmacist, a prominent businessman in Monroe, his status was impressive. Stacy looked remarkedly like his deceased wife in physical appearance, and she took it as a compliment, being that his former wife was quite attractive. In him, she saw the financial security she longed for and told herself that she would grow to love him over time. Shortly after the honeymoon period, she realized that all he wanted from the marriage was for her to be his surrogate first wife. He wanted her to dress like his first wife as he paraded her around at parties, cook his favorite meals, keep an immaculate house, and the list went on and on. She couldn't breathe and was rapidly suffocating in the marriage. She was sexually turned off by him and despised him for the misconception. Had she known his real intent, she never would have married him. Her delusions ended when his feet turned into clay. Wisconsin being a no-fault divorce state, she could expect to get half of his money in a divorce settlement—a tidy sum for a new start. After a year into the marriage, she started planning her exit strategy. If she had an affair, that would push him over the edge, easing the way for a quick divorce. Stacy didn't share all this with Cheryl, but Cheryl got the gist of her plan as she observed Stacy going after Herbert Milz.

Herbert Milz, on the other hand, was a henpecked weak man who had married into money, a tortured soul. He was a plain-looking man, someone who didn't stand out in a crowd. He dressed very conservatively and always had a fresh haircut. Linda Milz, his wife, inherited a large fortune after her parents were killed in a horrific airplane crash. Linda didn't have any siblings. The financial settlements from their life insurance policies, the airline payout, and their personal wealth left her with over a million dollars. Linda was twenty-two at the time of her parents' deaths, living at home, a spoiled bitch, and hard to get along with. Her parents were members at the Monroe Country Club, so the club put up with Linda's intolerable drunken behavior because she was a generous financial supporter of the club. The social aspects of the country club were her whole life. She didn't have any interests other than drinking and playing cards. Bridge was her passion, and she was good at it. She bought a small house in Florida and stayed there December through April to escape Wisconsin's brutal winters. Some of her women friends would fly down to Florida to spend time with her, drinking and sightseeing. She would book at least three Caribbean cruises every winter where her bar tab at the end of the cruise was higher than the cost of the cruise. After she came into her inheritance, she cut off all communication with any and all her relatives. "They are only after my money," she lamented after several drinks. "They are patiently waiting for my death rattle! Screw them all, I say!"

In spite of her wealth, she found precious few acceptable suitors for a husband. All the men she dated were very transparent with their happy talk and insincere intentions. It was her money that attracted them to her, and she saw right through the deceit. She would occasionally have sex with them to egg them on, but it was only a sport for her, giving her great amusement. Nothing else. The marriage market looked bleak when, at age thirty-one, she decided in earnest that she wanted a husband. She was lonely and didn't want to die a spinster like her two maiden aunts. She was used to getting what she wanted when she wanted it, and now was no exception. She didn't believe in love, so the idea of marriage needed to be transactional. As she cast her eye over the eligible men at the club, she took a second look at Herbert Milz. Was he fair game to suit her purposes? Herbert was thirty-three years old, a recent country club member, and owner of the Milz Auto Sales and Service business located in the 500 block of 10th Street. He was a bachelor who worked very hard keeping his business afloat. He was a shy, quiet man, but got along very well with his staff and customers. He had many friends, which impressed Linda. She convinced herself that he was the right man for her. A man she could control, keep her company, and look after her in her old age; someone she could trust. She stalked and pursued him like a tigress. He was overwhelmed by all the sudden attention. His friends immediately saw what was happening and encouraged him to marry her. It was like winning the lottery. Herbert wasn't so sure, but in the end, he cratered to all her high-pressure tactics and sexual advances. He married her. On their wedding night, she passed out drunk—a harbinger of things to come. As a wedding gift, Linda paid off all his debts and wanted him to sell the business and retire. He mustered enough backbone to say no and continued to manage the business. Many speculated that it was the only way he could get away from her and the verbal abuse he constantly endured. She would dig at him, criticize him, and jest at his expense at the country club, totally embarrassing him. He recognized stupidity and impertinence when he saw it. Over the years, Linda's drinking got out of control, and the marriage greatly suffered. Being raised a Catholic, divorcing her was out of the question, so Herbert suffered in silence. In every respect, they led separate lives. During her winter retreat to Florida to escape the harsh Wisconsin winters, Herbert flew to Florida during January and February. Two months was all he could stand without losing his mind.

From time to time, he shared some of his misery with Cheryl, whom he greatly admired and respected. He loved to sing and joined the church choir a number of years ago after becoming a lapsed Catholic, much to the consternation of his mother. He totally blamed himself for meeting his doomed fate with Linda. Cheryl was a good listener. He trusted her to keep his confidences, and she did.

Cheryl grew alarmed when the affection between Stacy and Hebert accelerated and became more visibly apparent. She could plainly see and highly suspected that they took the next step and were having an affair. It was the look in their eyes, the way they stared at each other. What should she do, if anything? Brian advised her to let it go. But the whole sordid drama playing itself out on Wednesday's choir rehearsals was causing her restless nights. Why was that? Why did it bother her so much? Brian was right, of course. It really wasn't any of her business. But she felt she needed to say something. Perhaps today was the day. Stacy told her Wednesday night that her husband would be at a bowling tournament in Milwaukee for the weekend with his Turner Hall league team. He was the team sponsor. Glancing over to Stacy's music folder, Cheryl decided to stop by her house on the way to New Glarus and drop it off. Then she could broach the subject of the affair with her. She expected some blowback, but she needed to say the words, clear the air and her own conscience.

Cheryl backed her car out of her driveway at 9:15 a.m. and drove to Stacy's house, plenty of time to meet with Stacy and still make her appointment in New Glarus on time. As her car sailed along on the picture-perfect day, she tried to think about what she was going to say to Stacy. She turned east onto the tree-lined Exeter Crossing Road and turned up the gravel driveway to the house. All was quiet as she exited her car with the music folder. She surmised that Stacy's car was parked in the closed detached garage. "I hope she is home," she said to herself. Cheryl climbed the porch steps and knocked on the front door. No response. She knocked harder. Still no response. She was disappointed. "Maybe she wasn't home after all." Cheryl turned the doorknob and gently pushed against the door. It opened easily. "I will leave the music folder with a note," she told herself. She flung the door open and went into the living room. What she saw lying on the floor froze her in horror. Her hand immediately flew to her mouth as she dropped the music folder. She starting gasping for air. Stacy's prone body lay on the floor like a fallen stone-cold statue. Blood had leaked from her chest and had stained the living room carpet. Her wide-open blank eyes stared into space. Her face was ghostly pale and still. Her gaping mouth was wide open. Cheryl immediately knew that Stacy was dead. She felt dizzy. As her head cleared from the shock, Cheryl reached down and touched her arm. Her insides were twisting with fear. The body was cool to the touch. She jumped up, raced to the telephone, and called the sheriff's department. Cheryl was shaking like a leaf.

CHAPTER 2

Monroe Police Detective Samantha Gates was sitting on her living room sofa, enjoying her Saturday. The time was one o'clock. Secure and snuggled in her arms was wee Karin Sue Nelson, peacefully sleeping. Her baby girl was nine months old and the joy of their lives. Karin had Drew's red hair and Sam's blue-green eyes. When Sam married Drew Nelson, the staff at the police department wanted her to keep her maiden name of Gates. For years, they knew her by her surname, so after her marriage, the name Nelson didn't seem to fit or work for them. Sam was surprised and amused at the suggestion, but she was okay with the idea. Drew didn't mind and went along with it as well. A wife with two names? He found some humor in that. Drew was employed as a physical therapist at the hospital.

Sam was tall, 5-foot-10 1/2; lithe; and wore her chocolate brown hair short. After the birth of Karin, she worked hard to get her figure back. She breastfed Karin for six months; after which, the baby went on solid food. Breastfeeding her baby was one of those moments in life that was beyond description. Sam felt less stressed and more confident when nursing. She would look into Karin's innocent loving eyes and talk to her. With the intimate touching, Sam and Karin connected in a unique way, a bond between mother and child that was strong. The joy and wonderment of being a mother for the first time overwhelmed her emotionally. Having her baby at her breast was exhilarating. Throughout her pregnancy, Sam couldn't wait to meet her little girl and welcome her into the world. As she gently rocked Karin, Sam couldn't take her eyes from her sleeping little angel, so sweet, so trusting. Karin was now sleeping through the night, which Sam and Drew very much appreciated. Parenthood was quite the adjustment for them. Being up at all hours of the night was a pain, but the rewards were well worth it. Drew was a doting father and hovered over his daughter like a mother hen. Their family circle was complete, and life was good.

Sam's colleagues at the PD were very supportive of her and volunteered to babysit little Karin anytime she and Drew needed a night off. Their good wishes and intentions were very much appreciated by Sam, but she already had a babysitter living two houses down from them. A retired farm couple had moved into the neighborhood two years ago, and they all got well acquainted. Martha and Henry Sturzenegger came from a large extended family and were very helpful when it came to raising and understanding babies and their needs. Martha volunteered to take care of Karin during the day and doted over her by gathering her up in her loving, secure arms. Karin took to Martha right away. Sam and Drew felt very comfortable leaving Karin at her house as they went to work, pursuing their own careers. The farm couple was quickly becoming part of the family, and they shared many meals together with Sam and Drew. Sam thought of her as a loving, caring neighborhood mom.

Sharon Gates, Sam's widowed mother, was at the Parkview Nursing Home. Sam's father had been a police officer who was killed in the line of duty when Sam was sixteen years old. She dearly loved her father, and his death launched her into a career in law enforcement. Sam loved her job and knew that her father would be very proud of her carrying on his legacy. Sharon had a wicked sense of humor that could shock her friends and unsuspecting strangers with outrageous caustic one-liners. She was at times a challenge for Sam when trying to interpret her mother's weird sense of humor. But one thing was crystal clear: She dearly loved her new granddaughter and couldn't wait for Sam to bring her to visit. Karin was a dream come true for Sharon—a miracle. Sam waited until she was in her thirties before getting married, and that had greatly concerned Sharon, who didn't think motherhood was in the cards for her detective daughter. But fate intervened and minted her a sweet little angel. Deep in her soul, Sharon thanked God for the blessing and the answer to her prayers.

A frequent visitor to Monroe was Sam's good friend, Janet Sonnenberg. They had known each other since their college days together at the University of Wisconsin in Madison. Janet was as excited as Sam about the baby. With each visit, she brought along a small baby gift. These gifts included a colorful striped baby onesie, a six-pack of socks, a knitted baby hat, and other such items to the amusement of Sam. She told Janet that all the wrapped gifts weren't necessary, but Janet ignored her. "I am Karin's godmother, and that is that—full stop!" Sam laughed as Janet held Karin in her arms, made funny faces, and talked to her in baby speak. Drew really enjoyed Janet's visits and all her enthusiasm.

Sam and Drew had afternoon plans taking Karin to the nursing home to see Sharon. Drew was busy finishing up some yard work and wanted to shower before they left for the nursing home. Sharon was expecting them at two o'clock. A sweaty Drew appeared at one thirty, on his way to the bathroom to freshen up. The telephone suddenly rang, and he answered the call. It was Chief Brandon Johns from the Monroe PD, wanting to speak to Sam. He put the telephone receiver down and took Karin from Sam's arms. He disappeared into the kitchen with her.

"Good afternoon, Chief. How are you?" Sam asked.

There was excitement in his voice as he hurriedly told her about the telephone call he just had with the Green County sheriff. It involved a murder at a farmhouse on Exeter Crossing Road near New Glarus. The person reporting the murder found the body around ten o'clock this morning. The sheriff's department was shorthanded and wanted the Monroe PD to help in the investigation. The chief readily agreed. He told Sam that he would pick up her in twenty minutes and drive to the crime scene together. He abruptly hung up. Sam was stunned. She sat back down on the sofa. A feeling of dread passed through her body. This was the moment that she had feared. Up until now, her work at the PD was light duty. No serious crimes to investigate. She was used to being home with Drew and Karin on a regular, scheduled routine. No stress, no fuss. After she hung up, Sam immediately knew what a murder investigation would do to her, disrupting her private life. She exhaled heavily as Drew returned to the living room with Karin and saw her face.

"What's up?" Drew asked, knowing the answer. "The chief never calls you on a Saturday afternoon."

Sam quickly explained the situation to him. Drew comforted her by telling Sam that it was a part of the job and he understood completely. He would take Karin to visit Sharon and explain Sam's absence. He also told Sam that he could handle the blowback from Sharon and not to worry. Sam kissed him on the cheek and flew into the bedroom and changed her clothes while Drew took a brief rinse-off shower. The chief's car pulled up, and Sam rushed out the front door, down the porch steps, and they hurriedly drove off. Drew and Karin waved to them as they watched the chief's car disappear around the corner.

The drive to the murder scene was short, with Johns doing most of the talking. Sam watched the landscape fly by as his car sped along State Highway 69. She barely paid attention to what he was saying. All she could think about was leaving little Karin. What would she think when she woke up from a nap and Mama wasn't there? She shook her head, trying to shake those guilty thoughts out of her mind. She needed to focus on the task at hand and deal with her maternal instincts later. When they arrived at the farmhouse, Johns slowed down and drove up the gravel driveway located on the south side of the road and parked beside two Green County sheriff vehicles, an ambulance and the medical examiner's car. Sam noticed a 3 x 2-foot white framed sign in the front yard that read, "Burr Oak Farm, est. 1841." Albert Swenson was also there to take the crime-scene photos. Yellow crime-scene tape was tied to the pillar posts on the front porch, fluttering in the breeze. Ducking under it, they entered the house. The sheriff greeted them and pointed to the body. Dr. Ken Anderson, Green County medical examiner, nodded to Johns. The sheriff and Johns were good friends.

Sheriff Thomas Wahl was a veteran law and order police officer, a man of high standards. He had been reelected Green County sheriff four consecutive terms. He was an affable man with a quick wit and a ready smile. Johns thought he would have made an outstanding politician if he hadn't chosen law enforcement as a career. His public-speaking skills were much in demand as he entertained the citizens of Green County on numerous occasions. He was tall, 6 feet 2 inches; had close cropped haircut; and in great physical shape. Behind his sky blue eyes was a keen intellect, and if you didn't know him, he could size you up and dissect you with the precision of a surgeon.

Stacy Leonard lay in the same prone position as when Cheryl discovered her body earlier that morning. Johns looked at the corpse for a long moment and then turned to the sheriff, who cleared his throat. "The preliminary report from Dr. Ken is that Mrs. Leonard died from two gunshot wounds to the chest at close range sometime last night. After the autopsy, we can confirm the approximate time of death and the caliber of the gun. I wanted you to see the body before we removed it to the morgue. Any questions?" Johns looked at Dr. Ken, who nodded in agreement with the sheriff's assessment, and then to Sam, who was intently staring at the corpse. She readily identified victim as someone she knew. Then she carefully looked at the crime scene, taking in all that she saw.

In all her years of experience as a homicide detective, she mentally processed every detail of the murder room. Once she was satisfied, she nodded to the chief. Johns told Swenson to take the crime-scene photos of the body. He readied his camera and took the photos from various camera angles as well as the room itself. Johns, Sam, and the rest of the assemblage watched him as he methodically took the pictures.

"Have you contacted Mr. Leonard?" Johns asked the sheriff.

"Yes. He is at a bowling tournament in Milwaukee, and we spoke to him about an hour ago. He should be here later this afternoon, around four o'clock."

"Good, we will need to speak to him," Johns replied and told the sheriff and Dr. Ken that the body could be moved.

Dr. Ken offered to begin the autopsy later that day and work through the night, if necessary, to determine the exact cause of death. Johns told him that he would accompany Paul Leonard to the morgue later that day to ID the body.

The two ambulance attendees lifted the corpse onto a gurney, wheeled it outside, and lifted it into the back of the ambulance. The ambulance slowly drove down the driveway, followed by the Dr. Ken's car turning west on Exeter Crossing Road, heading for Monroe. The deputy sheriff also left to continue his shift rounds.

"I will have my report on your desk Monday morning," Sheriff Wahl told Johns, handing him the key to the front door.

Before they said their goodbyes, Johns asked if the lights were turned off in the house when the body was discovered. He said they were. The sheriff left them, driving down the driveway and turning onto Exeter Crossing Road. Sam and Johns watched him leave and then looked at each other.

They reentered the house. "So what do you think?" Johns asked.

Sam was totally engaged and riveted on the crime scene as she once again studied the living room. "For starters, there wasn't a struggle. No sign of that. It seems that the killer entered the house sometime last night, confronted Mrs. Leonard, fired two bullets into her chest, turned out the lights, and left. No panic. The killer just picked up the shell casings and walked away . . ." Sam paused for a moment. "I would assume that Mrs. Leonard knew the killer, being that there wasn't any forced entry or any signs of a struggle. The autopsy report will give us the make of the gun used in the murder . . ." Sam paused again from her methodical thinking and added, "We will need the forensics team from Madison to go over the house."

"I have thought of that," the chief said, retrieving a black notebook from his pocket. "I will call Scott Brady. I have his home telephone number listed in my book."

"He will love that—being called out on a Saturday afternoon!"

"Remember, I called you out on a Saturday."

Sam grimaced. "I know, it's just part of the job. How about Mr. Leonard? Where should we talk to him?"

"I will interview him here, when he returns from Milwaukee. Would you like to sit in on the interview?"

"Yes. You know as well as I do that family members are prime suspects until eliminated. I will be curious as to what he has to say."

Johns made his way to the telephone in the kitchen, ignoring the one in the living room, and called Brady. Brady told him that his forensics team would be there at 5:00 p.m. After one more look around the living room, Johns and Sam went to the front porch and sat on two white rocking chairs, chipped and in need of paint, to wait for Mr. Leonard. They sat in a comfortable silence, looking out at the rich landscape and thinking. Sam noticed a house across the sun-drenched cornfield sitting on a bluff.

"Do you see that house?" she asked, pointing to it.

Johns followed her extended arm and nodded.

Sam continued. "There is a clear line of sight from that house to this one. I think we should interview the people living there to see if they can help us in the investigation. Maybe they saw something last night that could help us."

Johns agreed.

* * *

"What do you know about Mr. Leonard?" Sam asked.

"Not much. He is well-respected and owns a pharmacy on the north side of the courthouse square. His first wife died in an automobile accident a few years ago, and he remarried. Stacy Leonard was his second wife. Losing two wives will be traumatic to say the least."

Sam wrinkled her nose and squinted her eyes. "Was the marriage a happy one?" Sam asked.

Johns smiled at the question.

"I can't answer that one. I never heard of any marital issues, but of course, I am not a party to the extensive grapevine of local gossip." His comment made Sam smile.

"How about you?" Johns asked.

"I have seen her Sunday mornings singing in the church choir. That's about it. I can't say I have ever spoken to her. It must have been an awful shock for him when the sheriff told him about his wife over the telephone."

"I would think so. How does any human being react to the news that a loved one has suddenly— and without warning—been murdered? The gut punch had to be horrific. I can only imagine what's going through his mind as he drives home: sadness, anger, disbelief, despair, guilt. We will need to give him space. If he is too distressed and doesn't want to be interviewed, so be it. We can talk to him another time."

Sam nodded.

"I want to walk through what I think happened here," Johns absently said. Sam looked at him and remained silent. Johns steepled his fingers and began. "Okay, the killer comes to the farmhouse sometime last night with some sort of grievance. The living room lights weren't on this morning, so was the time of the murder early evening, before sunset? Or was it after dark and the killer turned out the lights? Next, the killer probably brought the gun with him. We will have to ask Mr. Leonard if he had a gun in the house. There doesn't seem to have been a struggle, implying that the killer produced the gun and fired two shots into Stacy Leonard's chest before she could react. Was the killer wearing gloves? What about fingerprints? Forensics will tell us that in the report. We will need fingerprints to match anyone who visited the house . . ." Johns paused. "Moving on, after he shot her, the killer had the presence of mind to turn off the lights in the living room, pick up the spent casings, close the front door, and drive away." Johns stopped talking and gave Sam time to reflect on his hypothesis.

"So you think the murder took place after dark?"

"I would think so. If you were intent on killing someone, would you drive here in broad daylight so any passing car could see your vehicle parked in front of the house?"

Sam nodded. "Makes sense to me. So you think the murder was premeditated?"

"For now, yes."

Sam raised her eyebrows. "Did you notice that there were no bullet casings at the crime scene?"

Johns nodded.

She continued. "The killer had the presence of mind to take them with him. It may prove your theory about premeditation."

Johns smiled.

"I noticed a dusk-to-dawn yard light near the barn. I wonder if it is working," Sam said.

"Good point. We should check it out. If it was working, perhaps a passing motorist noticed a strange car in the driveway close to the house."

"So are you assuming the killer was a man?" Sam asked.

"Not at all. Wherever the facts take us, as we uncover them, will answer that question. Killers aren't very smart people. They aren't as perfect or as clever as they think they are and will screw up somewhere along the line. All we have to do is catch them. But first, we need to find a motive. Remember, find the motive, find the killer."

Sam laughed. How many times had the chief used that line on her? "Well, we have theorized many what-ifs, so after we have apprehended the killer, it would be interesting to see how all this theorizing worked out," Sam mused.

Johns smiled at her. "Have you heard about the curse of this farmstead?" Johns asked.

Sam looked at him with a quizzical look on her face. "No, but I bet you are going to tell me."

Johns grinned at her. "When I was a kid, the curse of Burr Oak Farm was legendary. Starting in the early 1800s, many murders have been committed here: Indians being massacred, families being poisoned, and a G.I. suffering the effects of shell shock returning from World War II murdered his wife and hanged himself. In fact, there is a small pioneer cemetery located on the hill in back of the house. Some of the locals still swear that ghosts and weird noises are seen and heard on the farmstead from time to time, verifying the place is still haunted. A lot of people are convinced and still believe that. And now this murder will just add to and renew those sightings and superstitious beliefs."

"Do you believe it? I mean, that the place is cursed?" Sam interrupted.

Johns laughed. "When I was in high school, a carload of my friends and I would drive out here and park on the shoulder of the road after dark to see what we could see. Nothing ever happened other than hearing a distant hoot owl on a moonlit night. We double-dared one another to quietly walk up to the place and look around. It was a total waste of time, but some of my friends told our classmates that ghosts appeared and chased us back to our car, trying to kill us. The tall tale was funny for a couple of days."

"So why are you telling me all this?" Sam asked.

"As we begin our investigation, I am convinced that the curse will come up, and I want you to know the back story and not to get sidetracked. Believe me when I say that a psychic medium or a fortune-teller isn't going to solve this case."

Sam shook her head and snorted. "In other words, this homestead is haunted by the horrifying memories of the past."

"Exactly!" Johns replied.

Another silence fell between them. The chief slowly rocked in his chair, staring out at the lush green landscape. The temperatures were comfortably warm, the song birds were singing their hearts out, and the squirrels were scampering across the yard. The afternoon was magical and idyllic. What a contrast to what Mr. Leonard must be feeling as he raced home to the horrific tragedy awaiting him here. Sam looked at and admired the very tall burr oak tree with distinctive and colorful bristle-tipped lobed leaves located on the edge of the grove. As she stepped off the porch and gazed up, she figured that the grand tree must be at least 150 feet tall and over a hundred years old. The tree was huge and located on the east side of the house. She also noticed a small family plot on the hillside overlooking the house, a pioneer grave site. She told the chief that she was going to take the short walk to investigate the cemetery. Johns nodded.

Sam made her way up to the pioneer cemetery. Even though the day was warm, the cemetery seemed cold and damp in the shade. It was surrounded by a low wrought-iron fence and dense weeds. The gravestones were weathered and barely readable, surrounded by tall native grasses. The gravestones were crookedly aslant, shaped by time, gravity, and neglect. Sam felt a cold chill run down her back. She abruptly turned around and left the small cemetery, rejoining the chief on the porch. He inquired how her visit went.

"Chilling" was her response.

am looked at her watch. It was 4:00 p.m. She left the porch and walked into the kitchen to call Drew before Mr. Leonard arrived. When Drew answered the telephone, she could hear Karin crying.

"Is everything okay?" she asked.

"Karin just woke up from a nap, and she is a little cranky. I changed her diaper, and I am warming a bottle of milk for her."

Sam's immediate reaction was that she should be home with her daughter. A sharp pain of guilt shot through her body. "How did it go with Mother this afternoon?"

The crying stopped, and Karin was cooing in Drew's arms. "Sharon held Karin most of the time we were there. They both enjoyed the visit, but Sharon couldn't stop herself and kept asking why you weren't with us. I wouldn't worry about it though. Karin covered for you."

The affirmation made Sam smile.

"When do you think you will be home?" Drew asked.

"We are expecting Mr. Leonard any minute now. I would guess I should be home by 6:00 p.m. at the latest."

"Good, I will warm up some leftovers for supper. Say goodbye, Karin." Drew placed the telephone receiver next to Karin's head, and Sam could hear her making gurgling sounds. "I love you," Drew said."

"Love you back," Sam replied, hanging up the telephone receiver.

At 4:20 p.m., Sam and Johns watched from the porch as Leonard's car slowed and turned up the gravel driveway. They walked to his parked car next to the garage and introduced themselves. He looked very pale and tired. He said he needed a drink of water. They took him to the porch and pulled up a wooden chair alongside the two rocking chairs. He grimaced as he ducked under the yellow crime-scene tape. The tape seemed to unnerve him. Sam went inside the house to fetch him the glass of water. When she returned, he was seated next to Johns in one of the rocking chairs. Sam handed him the water and sat down on the extra chair. Leonard took a big swallow and stared at the chief. Leonard was 5 feet 9 inches tall, average build, with straight brown hair parted on the side, dark brown eyes, and had a distinctive Greek nose. He kept looking at the front door of his house.

"First of all, I am sorry for your loss. It must have come as a big shock to you."

Leonard nodded, looking at Sam and Johns. The numbness in his face was very apparent. He was in a state of shock.

"Do you feel well enough to answer a few questions? If not, we can reschedule for another time."

"Tell me what happened," Leonard softly said. "The sheriff told me on the telephone that my wife was found this morning, murdered in my house. She was shot in the chest. I just can't believe it."

"For clarification, the sheriff's department has turned the murder investigation over to the Monroe Police Department, being that they are understaffed at this time. Detective Gates and I will be handling the investigation." Johns paused. "Are you feeling okay? You look unwell."

"I will be fine."

"Okay, tell us about your movements last night."

"Why?" Leonard asked, startled by the question.

"Just standard police procedure when questioning a family member. We need a clear picture of your whereabouts."

Leonard shifted in his chair and spoke in a low monotone voice. His face was very pale. He kept glancing at the crime-scene tape. "I ate something disagreeable last night at the hotel, and my lower GI tract was causing me fits. I think it had to do with some greasy mystery meat. Anyway, I had a hard time trying to bowl, and I went to bed around

7:30 p.m. I told the team to find a sub for me. I was in my room this morning when the call was put through from the sheriff."

Johns squinted. He was thinking. Leonard's body language was interesting. He couldn't read it. Was he stunned, numbed, or what?

"Can I see where my wife's body was found?" Leonard asked.

They stood up, and Johns led the way into the house. He stopped before entering the living room and pointed to the spot on the floor where the body was discovered by Cheryl Kubly-Schultz. Traces of blood were visible on the carpet. Leonard stared at the carpet for a long moment in silence.

"We can't go into the living room because the forensics team from Madison will be here later today to go over the living room and the house, looking for physical evidence."

Leonard slowly nodded. "Thank you."

They went back to the front porch and sat down. Leonard looked nervous as he clasped his hands together.

"We need to ask you some more questions. Are you sure you are all right?" Johns asked.

Leonard nodded.

"When did you leave for the bowling tournament in Milwaukee?" Johns asked.

"The team carpooled Friday morning, and I drove myself after work. I left here around 3:30 p.m."

"Where you alone?"

"Yes."

"Did you see your wife before you left?"

"Yes. She was here at the house and wished me well at the tournament."

"How did she seem to you?"

"What do you mean?"

"Was she anxious or upset about you being gone for the weekend?"

"No. I don't think so. The tournament is an annual event, and she never expressed an interest in going. In fact, she wasn't a bowler. She was musical and taught music at the high school in Monroe. Also, she liked to sing in the choir at the First Christian Church."

"Did you call her when you arrived in Milwaukee to check in?"

Leonard flinched. The question seemed to rattle him a little. He felt a bead of sweat cascading down his armpit. "No."

The one-word response surprised Johns. "Did she call you?"

"No."

A long pause followed. "So to recap, the last time you saw your wife alive or talked to her was yesterday afternoon, and all was fine. Then she was murdered sometime last night. Does that strike you as odd?" Sam intently watched Leonard's face as the chief questioned him.

Leonard could feel both armpits getting damp. "Look, if she was having any personal problems, she didn't share them with me."

"I am only trying to get a clear picture of your relationship with your wife. Would you say that your marriage was a happy one?"

The muscles in Leonard's face tightened. He hesitated for a long time, thinking. He felt that he was in a kind of purgatory, trapped and damned. He couldn't have his deceased first wife, whom he loved, and he couldn't live with his second wife, who betrayed him and was unfaithful. And now he suddenly realized, only too late, that his fond memories of his first wife had him stuck in the past. He desperately wanted to relive those happier times with his new wife Stacy, but it turned out to be a catastrophic mistake. All these thoughts were cascading and racing through his mind. Should he tell the chief that he had recently been to a lawyer to seek legal advice for a divorce? Would that admission make him a suspect? Finally, he spoke.

"Like all marriages, we were having issues. I will leave it at that," Leonard said.

"How long were you married?"

"Two years. Is that important?"

"During a murder investigation, the police need to get as clear a picture as possible about the victim and the family. These routine questions will give us a starting point for our inquires and to eliminate any possible suspects."

"Am I a suspect?"

"I am not saying that. But your truthful answers today will help us with the investigation and help bring to justice the person who murdered your wife."

Leonard's shoulders slumped.

"Do you want to continue?" Johns asked.

"Yes."

"How are you feeling?"

"Okay."

"Do you know of anyone who would want to harm your wife?"

Leonard shook his head. He secretly suspected that his wife was having an affair, but he didn't know who it was for sure. If he offered a name and he was wrong, the speculation could boomerang back on him. "No one I can think of."

Johns knew he was lying. "Take your time. Someone killed your wife, and we are looking for a motive. Think hard. Does anything at all stand out to you? Maybe a comment from your wife that may have seemed unimportant or a noticeable change in her behavior."

Leonard shook his head. "No one comes to mind."

"This next question will seem jarring to you, but we need to ask you based on years of investigating experience . . ." Johns paused for a moment, letting his words sink in. "Given your martial problems, do you think your wife was having an affair?"

The question was a gut punch to Leonard. He heavily exhaled. A flash of anger crossed his face, causing an involuntary muscle response. Both Sam and Johns noticed it.

"I don't know."

"In my experience, a spouse always knows or suspects when their partner is being unfaithful. Sometimes they go into denial, but nevertheless, they know. I will ask you again, do you think your wife was having an affair?"

Leonard lowered his head and looked at his shoes. "Yes," he said in a deflated tone of voice.

"Do you know the man she was having the affair with?"

"No. You are right that our marriage was on the rocks. We stopped having sex. You are also right that her behavior suddenly changed. She was distant, stopped speaking to me. And then about three months ago, she seemed happier. She had a bounce in her step. I knew it wasn't because of me."

"How did that make you feel?"

"I was devastated. I realized, only too late, that I made a horrible mistake marrying someone younger than me. I sorely missed my wife, and I was lonely. When I met Stacy, she made me laugh and live again. The sex was great. The harsh reality is that it was all a foolish fantasy, and it has unnerved me."

Johns and Sam glanced at each other. "So you have no idea who may have wanted to harm your wife?" Johns asked again.

Leonard shook his head.

"So tell me about your timeline in Milwaukee from the time you left here on Friday until the time you left Milwaukee today after the sheriff called you."

"Like I said, I came home from work Friday afternoon, packed my suitcase, said goodbye to Stacy, and drove to Milwaukee."

"Did your wife have a job? Did she keep regular hours?"

"Yes, like I said, she was a music teacher at Monroe High School. Her day usually ended at 3:00 p.m."

"And she was home when you arrived from work?"

"Yes."

"You stated earlier that she wished you a good trip to Milwaukee. But neither of you called each other to check in. Is that correct?" Johns asked.

"Yes, that is correct."

"Then why did she wish you a good time in Milwaukee? You must have known she didn't mean it. Do you think she was meeting someone, her lover for instance, during your absence?"

Leonard hung his head. "The thought did occur to me."

A long silence followed. Johns looked at his watch. The forensics team would be here soon.

"Okay, moving on, you said that you ate dinner at the hotel Friday evening that made you ill."

"That's correct. I think it was the greasy meat entrée. It was a buffet."

"And the discomfort was such that it caused you to bowl so poorly that you couldn't finish and went to bed early Friday night. You told the team to find you a sub for Saturday as well. Is that correct?"

"Correct."

"Did any of your friends check in on you after you went to bed?"

"Not that I know of. They could have come by when I was sleeping."

"I am assuming you had a room all to yourself."

"Yes. Some of the other team members shared a room to save on expenses."

"How about Saturday morning? Did anyone drop in to check on you?"

"Yes. Brian Hoffman came to my room about 8:30 a.m."

Sam recognized the name. She knew him from church.

"So after you went to bed at approximately seven thirty, Friday night, feeling unwell, no one can verify your movements until eight thirty, Saturday morning?" Johns asked.

The blood drained from Leonard's face. He looked like he was going to faint. The sudden realization that he might be a suspect made him feel very nervous and nauseous. He gathered himself enough to answer, "That is correct."

"One more question," Johns said. "Was there a life insurance policy on your wife?"

Leonard gasped. "We both had one for $10,000."

"Also, do you or your wife own a handgun?"

"No," Leonard replied.

Johns turned and saw Scott Brady and his team drive up the gravel driveway. The trio on the porch watched the vehicles approach.

"Do you have someone to stay with tonight? The forensics team will be working here quite late," Johns said.

"I can stay with my sister in Monroe," Leonard replied.

"Good. You can't reenter the house until the forensics team is finished."

"I can borrow some clothes from my brother-in-law, we are the same size," Leonard offered.

Johns nodded. "We will be contacting you again. So if you plan on leaving Monroe, let us know."

Leonard nodded. "Anything else?"

"Yes. One other thing, please drive to the morgue located in the basement of the hospital and wait for me. I want you to positively identify your wife's body. Dr. Ken will be there, so request to see him when you arrive."

A visibly shaken Leonard stood up and slowly walked to his car. Johns greeted his friend Scott Brady and his team, introduced Sam, and took them into the house. As Leonard drove down the driveway, Sam watched his car turn west on Exeter Road. Johns and the forensics team quickly disappeared into the house. Shortly, Johns returned to Sam, who was sitting on the porch in a rocking chair.

"Let's go," he said.

On the drive back to Monroe, they discussed their impressions of Leonard. They agreed that he was lying and that he may be withholding important information. Also, they theorized that he could have driven to the farmplace from Milwaukee Friday night, murdered his wife, and returned. It certainly was a possibility, but was it plausible? Only time would tell. Sam commented on the fact that the suspicion of an affair can destroy a man. If Leonard thought his wife was having an affair, could that be a motive for murder? Johns agreed. The house on the bluff overlooking the farmstead intrigued Sam, and she told Johns that she was going to interview the people living there Monday morning. Johns said he thought it was a good idea and that it was a good place to start. They scheduled to meet again Monday afternoon to debrief the murder and to plan their next steps. By then, they should have the sheriff's incident report and, hopefully, a report from Brady's team. Johns dropped Sam off at her house and drove straight to the hospital. He was curious to see Leonard's reaction when he viewed his deceased wife's body.

CHAPTER 4

I t was Monday morning, May 20. Agnes Keel paced around the living room floor of her ranch-style house like a caged animal. Detective Gates called her at eight thirty and set up an appointment to visit her at eleven o'clock. Agnes was seventy-nine years old and a widow. She lived alone. Her husband, Jeffery Keel, died two years ago in their home from heart failure. Agnes was short, 5 feet 1 inch, overweight, had shoulder-length gray hair, brown eyes, and wore wire-rimmed spectacles that sat on a pug nose. She rarely left the house and was something of a recluse living in a safe place for an old woman who had forgotten the fragile magic of her youth, morphing into old age, afraid of change, and stiff in her thinking. A concerned and kindly neighbor lady ran errands for her, taking her to doctor appointments, doing the grocery shopping, and tending to her everyday survival needs. When her husband was alive, Agnes depended heavily on him. After he passed, she had no social life and lived in the constant fear of the outside world. She was mentally challenged and perpetually scared that Mr. Death was stalking her, waiting for the right moment to take her. She had three deadbolt locks installed on her front door after Jeffery died. If she heard three distinct knocks on the door, it was a sure sign that Mr. Death had come to take her away. Her neighbor would knock only two times, a prearranged signal; after which, Agnes could safely open the door.

Agnes was afraid of the dark, and the night sounds outside her bedroom window were both eerie and unnerving. They terrified her

31

down to the marrow in her bones. She slept with her bedroom lamp on. She had retreated into a silent world of darkness. Her house was like a cave, where no one could see her. She didn't fit into society like normal people, which caused her great anxiety and confusion. A reoccurring dream that started about a year ago haunted her. In the dream, she was in a small town all alone, no people. Where was everybody? Wandering through the streets and empty buildings, finding no sign of life, she panicked. She raced from house to house, building to building, desperately searching for someone, anyone. Then she would suddenly wake up in a cold sweat. She was terrified and scared out of her wits. Was she going crazy? But, she thought, was the nightmare telling her something she couldn't interpret? Perhaps it came from beyond the grave? A message telling her that all her sleepless nights of waiting was a slow walk to death and held something far worse for her than this world had to offer. Was she going insane? The call from Detective Gates had totally unnerved her.

At 11:00 a.m., she heard the gravel crunch on her driveway. She looked out her front window and saw Detective Gates exit her car. She watched as Gates made her way to the front door. She knocked three times, throwing Agnes into a fright. Was Mr. Death knocking? She froze. Three more knocks. She didn't move.

"Mrs. Keel, are you in there?" Sam asked through the door.

"Who are you?" came the nervous reply.

"I am Detective Gates from the Monroe Police Department. We had an appointment for 11:00 a.m., remember?"

"Do you have any identification?"

"Yes."

"Show me through the window."

Sam walked to the picture window and pressed her badge against it. Agnes appeared and stared at it.

"Knock on the door again but only two times."

Sam rolled her eyes. "Okay." She went to the front door and knocked two times. Sam could hear the clatter of the dead bolts as Agnes unlocked the door.

"Come in quickly," Agnes said.

After Sam entered the house, Agnes took a quick looked outside, slammed the door shut, and locked it.

Sam looked around the small three-bedroom ranch-style house. The living room was neat and tidy, furnished in antiques. The pendulum of a grandfather clock had stopped, and the time was 6:15 a.m. or p.m.? Looking through to the dining room, Sam could see a large picture window facing south with a wooden table and two chairs pushed up against it. Looking through the window, Sam could clearly see the Leonard house across the field. On the table was a pair of binoculars, glossy magazines, a spiral notebook, and a pencil. Agnes suspiciously eyed Sam as she surveyed the layout of the house.

"May I sit down?" Sam asked.

"Of course, my dear," Agnes said, pointing to a faded burgundy sofa. Agnes sat across from her in a cushioned high-backed armchair.

"When I telephoned you this morning, I was curious if you heard that Mrs. Leonard, your neighbor across the field, was murdered sometime Friday night. I can see that you have a table pushed up against a window, giving you a clear line of sight to her farmplace. Also, I noticed a pair of binoculars sitting on the table. Can you help me?"

Agnes intently stared at her. "Are you sure you are a police detective and not someone else?"

"Like who?"

"Mr. Death!"

Sam was taken aback. She reached into her pocket and handed her ID to Agnes. She stared at the ID for a long time through her spectacles. Satisfied, she handed it back to Sam.

"Your picture is awful. You should have a new one taken."

A slight, almost imperceptible smile crossed Sam's face. "Can we go and sit at the table by the picture window?" Sam said, pointing to the dining room.

Agnes nodded and stood up. Sam followed her to the table. They sat down at opposite ends of the wooden table, looking at each other. They both had a clear view of the Leonard house from their chairs. The glossy magazines on the table were a collection of *Car and Driver* and *Road and Track*. Sam could see a list of cars written in an open spiral notebook in front of Agnes.

"I am curious. Are you interested in cars?" Sam asked.

Agnes smiled, ignoring her question. "My husband, Jeffery, died two years ago in this house at exactly 6:15 a.m. He wasn't in the best of health, but he firmly believed, when the pendulum on our 8-foot antique grandfather clock stopped, he would be dead."

Agnes turned in her chair and pointed to the clock standing along the north wall of the living room. Sure enough, the pendulum was stopped and the time was six fifteen. She continued. "Jeffery would tell me that the pendulum swinging back and forth represented life and death. Tick, tock, tick, tock. If you forgot to wind the clock, the pendulum would gradually slow down and stop, announcing a time of death. The clock killed him at 6:15 a.m."

Sam wrinkled her nose. *He probably forgot to wind it,* Sam mused to herself.

Agnes turned and looked at Sam. "He was the love of my life. He owned a filling station and auto repair shop in New Glarus. Well, anyway, we would sit here for hours, watching the cars traveling along Exeter Crossing Road, and identify the people driving them. It was great fun for Jeffery knowing the comings and goings of the local people. Being in the auto repair business, he had an intimate knowledge of the cars and their owners."

"Did you share his enthusiasm about the cars?"

"Heavens no."

Sam noticed that Agnes occasionally glanced at the front door as if she were expecting someone, Mr. Death, for instance?

"So what interests do you have apart from cars?"

"The ghosts, of course."

"The ghosts?"

"You must know, young lady, that the property the Leonard house sits on is haunted and cursed. I told Jeffery that the ghosts I saw there were from the afterlife, looking for some peace. He wasn't so sure. You have heard the stories, I assume?"

34

"Yes, I have heard about the ghosts. Are the stories true?" Sam asked.

"Absolutely. I have seen the ghosts. The farmplace is cursed with them. I sit at this table night after night, watching and waiting to see them appear."

"Do you do this every night?"

"Yes. I gaze through my binoculars and look for sightings of any ghosts from the past, looking for peace, like I said. I have seen a woman wearing a white dress at dusk and shadows moving in the moonlight. I have even seen blood on a full moon." Agnes hesitated, thinking about her sightings. "Jeffery told me that the farmplace was, indeed, haunted because of all the unnatural deaths that occurred on the property after the Indian massacre by U.S. troops in the early 1800s—murders, disease, and suicides. Many, many ghosts linger and haunt the place, looking for peace."

A short silence passed between them.

"Were you aware that Mrs. Leonard was murdered sometime Friday night?" Sam said, getting Agnes's attention.

"Yes, and I predicted it."

"What? You knew that Mrs. Leonard was going to be murdered? How?"

"I was watching the cars on the road through my binoculars and heard the sound of a hooting owl sitting on the peak of their farmhouse roof—a sure sign of an impending death."

"So you weren't surprised?"

"Not at all."

"Can I have a look?"

"Of course," Agnes said, picking up and handing the binoculars to Sam.

Sam looked through the two small telescopes at the burr oak tree, the white house, and the white framed sign in the front yard.

"Do you remember the cars that were at the house or passed by Friday night?"

"Of course."

Agnes picked up her spiral notebook and handed it to Sam. She was surprised. On the top of each page was the date and the time of the entries. She easily found Friday. Starting at noon, she read the entries of a "Blue Chevrolet Nova" and a "Copper-tone Chevy Camaro" at the house. Then a series of cars followed that drove up and down Exeter Crossing Road: "Light Blue Oldsmobile Cutlass," "Blue Ford Pickup Truck," "Green Dodge Pickup Truck," "Blue Ford Pickup Truck" again, and "Red Ford Pinto." At 3:30 p.m., "Blue Chevrolet Nova to the house." At 3:45 p.m., "White Plymouth Valiant to the house." After that, another group of cars. At 7:00 p.m., "Blue Chevy Nova to the house." A few more cars were recorded after that, including the initials "B. R.," whatever that meant. Then at 9:30 p.m., unknown car to the house with a question mark. Sam ignored the other entries, just cars traveling up and down the road with drivers going about their daily lives. She was only interested in the cars that went to the house.

"I am assuming that the Nova and the Valiant belong to Mr. and Mrs. Leonard."

"Correct."

"Who owns the Camaro?" Sam asked, showing the Friday entry to Agnes.

"I don't know. Some man was driving it."

"Your log only records the times that the cars arrived at the house."

"Correct."

"So on Friday afternoon, Mr. and Mrs. Leonard arrived home, and she must have left again because according to your log, Mrs. Leonard returned home again at 7:00 p.m. So Mr. Leonard must have been at home. So just to be clear, is that correct?"

"No," Agnes said, shifting in her chair. "Mr. Leonard left shortly after he got home on Friday and didn't return."

"Okay. Then Mrs. Leonard must have driven away and returned again at 7:00 p.m."

"If that is what my log says, then that is correct."

Sam took a moment, trying to get the confusing time line straight in her head.

"So why are you keeping this log if it was your husband's hobby?"

"To keep his legacy alive, of course," Agnes quickly responded with authority.

"Which of these cars are owned by Mr. and Mrs. Leonard?" Sam asked, handing Agnes the notebook.

Agnes wrinkled her nose as she stared at the page. "Like I said, the blue car was driven by Mrs. Leonard, and the white car by Mr. Leonard. Are you deaf?"

"Please tell me again what you saw."

"Okay. You should be taking notes, young lady. As you can see, on Friday, Mrs. Leonard came home in her blue Chevy Nova about 3:30 p.m. and parked it in the garage. Then Mr. Leonard came home and parked his white Plymouth Valiant in front of the house. He came out a little later, placed a suitcase in the back seat of his car, and drove off."

Looking at the log book again, Sam asked, "Were these the only cars that drove into the farmplace on Friday that didn't belong to either Mrs. or Mr. Leonard?"

Agnes looked exasperated. "How many times do I need to repeat myself? A Chevy Camaro came at noon, and the blue Chevy Nova was also there. Then the unknown car came around 9:30 p.m.," Agnes said, pointing to the entries.

"Okay, okay. Mrs. Leonard and the guy driving the Camaro were the only people at the house at noon?"

"Yes."

"Did you recognize the driver of the Camaro?"

"No."

"Okay, so tell me again about that Friday night. I apologize for the repeated questions, but I am only trying to get a better picture of what you observed."

Agnes slumped down in her chair. "Well, I usually sit here until midnight if I can stay awake waiting and watching for ghosts. Friday night, at dusk, I saw a car enter the driveway and park in front of the house."

Sam felt her pulse quicken. "Did you see the make and model of the car?"

"No. Read the entry. Car unknown. It was a dark cloudy day. A day without sun. Well, anyway, it was too dark by then to see properly. I only saw the headlights."

"Could you recognize it by the headlights or taillights in the dark?"

"I wasn't paying that much attention. Remember, I was looking for ghosts."

"Was the dusk-to-dawn light on?"

"That light hasn't worked for months."

"How about the porch light? Was it turned on?"

"Yes, but it didn't help me see the car."

"What else did you see?"

"Another car drove up and parked on the shoulder of the road and turned its headlights off."

"Another car? Was the first car still was parked in the driveway of the house?"

"Yes."

Two cars? Sam mused. "What happened next?"

"About ten minutes later, the lights in the house and the porch were turned off, and a person left the house, jumped into his car, and sped down the driveway. The car turned west toward State Highway 69."

"Was it a man or a woman driving the car?"

"Can't say."

"Did that strike you as odd? That the lights were turned off and only one person exited the house?"

"Not really. I didn't think about it. The Leonard house had people and cars coming and going all the time."

"How about the second car sitting on the shoulder of the road?"

"Let me think . . . Oh yes, after the first car sped down the driveway and headed west, he switched on his headlights and drove away in the same direction as the first car."

"How far was he parked from the driveway?"

"I don't know, maybe 30 or 40 feet."

"Close enough to see the driver of the first car?"

"I suppose so. You would have to ask him."

"Did you find it unusual to see a car parked on the shoulder of the road, lights switched off, looking at the house?"

"Not at all. People have been doing that for years, hoping to see a ghost."

"When did you hear about the murder?"

"Saturday afternoon, when my neighbor delivered my groceries."

"Did you see a car pull up at the house around ten o'clock, Saturday morning?"

"Of course."

"Then did you see any other cars after that?

"Yes. Green County sheriff cars and a variety of others."

"What did you think?"

"I assumed that another murder occurred at Burr Oak Farm. Like I said, my neighbor confirmed it later that afternoon."

Sam was floored. Who was this woman sitting across her?

Agnes was staring straight at Sam.

"Do you believe in ghosts?" the old woman asked.

"I have never seen one."

"My aunt Mildred, who died twenty-five years ago, believed in ghosts. She saw them all the time. When her husband died from the fever, she had the undertaker remove his head, and she placed his skull on her bedstand. She rubbed it at night before going to sleep to remain close to him. Now that woman was a true believer and a real oracle."

A cold shiver ran down Sam's spine. "Anything else to add that you can remember?"

"I don't know if this is important, but after Mr. Leonard left Friday afternoon, Mrs. Leonard came out of the house, backed her car out of the garage, and drove away."

Agnes was repeating herself, but her comment got Sam's attention. "How long was it after Mr. Leonard drove away?"

"Now let me think . . . maybe a half hour, an hour, or so."

"How long was she gone?"

"She returned around 7:00 p.m."

"I can see that it isn't written in your log book, the time she left," Sam said.

"Why should it?"

Sam ignored her sarcasm. "Did it ever occur to you that you may be a witness? That the car you saw parked Friday night in front of the house could have been the killer?"

Agnes gasped. She turned pale as she clasped her arms around her chest. "He is going to come here and kill me! Mr. Death!" she shrieked.

Sam was stunned by her reaction. She gave her a moment to calm down. "No, I am not saying that at all. I think you are perfectly safe. I will only share this interview with Police Chief Johns. No one else will ever know what we talked about here today in the privacy of your home."

Agnes started shaking. She jumped up from her chair, backed away from Sam, and stared at her like a frightened animal. "You lied to me! You are Mr. Death! You tricked me into letting yourself into my home!" she screamed. She was shaking like a leaf.

Sam was flabbergasted. "I am not Mr. Death, and I didn't trick you. You have to believe me. I am who I said I was, a police officer, and I promise you that I will keep you safe."

Sam noticed that Agnes's shoulders relaxed a little, but her face was frozen in fear. "What do you want from me?" she asked.

Sam glanced down at the notebook. "I will need your spiral notebook. I promise that I will return it after I have thoroughly gone through it in a couple of days, then I will give it back. Is that okay with you?"

Agnes stared at her. "What choice do I have?"

Sam picked up the notebook and stood up. She thanked Agnes for seeing her and walked to the front door. Agnes followed her and watched as Sam unbolted the door. Once Sam was outside, she heard the sound of the bolts being shoved back into place.

CHAPTER 5

After leaving Mrs. Keel, Sam drove to the hospital to have lunch with Drew. She went to his office in the Physical Therapy Department, and Drew told her to go to the cafeteria. He would join her in fifteen minutes. The cafeteria was busy, but she found an empty table along the north wall to wait. She couldn't get Mrs. Keel out of her head. It was her state of mind that concerned her. The woman was obviously suffering from loneliness, anxiety, depression, and fear living in isolation from the rest of the world after her husband died. Her fixation on death was worrisome. But on the other hand, she had it together enough to chronicle the cars she saw traveling along Exeter Crossing Road and the comings and goings at the Leonard house. Sam briefly mulled over the idea of sending Social Services to check on Mrs. Keel.

Drew suddenly arrived with a big smile on his face, interrupting her thoughts. "Good to see you," he said.

Sam stood up, and Drew gave her a big hug. They each grabbed luncheon trays and went through the food-serving line and returned to the table with chicken salad sandwiches, Jell-O salad, and a glass of water. It was the same table that Sam had been sitting at, which afforded them some privacy.

They talked about Karin as they enjoyed their lunch. Sam was in love with the joy in her life and daddy's little princess. Her smiles and developing personality were bewitching. They could watch her for hours and marveled at their little miracle. She was now sitting and pulling herself up. She had a mischievous look in her eye as she tried crawling. When eating, she loved picking her food up with her index finger and thumb. And most importantly, she was sleeping through the night. As proud parents, they could talk for hours about her. When they finished eating lunch, Drew looked at his watch.

"I have ten minutes, so how did your interview go this morning?"

Sam quickly filled him in on the mental health of Mrs. Keel and her concerns for the elderly woman. Drew volunteered to help with Social Services by asking some of his hospital colleagues for advice. Sam was grateful for his interest. She also told him that she and Chief Johns were going to debrief the murder case in the afternoon and she should be home in time for supper. Drew told her that he would pick Karin up from Mrs. Sturzenegger at 4:30 p.m. and they could heat up some leftover pot roast for supper. After she left Drew, Sam's spirits were lifted. He had an aura, a confident way about him, that screamed that all was right with the world and not to worry. She dearly loved him for that.

When Sam arrived back at the PD, she went to her desk and wrote up her interview with Mrs. Keel. After she finished, she picked up and reviewed the spiral notebook pages that she borrowed from her. She was, after all, the "eye in the sky," doing surveillance on the Leonard home. Sam was convinced that the unknown car that came to the house after dark on the night of the murder belonged to the killer. *Find the owner of that car, find the killer,* she mused to herself.

At 2:30 p.m., Johns approached her desk. "Ready?" he asked.

Sam nodded and followed him into his office, taking the spiral notebook with her. He shut the door behind them and sat at his desk. Sam sat across him, staring at a manila file folder located on his desk. Johns picked it up and handed it to Sam.

"This is the sheriff's incident report, Dr. Ken's autopsy findings, and the forensics report. Take your time and read through them."

Sam took the folder, opened it, settled back in her chair.

After she finished reading the information, she handed the folder back to the chief.

Johns asked, "How did it go with Mrs. Keel?"

Sam spent the next few minutes filling in the chief on her visit to Mrs. Keel. He found it somewhat amusing, given the old lady's advanced age, state of mind, and that she was somewhat lucid. After she finished with her brief update, Sam asked for the file again and started reading, this time more slowly.

The sheriff's report didn't reveal anything new: the call from Cheryl Kubly-Schultz finding the murdered body of Stacy Leonard Saturday morning; the crime scene being secured; Dr. Ken confirming the approximate time of death; Albert Swenson taking crime-scene photos; the investigation being handed over to the Monroe PD; tracking down and telephoning Paul Leonard in Milwaukee, telling him of his wife's murder; Johns telling Leonard that he needed to go to the morgue and identify the body of his wife; and Dr. Ken performing the autopsy. Sam put the report down on her lap and sighed. Then she read through Dr. Ken's report. It stated that Mr. Leonard positively identified the body of his wife. It went on to say that she died sometime between 9:00 p.m. and midnight Friday. She was shot in the heart and chest by two bullets from a lightweight Smith and Wesson 9mm handgun at close range. Death would have been instantaneous. He added that the bullets were fired from the small-caliber pocket pistol with little recoil but capable of killing someone. He was handing the bullets over to the forensics team for their analysis. Otherwise, Stacy Leonard was in good health and had recently had sex. That last comment caught Sam's attention. *So according to Mrs. Keel, after Mr. Leonard left for Milwaukee Friday afternoon, Stacy also left the house and drove somewhere to meet her lover and returned home at 7:00 p.m.* She handed the folder back to Johns, who was watching her.

"I can see, by the expression on your face, that you found something interesting."

Sam smiled. "Am I that obvious?"

"So what did you find?"

"Something that Mrs. Keel told me. She said that after Mr. Leonard departed Friday afternoon, she watched Mrs. Leonard get into her car and drive off. She returned around 7:00 p.m. What piqued my interest was that she must have had sex during the time she was gone.

Remember Mr. Leonard saying that he hadn't had sex with his wife for quite some time?"

Johns nodded.

"Was she on the pill?" he interrupted.

"Good question. We will need to find out. Then as Mrs. Keel watched through her binoculars, an unidentifiable car arrived at the house around dusk. The driver entered the house. The visitor was there but a short time. The lights were then switched off in the house and the porch. The visitor then left in his car and drove off in the direction of State Highway 69. So according to Dr. Ken's report and the time of death, I am assuming that the driver of that mystery car must be the killer."

Johns leaned back in his chair and steepled his fingers. He was thinking. "Sounds plausible to me. So the person entering the house wouldn't have the time to have sex with Mrs. Leonard, kill her, and abruptly leave, turning out the lights?"

"Not according to Mrs. Keel."

"Were there any other cars accounted for at the house after the killer left?"

"No, but Mrs. Keel said that a car slowly drove up and parked on the shoulder of the road opposite the house about the same time of the murder. The driver switched off the headlights and waited."

"So this was at the same time the presumed killer was in the house?"

"Yes. I would think so."

"Why would he do that?"

"Mrs. Keel speculated it was one of those curious people who would show up from time to time at dusk, hoping to see a ghost."

"How long was the car sitting on the shoulder of the road?"

"Not long. The car drove off after the killer's car left the house."

Johns leaned back in his chair. "Curious," he said out loud, more to himself than Sam. "So tell me about Mrs. Keel," Johns said.

Sam glanced at the ceiling and paused for a moment, gathering her thoughts. "She is a sad case. Mrs. Keel has been a widow for two years and has isolated herself in her house from people and human contact.

She has a neighbor who buys her groceries, runs her errands, and drives her places she needs to go. Otherwise, she leads a lonely existence. She is terrified of death and has some bizarre thoughts about it, mostly centered on a Mr. Death, who, she is convinced, is waiting for her. She has three dead bolts on her front door to keep Mr. Death at bay."

Johns rolled his eyes. "Mr. Death? Was she coherent? By that, I mean, clear and sensible during your interview?"

"Yes, to some extent."

"So what is that spiral notebook in your lap all about?"

Sam handed it to the chief. "Mrs. Keel has an odd way of passing the time. When her husband was alive, they would sit a table overlooking Exeter Crossing Road and record the make and model of the cars that passed. To help them identify the cars, they looked through a pair of binoculars. They would keep a log of the comings and goings of their neighbors in the notebook."

Johns sighed. "Continue."

"I know, it sounds like a total waste of time. However, in this case, I think it might prove to be most helpful. They identified people by the cars they drove. In a way, they were like a hidden camera in the sky surveilling the road. For instance, Mrs. Keel knew the time when Mr. Leonard came home from work and left for Milwaukee, around 3:30 p.m., on the day his wife was killed."

Johns leaned forward in his chair. Sam had his full attention.

"She also remembered that a short time later, Mrs. Leonard left the house and returned around 7:00 p.m. Dr. Ken's report stated that she recently had sex. To my mind, that would suggest that she drove off to meet someone to have sex and returned home again at 7:00 p.m."

"Anything else?"

"Not really, unless you are interested in ghosts."

Johns laughed out loud. "I warned you. Okay, let's review what we have here. Oh, by the way, Scott Brady called and wants Mr. and Mrs. Leonard's fingerprints and anyone else who could have been at the house. He lifted five distinct fingerprints that need identification."

"Did he say anything else?"

"Not really, he was mostly concerned about the fingerprints. They didn't find anything of interest in the house."

"So where do we begin?" Sam asked.

"I find your notebook intriguing. We need to match any cars that were seen and logged at the farmhouse as to who their owners are. I think if we go back a month or two, that should be sufficient. It's imperative that we find Mrs. Leonard's lover. He could be a suspect or knows who the killer is. Also, we need to reinterview Mr. Leonard after his wife's funeral. I read the obit in the paper this morning. The Rettig Funeral Home is handling the arrangements, and the funeral service is this Thursday at 11:00 a.m. at the First Christian Church. We should attend."

Sam momentarily glanced at ceiling, remembering something. "What was Mr. Leonard's reaction when he identified the body?"

"Sorry. I should have mentioned it earlier. Well, he had no reaction."

"What do you mean?"

"When Dr. Ken drew back the corner of the sheet, exposing her face, Leonard just stared at her, fixating on her face. He showed no hint of emotion. I couldn't help but wonder what he was thinking. After less than a minute, he nodded and told us that the deceased was, indeed, his wife."

"That's all?"

"He turned around and left the viewing room without another word."

"What was your immediate reaction? Did you think he was numb seeing her body?"

"No. I was thinking it was something else."

"Guilt?"

"More like surprise, shock, I guess. He couldn't believe what he was seeing. If he had any emotional feelings toward his wife, he kept them well hidden."

Sam nodded. How strange. Was it shock, or was it guilt? "Moving on," Sam said, "how about Cheryl Kubly-Schultz? She may know something important, having Stacy Leonard as a choir member."

Johns agreed. "Can you schedule an interview with her?"

"No problem."

"Anyone else come to mind?" Johns asked.

Sam was thinking. Other than interviewing Mr. Leonard again and Cheryl Kubly-Schultz, is there anybody else? Perhaps Pastor Carl Peterson at the First Christian Church? Maybe he could shed some light on Stacy Leonard.

"I will speak to Pastor Carl about Stacy. Maybe he could be helpful," Sam said.

"Good. I will call Dr. Ken to get an impression of Mrs. Leonard's fingerprints. I have a meeting in La Crosse tomorrow afternoon and Wednesday morning about the status of state crime prevention. I will be staying overnight. I want you to schedule the interviews with Cheryl Kubly-Schultz and Pastor Carl during my absence. We can debrief when I get back later in the week. Does that work for you?"

Sam nodded. "I will make the appointments."

"By the way, how is little Karin doing?" Johns asked.

For the next fifteen minutes, Sam brought the chief up to date on the brilliance of the exceptional little girl she and Drew were raising. Chief Johns was all smiles as Sam rattled on.

CHAPTER 6

C heryl Kubly-Schultz was sitting in the living room of her home, waiting for Detective Gates to arrive. It was Wednesday morning, and the appointment was scheduled for ten o'clock. Cheryl awoke early, vacuumed, and freshened up her house for the visit. She baked some scones with dried cranberries to be served with coffee. Gates called her late Monday afternoon for the interview. After Cheryl discovered the dead body of Stacy Leonard last Saturday, she was badly shaken by the experience and the shock. She requested a week's vacation from work to sort herself out. She and Pastor Carl collaborated on the funeral music for Stacy. Tonight's choir rehearsal would practice and focus on the music requested by the family. Cheryl would sing a solo, "Amazing Grace," an uplifting funeral song specifically asked for by Stacy's parents. After tomorrow's service, a luncheon was going to be served at the First Christian Church for the grieving family, relatives, and friends of the deceased. Cheryl's heart was heavy as she sipped a cup of coffee, waiting for Gates to arrive. She was feeling a sense of loss, grief, and guilt.

She took her job as choir director very personally. Getting to know each choir member individually and their musical range and talent was important to her. They were family. When it became obvious to her that Stacy and Herbert were getting on more intimate terms with each other, should she have intervened? That thought now haunted her. Could she have helped in some way? Finding Stacy's body was devastating. How could she direct the choir without Stacy's sense of humor and smiling face? How about the other members? How would they be affected? When Detective Gates called for the interview, it threw her for a loop. She was now a part of the investigation. She talked to her husband Brian about the interview, and he volunteered to sit in on it with her for moral support, but she refused his offer. This was something that she needed to do on her own. Stacy had spoken to her in confidence about her failing marriage. How much of that should she share with Gates? After all, Stacy confided in her and trusted her. Then what about Herbert? He also shared his marital woes about Linda. What if Gates asked about that as well? How much did Gates already know? Cheryl once heard that police detectives often ask questions, when they already know the answers, to test people. Should she only answer the questions asked and not volunteer anything? If Gates later discovered that she had withheld critical information, would that put her in jeopardy? All these thoughts swirled around in her head as she waited. She was very nervous. Her hands were shaking. The striking gong of the teardrop pendulum antique clock sitting on the fireplace mantel rang out ten times. Cheryl stood up and walked to the picture window overlooking the street. A moment later, she saw an unmarked police car drive up and park. Detective Gates exited the car. She watched as Gates made her way up the sidewalk to her house. Cheryl went to the front door and opened it as the door chimes rang out. She invited Sam into her home. They went into the living room. Sam could hear the squeak of the white oak hardwood floors under her feet. She sat down on a high-backed cushioned armchair across from the sofa. Cheryl excused herself and went to the kitchen to fetch Sam a cup of coffee and a plate of scones. She returned and gave the cup of the hot black liquid to Sam and seated herself on the sofa. Sam picked up a scone and took a small bite. "Delicious," she said.

Cheryl waited for Sam to speak.

"Thank you for the coffee and the scones," Sam began.

She immediately observed that Cheryl was nervous. Maybe small talk was needed to calm her. She and Sam talked about the weather and the chance of rain. This inane conversation seemed to calm Cheryl.

"I know this is a difficult time for you, and I appreciate you seeing me today," Sam began.

Cheryl took a sip of her bitter coffee and nodded. "How can I help you?"

"I have read the sheriff's report of you finding Mrs. Leonard's body. It must have been quite a shock for you."

Cheryl placed her coffee cup down on the coffee table in front of the sofa. "Yes," she answered in a soft voice.

"Can you tell me why you went to see Mrs. Leonard Saturday morning?"

Cheryl shifted in her seat. "Stacy, Mrs. Leonard, forgot her music folder after our last choir practice. I had a meeting scheduled in New Glarus Saturday morning, and I was dropping off the folder at her home since it was on my way."

"When you got there, did you see her car?"

"No. I assumed that either she wasn't home or the car was in the garage."

"You didn't call her before you left your house to verify whether or not she was at home?"

"No. I didn't think of that. If she wasn't at home, I would just leave the folder on the front porch with a note."

"Did you know that her husband was in Milwaukee at a bowling tournament for the weekend?"

"Yes. She told me after choir rehearsal Wednesday night."

"Was that the last time you saw her alive?"

"Correct."

"Could anyone else have overheard Stacy telling you that Mr. Leonard was going to be out of town?"

The question caught Cheryl by surprise. "I suppose so. It was just part of a conversation I had with her. The other choir members were chatting and milling about ready to go home."

"So anyone of them could have overheard your conversation?"

"Yes."

"My next question is a sensitive one. Take your time and think carefully before you answer it. Okay?"

Cheryl nodded as she stared at Sam.

"Dr. Ken performed the autopsy. As part of his report, he stated that Stacy had sex prior to her death. Apparently, she and her husband were estranged, so do you have any idea whom she had sex with?"

Cheryl gasped, and her right hand flew to her face. She turned pale.

"Are you all right?" Sam asked, surprised by Cheryl's reaction.

Herbert! Cheryl immediately thought.

Sam waited, watching her closely. She had struck a nerve. Cheryl was thinking. A long moment passed.

"What was she thinking?" Sam asked herself. Finally, Cheryl seemed to compose herself, took another sip of coffee, and looked Sam in the eye. "I think I know who Stacy had sex with before she was killed," she stated in a low, sad, flat voice.

"Please tell me who and why you think so."

"I am 90 percent sure that it was Herbert Milz."

Sam squinted. "The owner of Milz Auto Sales?"

"Yes."

"Why do you think she had sex with him?"

Cheryl felt conflicted. She loved her choir members and wasn't bound by any confidentially agreements for what they shared with her. But in a way, she felt a strong sense of loyalty to them. But on the other hand, this was a murder inquiry of grave importance. She spoke slowly, measuring her words. "Both Stacy and Herbert sang in the choir. About three months ago, I noticed that their behavior changed. That was after Herbert returned from Florida."

"Was he there for a winter vacation?"

"His wife owns a house in Florida, and she resides there over the winter. Herbert only spends January and February with her because of his business interests here in Monroe."

"Did he return alone in March, leaving his wife in Florida?"

"Yes."

"And you believe that Herbert and Stacy started having an affair after he returned?"

"That was my impression. Stacy stands in front of him at choir practice, and I noticed her flirting with him and occasionally touching his hand. From where I stand directing the choir, I can see such things. Herbert was thoroughly enjoying the attention. It really lifted his spirits."

"So once again, did you think they were having an affair?"

"Yes, I was certain of it. It's like something you know without really knowing it. I was also aware that they both were in unhappy marriages."

"How did that make you feel?" Sam asked.

"Very concerned. They were wonderful Christian people, and the idea of an affair greatly distressed me."

"Did you take any action? For instance, talk to them about your concerns?"

Cheryl paused. Sam sipped her coffee, watching her. "On the morning I found her body, I had decided to express my feelings with her. If I knew about the affair, then other people probably knew as well. I needed to say the words, more for myself and to ease my own conscience."

Sam could visibly see her pain. Not only the horror of discovering the body, but also her personal connection to Stacy.

"Do you think either Paul Leonard or Linda Milz knew about the affair?"

"I don't know. If they did, I was unaware of it."

Paul Leonard suspected it, Sam mused to her herself.

Cheryl stood up to stretch her legs. "Can I get you another cup of coffee?"

Sam picked up her empty cup from the coffee table and handed it to her. Cheryl disappeared into the kitchen. Sam looked around the well-kept living room and admired a Steinway baby grand piano. When Cheryl returned with the cups of coffee, Sam asked her about the piano.

"My husband Brian bought it for me about three years ago. He had a client in Madison who sold it to him at a reduced price. We had it tuned up, and I spend hours playing it. I love the rich, deep tones. While I am playing, I am filled with joy."

"Will you play something for me after the interview?"

"I would be happy to play you something." Cheryl seemed more relaxed as she settled back into the sofa.

"Do you know of anyone who would want to harm Stacy?" Sam asked.

Cheryl shook her head. "Stacy was a fun-loving young woman. She admitted to me that she made a horrible mistake marrying someone older than herself. After the euphoria of the honeymoon had lifted, she saw his clay feet. Other than that, she loved her job being a music teacher at the high school."

"How about Herbert Milz? What do you know about him? Could he have killed her?"

Cheryl gasped. "Herbert?" she said in disbelief.

"I have to ask these questions as a part of our inquires. We need to eliminate people as possible suspects."

"Herbert is a kind, wonderful, caring man. He is well respected in the community. I will admit that he is somewhat shy and reserved, but a killer, absolutely not!"

"What prompted him to share some of his marital problems with you?"

Cheryl hesitated. "I was always kind to him. I suppose that he felt he could trust me. Everybody needs at least one person to confide in. For me, it's my husband Brian. By the way, do you know Linda Milz?"

"I have seen her a couple of times but never spoken to her," Sam replied.

Sam totally agreed and completely understood that trust was the basis of a relationship. Drew was her rock, and she trusted him with everything.

"How about Mrs. Linda Milz? What can you tell me about her?"

Cheryl shifted in her seat. "The only thing I know about her is town gossip and thirdhand information. I have seen her around the historic square, but I have never spoken to her."

"What have you heard?" Sam asked.

"Well, that she is a bitch of the first water. She is very rich and a country club member, a self-proclaimed diva. The rumor is that she can drink any sailor under the table with brandy old-fashions and walk away. My friends who know her can't stand her but apparently have found a way to tolerate her rudeness and bad behavior. After all, we all live in a small town."

"Why did Herbert marry her?"

"That's a very good question. The general consensus, for those who care to comment, is that she bullied him into the marriage."

"But why?"

"I suppose she panicked. Linda was getting older and decided that she needed companionship."

"Why not buy a dog?" Sam asked.

Cheryl laughed out loud. "Why not, indeed? This is hard to say, but Herbert is her punching bag. His only joys in life are managing his business and singing in the choir. He has an excellent tenor voice."

"Did Linda ever come to church to hear him sing?"

"Never. And I think that was okay with him."

"Do you think Linda knew about the affair?"

"I don't know. You would have to ask her."

"What do you think?"

"If you want my honest opinion, if she knew, she wouldn't care a jot or a tittle. From what little I know about the marriage, it was transactional and reeked of indifference. There is an old saying that goes something like to know yourself is to know what you have done. I don't think Linda has a clue."

"Harsh words," Sam replied.

"Sorry. I was only thinking of Herbert."

A sudden thought flashed across Sam's mind. She needed to learn more about Paul Leonard and his relationship with Stacy. She liked Cheryl for her honesty.

"One more thing before I go, do you have any thoughts about Paul Leonard?"

"Other than the fact that he is a very good pharmacist?"

"Yes, but more specifically, his marriage to Stacy."

Cheryl cast her eyes to the ceiling. "Here again, I only saw him at the pharmacy and heard the thirdhand tittle-tattle. Apparently, he was madly in love with his first wife. When she suddenly died in a tragic automobile accident, he was devastated. Two years later, he dated Stacy.

From what I understand, he was looking for a replacement wife, and Stacy had many of the attributes of his deceased wife. He was older than Stacy, but he overwhelmed her with outrageous expensive gifts and flattery. After the marriage, I didn't hear much until Stacy began speaking to me about him after choir practice. I was surprised by her candor."

"Do choir members normally speak to you about their personal lives after practice?"

"No. But sometimes they will share things with me. A choir director has a certain intimacy with the chorus. I often stay after practice for half an hour or more to talk, if someone wants to speak to me. I am a very good listener."

"What did Stacy say about her husband?"

"Only that he was fixated on his dead wife. Sometimes he would unwittingly call her Alice, the name of his first wife. His true intentions were soon revealed to her after their honeymoon. He was still in love with Alice. He got very angry when Stacy tried to exert herself as her own independent woman. They would often row over it."

"Was divorce in the future?"

"It was for Stacy. She told me she was looking for an exit strategy to end her unhappy marriage."

Sam leaned back in her chair. "Do you think that Herbert Milz was a part of her plan?"

"The thought did occur to me. He never would have divorced Linda because of his religious beliefs, so—and I hate to admit this—Stacy probably figured he was ripe for the picking, a means to an end."

"Thinking about it now, do you think that Paul Leonard found out about the affair and killed his wife?"

Cheryl heavily exhaled. Detective Gates had a way, through the probing questions she asked, to clear the mind. Was Paul Leonard, a highly-respected pharmacist, capable of murder? The question blindsided her. She didn't know what to think or say. Sam gave her the time she needed to puzzle it out. "I just don't know," Cheryl finally answered.

"That's okay," Sam responded. "This next question just occurred to me while I was talking to you. Please bear with me."

Cheryl curiously looked at her. "Fire away."

"I know this may seem far-fetched, but do you think that Stacy may have met someone else while having her affair with Herbert?"

Cheryl was taken aback. "What do you mean exactly?"

"Well, this is just a thought, but would it seem possible to you that Stacy could have been dating two men at the same time?"

Cheryl was floored. The idea was totally absurd. "So are you asking me if Stacy could have had two lovers at the same time?"

"Something like that."

"Absolutely not! First of all, she wouldn't do anything that awful to Herbert, and second, if she did have a second lover, she never mentioned it to me."

"But remember, she was having a secret affair with Herbert."

"It's not the same thing. Herbert is a kind gentleman. Why cheat on him?"

"You are probably right. After all, it was just a thought."

Sam's reply seemed to settle Cheryl down.

"I don't have any more questions," Sam said. A moment of quiet passed. "Anything that you might want to add?"

"Only that I wish I could have been a better friend to Stacy."

"Thank you for seeing me today and for the coffee. A hint of hazelnut? The scones were fantastic."

Cheryl smiled.

"Before I go, I want you to contact me if you think of anything else that may help our inquires, no matter how small or insignificant."

Cheryl nodded as Sam handed her a business card.

"One more thing, could you play me your favorite piece on the piano?"

Cheryl's face lit up as she slowly rose from her seat and headed to the piano. Sam turned in her chair to give Cheryl her full attention. She searched through several pieces of sheet music until she found what she was looking for and started to play "Moonlight Sonata" by Beethoven. Sam was immediately mesmerized, triggered by an unexpected emotional response to the beautiful music. As she listened, she was getting goosebumps. Her whole body relaxed. The music was transporting. It was like wave after wave of pure pleasure rushing over and through her body. Cheryl's performance was flawless and moving. After she finished, Sam stood up, broadly smiled, and clapped in appreciation.

"That was heavenly," she said almost teary eyed.

CHAPTER 7

I t was Thursday morning, the time was ten thirty, and Sam was sitting in the back row of the First Christian Church. The multicolored sunlight was shining brightly through the stained-glass windows, reflecting an array of rainbow colors across the sanctuary. Stacy's funeral visitation started at ten o'clock. Sam gave her condolences to the family and sat down to observe the mourners from the back pew. Family and friends were holding hands, hugging one another with teary eyes, saying their last goodbyes. Paul Leonard and Stacy's family welcomed the well-wishers in the rear of the church. An open casket was positioned in front of the sanctuary, near the altar, for people to file by and pay their last respects. Mary Peterson, Pastor Carl's wife, was softly playing familiar church hymns on the organ as a steady line of people slowly passed the casket. Sam recognized several schoolteachers and administrators standing in line to greet the family, as well as members of the congregation. Death has a way of bringing a community together. Sam watched as the funeral directors closed the casket and placed a mixed wreath of funeral flowers on the top. The fresh bouquet included roses, daisies, carnations, and gladiolus.

The choir processed up the aisle in their burgundy choir robes at 11:00 a.m. led by Cheryl Kubly-Schulz and followed by Pastor Carl Peterson. Cheryl and the rest of the choir looked sad and forlorn as they grieved the death of a good friend and a talented singer. The alto section would never be the same again without her voice. The church became quiet, earnest, and solemn. Missing from the choir loft was Herbert

Milz. Sam looked around the church, wondering if he would attend the funeral. A last-minute emergency prevented Chief Johns from attending with her, so Sam was on her own. *Was the killer in attendance?* That was the question Sam pondered as she surveyed the people crowded into the pews.

The pews were filled to capacity with mourners waiting for the service to begin. Pastor Carl gave a very emotional sermon, lifting up Stacy's short life and the resurrection. Tissues were plentiful, drying many wet teary eyes. Cheryl's solo of "Amazing Grace" was transporting and beautiful. The choir was impressively superb singing their hearts out for Stacy. Paul Leonard, the family, and the relatives all sat together in the first three rows. From where she was seated, Sam could see Paul and his stoic face. *What was he thinking? What was he feeling?* Sam thought to herself.

After the service concluded, the casket was wheeled out, followed by the family. There was going to be a short graveside service, followed by a luncheon in the basement of the church. After the family filed out, Sam went to the basement to wait, to listen, and to observe. The fellowship committee women had prepared potato casseroles, sandwiches, deviled eggs, salads, and fruit trays. Coffee, milk, and lemonade where at the ready. For those mourners not attending the graveside service, they got their food and sat at tables to converse and wait for the family to return. Sam joined them.

The talk around the table was one of shock and disbelief. "How could such a terrible thing happen to such a young, beautiful, and talented person?"

"The children are going to miss their beloved music teacher."

"That poor man. He is now grieving the loss of a second wife."

"He should burn down that damn haunted house and move to Monroe. The homestead is cursed. Everyone knows that!"

"Who could have done such a horrible thing to Stacy? Everyone loved her."

As the chatter droned on, Sam looked around the room. *Was the killer hiding in plain sight? Someone that everyone knew or thought they knew?*

The family returned from the cemetery and went through the food line. The volume in the room picked up as a number of people waited to offer their sympathies to Paul Leonard and the family. Sam excused herself and left the church. She decided to stop by Martha Sturzenegger's house to see little Karin before going back to the station.

Martha quickly answered the door and invited Sam in. She put her index finger to her lips. "Karin is down for a nap," she whispered.

Sam nodded. "I have just returned from Stacy Leonard's funeral."

"Can I get you a cup of coffee? I have just made it."

"That would be nice," Sam said as the aroma of freshly-brewed coffee filled the air. "I will look in on Karin while you are getting the coffee."

Sam went to a spare bedroom located on the first floor and gently pushed open the door. She tiptoed toward the crib sitting under the north window. Karin was fast asleep on her back. Her head was fully exposed with a light comforter covering her tiny body. Karin's little hands and feet were slightly moving with uncoordinated innocence. Was she dreaming? As Sam stared at her little darling, Karin was making funny, weird noises as she slept. Was she snoring? Sam was mesmerized as she watched her little angel fast asleep. Suddenly, Sam felt a slight tug at her elbow. She turned and saw Martha standing behind her. "I can stand here for hours watching Karin sleep," she whispered to Sam. Sam agreed.

Back in the living room, Sam and Martha sat enjoying their coffees. "I heard about the death of Stacy Leonard," Martha said.

"Did you know her?"

"Not really. I know more about her husband."

"Paul Leonard?"

"Yes."

"What can you tell me about him?"

"Well, he comes from a very nice farming family. We went to the same country Lutheran church. He got into a bit of trouble in high school."

Sam sat up in her seat and looked directly at Martha. "What kind of trouble?" Sam asked.

"Oops. Maybe I shouldn't have mentioned it."

"That's okay. What happened?"

"Well, it was girl trouble," Martha replied, sipping her coffee, wondering if she had spoken out of turn.

"Can you explain?"

"Well, from what I remember, he was dating a girl and another guy became interested in her. According to Paul's mother, who told me in confidence, he became jealous and confronted his rival at school. As you can imagine, one thing led to another, and they ended up in a fistfight. The police were called in, and they were both found guilty of disturbing the peace or something like that and given a sealed juvenile record and a number of hours of community service work to perform. It was the second offense for the other teenager."

Sam's eyebrows narrowed. "I interviewed Paul Leonard concerning the death of his wife, and he didn't strike me as being a violent sort of man."

"I don't think he is either," Martha quickly replied. "After that unfortunate incident in high school, he turned out very well, going to college and becoming a pharmacist."

There was a pause in the conversation as Martha finished her cup of coffee.

So when provoked, Paul Leonard could become violent, Sam thought to herself. She looked at her watch and stood up. She needed to leave for the police station to meet with the chief. Before she left, she thanked Martha for the coffee. Then she looked in on Karin who was still peacefully sleeping. Her little darling was purring like a kitten. She reached down with her index finger and softly stroked Karin's soft pink cheek. Touching her child so tenderly brought on an overwhelming feeling of love and sweetness to her heart. It was hard for her to leave. The bond between mother and child was strong. Tearing herself away,

Sam gave Martha a hug, thanking her again for taking such good care of her daughter.

When Sam arrived at the station, Chief Johns was waiting for her. They went into his office and closed the door.

"How was the funeral?" Johns asked, sitting back in his chair.

Sitting across him, Sam paused for a moment, letting her last image of Karin's face fade from her memory. "The funeral was sad but nice. Pastor Carl was at his ecclesiastical best, and the choir sounded heavenly. I didn't see anyone in attendance who stood out as not belonging there. If the killer was in the church, he didn't stand out."

"Was Herbert Milz there?"

"No, he wasn't."

"We urgently need to interview him. He could become a prime suspect."

"I agree. You know how complicated these love triangles can be. By the way, what was the emergency that kept you away from the funeral?" Sam asked.

Johns laughed. "The mayor called and said that his next-door neighbor's house had been broken into last night. He wanted me to investigate."

"Why did you laugh?"

"Politics. Well, anyway, as it turned out, the teenage son of his neighbor stole some money from his father and made it look like a burglary."

"How did you figure that out?"

"When I talked to the kid about the break-in, I immediately knew he was lying. After all, I have teenage kids myself. I gave him that 'I am going to send you to prison for the rest of your life look if you don't tell me the truth,' and he immediately cracked. He was very nervous and confessed to the whole thing."

"Did you arrest him for wasting police time?"

"I should have. But he got off with a stiff warning. Changing subjects, I spoke again to Scott Brady, and there wasn't much forensics evidence at the scene of the crime. However, he came up with four identifiable sets of fingerprints. He was able to match Paul Leonard,

Stacy Leonard, Cheryl Kubly-Schultz, and found one unknown print on a bottle of Brandy."

"Where was Cheryl's fingerprints?"

"On the front doorknob and the living room telephone."

"Where was the Brandy bottle located?"

"In the liquor cabinet."

"So it probably wasn't the killer's prints," Sam thoughtfully replied.

"Hard to say for sure, but I don't think so."

"Did the killer wear gloves?"

"Good question. Either that or he wiped everything clean before he left. Now your witness, Agnes Keel, said the killer was there for only about ten minutes. Do you think the murder was premeditated? Planned? After all, the killer had a gun with him."

"Or her, if you will."

Johns smiled. "Okay, her."

"The gun was a small Smith and Wesson 9mm pistol. In many respects, a woman's handgun. Small enough to carry in a purse," Sam said.

"Very true."

Sam cast her eyes to the ceiling. "Just think about this for a moment. Perhaps the murder wasn't premeditated. The killer brought the gun to scare Stacy, but something went terribly wrong, and Stacy was accidently shot. It's been known to happen."

"Okay, if it was an accident, why didn't the killer report it?"

"Good point."

"Either way, Stacy is dead, and we need to find the killer. Anything else?" Johns asked.

"Yes. Agnes Keel said that a car pulled up and parked on the shoulder of the road across the Leonard house and turned off the headlights about the same time that the killer's car was at the house. She assumed it was just another person interested in seeing ghosts. After the killer fled the scene, the car turned its headlights on and drove away in the same direction as the killer. Is it a coincidence that a car parked on the side of the road is there at the exact same time of the murder?"

Johns steepled his fingers. He was thinking. "We need to find the driver of that car. I will contact the newspapers in New Glarus and here in Monroe to run a notice requesting help from anyone who was on Exeter Crossing Road at the time of the murder. Hopefully, someone will read it and come forward."

"Sounds like a plan," Sam said.

"By the way, how did your interviews with Pastor Carl and Cheryl Kubly-Schultz go?

"Pastor Carl didn't have anything new to offer. Cheryl confirmed the affair but couldn't come up with anyone who wished harm to Stacy. Cheryl is riddled with guilt. She feels she could have done more to prevent Stacy's tragic death."

"Okay. I want you to interview Herbert Milz. From what we know, he was having an affair with Stacy. I want you to confirm that. Also, did something go sideways during the affair that caused her death? Passions normally run white hot when sex is involved."

Sam nodded. "So what about another interview with Paul Leonard? I think we need to take a closer look at him."

"Let's wait until next week. He buried his wife today, and we need to give him some time and space. So what about Milz?"

"I will call him later this afternoon to schedule the appointment. I can do it tomorrow, if he is available."

"Good idea. Anything else?" Johns asked.

"I copied Agnes Keel's spiral notebook. I plan to match cars and names of people together to get a better idea who visited the Leonard house. I must admit, though, the mysterious car parked on the side of the road at the time of the murder has me spinning out different theories."

"Do you care to elaborate?"

"Maybe later."

"I will schedule the appointment and interview Herbert Milz," Sam said.

CHAPTER 8

fter their meeting on Thursday, Sam placed a call to Herbert Milz at his business. She could hear the nervousness in his voice as she asked for an appointment to interview him about the death of Stacy Leonard. He wanted to know if it was necessary. Sam told him that his name came up during their investigation and that he may have information pertinent to the case. After a long pause, he agreed, but he didn't want to meet at the police station, his place of business, or his home. He was most emphatic about where the meeting wasn't to take place. His defensiveness surprised Sam. He offered to meet her at his tiny cabin overlooking Lake Beckman in Cadiz Springs on Friday at 5:00 p.m. He felt it was a safe place to meet and wouldn't bring any unwanted attention to the interview. Sam thought about it for a moment and agreed to meet him there. He gave her directions. After she hung up, Sam felt very uncomfortable about going to Cadiz Springs alone and asked the chief to accompany her. Johns readily agreed, thinking her request made sense. After all, it would be better having two officers present being that Herbert could become a prime suspect. But Milz called her back to reschedule the meeting for Saturday morning. Sam reluctantly agreed and was glad the chief was also available on Saturday.

On Friday, Karin had her routine nine-month physical checkup at the hospital. The interview with Milz being delayed until Saturday worked out well for Sam, so she could have the whole day off, attending to Karin's needs. The appointment was at 11:00 a.m. with a woman pediatrician who was tracking Karin's growth and development. Karin was up for the task as the doctor checked her measurements, heart, lungs, reflexes, joints, eyes, ears, and mouth. The doctor was gentle during the examination, talking to Karin as she went about her work. Karin was cooing and seemed to enjoy the attention. The doctor also checked the shape of baby's head for soft spots to make sure they were developing properly. At the end of the examination, blood was drawn to check for iron and lead. Karin gave out a yelp when she was jabbed. She clearly didn't enjoy this part of the exam. Sam scooped her up in her arms and comforted her by drying the tears away. The news was all very good, and Karin was declared a healthy baby. After she left the doctor's office, Sam went to the Physical Therapy Department to see Drew. Her hopes to have lunch with him were dashed. Drew's supervisor was to attend a scheduled meeting at the Parkview Nursing Home, but at the last minute, Drew was tapped to fill in for him. Sam was disappointed but understood. She gave him a quick summary of Karin's doctor visit and told him more details would follow at supper. She went home and spent a delightful afternoon with her daughter.

Johns arrived at the station at 9:30 a.m., Saturday. Cadiz Springs was an easy fifteen-minute drive from Monroe, so they had time to discuss the tenor of the interview. It was decided that Sam would take the lead and Johns would observe. Johns felt that Sam could put Milz at ease during an intrusive interview. Johns told Sam that he was familiar with Lake Beckman and Zander Lake, being that his father took him there fishing in his youth. It was a peaceful place where fishing and relaxing made for an idyllic day. They left the station in the chief's car and headed west on State Highway 69 to Cadiz Springs Road on a sun-drenched warm day. Turning south, they traveled a half mile through a stand of mature tall pines along a windy road to the cabin Milz owned that was located on the east side of the road. A light-yellow Pontiac Firebird was parked next to the cabin. Johns slowed down and tuned up the short gravel driveway, parking next to the Firebird. As they exited the car, Milz came out of the log-style cabin with a tin roof and waved to them. He greeted them on the front porch and ushered them inside.

The cabin was small but comfortable, about 800 square feet of living space. A grouping of comfortable cushioned chairs in the living room surrounded a large picture window facing west to Lake Beckman. The lake was barely visible through the pines and leafed-out trees. The red oak hardwood floors were covered with throw rugs. A small kitchen, bathroom, and bedroom completed the floorplan of the cabin. A well-used blackened stone fireplace was located along the north wall. Milz offered them a cup of coffee after they had seated themselves on the chairs. He seemed very nervous, but fetching the coffees seemed to calm him. After he distributed the steaming coffee in ceramic mugs, he joined them and set his cup on the coffee table in front of him. His hands were shaking. He glanced at the chief and then back to Sam, waiting for one of them to speak.

"This is a very nice cabin," Sam began. "How long has it been in your family?"

Johns smiled.

A visible wave of relief swept over Milz. He was delighted with the question and immediately responded. "My grandfather purchased this piece of land some fifty years ago. My father helped clear the pines, and they both built this cabin. It was a labor of love. I spent many hours here during my youth, fishing and boating on Lake Beckman. If you are interested, I could tell you about the area."

Sam nodded. "Please continue, it is really beautiful here."

Milz smiled. "Well, there is a spring-fed creek that runs through this driftless area. The creek was damned up, causing a reservoir covering approximately 90 acres. The lake isn't very deep. I would say about 6 feet. Every year the lake is stocked with fish. I have caught northern pike, yellow perch, and largemouth bass to name a few. We clean and pan fry them. Absolutely delicious!"

Milz paused. Sam and Johns were paying close attention, so he continued. "My father was very interested in the many varieties of birds and kept a list of them. They included sandhill cranes, killdeer, great blue heron, wood ducks, mallards, and Canada geese. At night we could hear the common loons on the water." Milz stopped talking for a moment, reliving the good memories.

Sam interrupted his thoughts. "Thank you for seeing us today," Sam said, jerking Milz back to reality.

He sat straight up in his chair, staring at her with wide-open eyes.

"We are here today to interview you in the hope of shedding light on the death of Stacy Leonard. Like I said on the telephone, your name came up, and we need your help."

Milz took a sip of coffee. "So what do you want to know?"

"When did your affair with Stacy start?"

The question was a gut punch. Milz felt light-headed. *Should I tell the truth?* He hesitated, thinking about his dilemma. He decided to tell the unvarnished truth as painful as that may be.

"We both sang in the choir at the First Christian Church. I was a tenor, and she was an alto. She stood directly in front of me at choir rehearsals on Wednesday nights. Late last fall, before I went to Florida for two months, Stacy and I became acquainted."

"Acquainted?" Sam asked.

"By that, I mean that Stacy suddenly became interested in me, and we flirted with each other, just for laughs. I do not love my wife—in fact, I loathe her—and the attention Stacy gave me was life-saving. She was very cute and reminded me of a high school cheerleader that I fell in love with from a distance. Anyway, something awakened inside me, and I felt like a little kid full of fun and laughter. I really can't explain the feeling, but she was very kind to me and showed me the respect I desperately needed . . ." Milz paused.

"Explain," Sam said.

Johns was focused on Milz whose face was flushed red.

"My wife Linda is a bitch. For some reason, she decided to marry me after she turned thirty. She is a very strong-willed woman and always gets what she wants. She is filthy rich and an alcoholic. To give you some idea of our unhappy marriage, I will tell you that I have been shrieked at, berated, humiliated, and stepped on like an old rug—a living hell. She takes great pleasure in living out her life in a gleeful rage against society and me. By contrast, I admit that I am a weak-willed man by nature with a pleaser personality. Well, anyway, she bullied me into marrying her. I sold my modest house and moved in to her gigantic house located on the golf course at the country club. She paid off all my personal debts, but I had the gumption to stand up to her to keep and manage the auto business." Milz stopped talking. He looked tired. The bitterness in his voice was clearly visible. This was way more information than Sam expected.

"So why did you marry her?" Sam gently asked.

"I hate to admit this, but I was weak. I knew what I was doing, but what was I thinking? Before we married, occasionally, we would play golf together in a foursome. She was a terrible golfer, swearing constantly and cheated in every way possible to break 120 on her score card and then laugh about it after the round. It was disgusting. I am a bogey golfer, and I hate it when someone cheats to improve their score. Anyway, back to your inquiry, that was the question that I have asked myself over and over and over again to the point of madness. I will tell you this, I can remember my wedding day like it was yesterday, and if it was tomorrow, I wouldn't have shown up."

Johns chuckled at his remark.

"Well, anyway, I figured out, only too late, that Linda was desperate and wanted a husband, not a relationship. I was easy prey for her and her diabolical scheme. I sold my soul to the devil, sacrificing my pride for shame these past four years." Herbert looked terrible.

Sam let the moment pass. "So let's get back to Stacy."

"When I returned to Monroe in March, Stacy and I picked up where we had left off. Linda was in Florida until mid-April, so I was alone to enjoy the flirting. It was a euphoric feeling. She gave me wings to fly, if you know what I mean, a reprieve from my life-sentence marriage to Linda. After a couple of choir practices, Stacy stayed behind and kissed me on the cheek in the parking lot. My whole body reverberated with exploding fireworks. I was in love. The unimaginable just happened. I couldn't sleep at all that night."

"Did you ask yourself why Stacy was interested in you?"

"No. It didn't matter. My whole body was quivering with excitement, and I couldn't wait to see her again. After church services that following Sunday, she asked me if there was any place we could meet in secret. I was stunned. I suggested we meet here at the cabin on Tuesday. No one would know or care driving along Cadiz Springs Road. Her teaching hours at the high school varied, so she said she would call me at the sales office and tell me what time we could meet. However, she needed to be home by 5:30 p.m."

"How did that make you feel?"

"It was like I was in a dream because I couldn't believe what was happening to me. My emotions were in overdrive. I was blinded by the idea that she really cared for me. I couldn't concentrate at work. She called me on Tuesday at work, and we arranged to meet that afternoon at three thirty. I got here early and waited, pacing around the cabin. Was she really going to show up? At the appointed time, I saw her blue Chevy Nova slowly coming down the road and parked next to my car. She gave me a big hug and a kiss. As you can imagine, my hormones were flying off the chart. I made her a gin and tonic, and we briefly chatted. What happened next put me in a daze. We rushed into the bedroom, stripped off our clothes, and made love. She was like a goddess. When I embraced her, there was no other sound in the world but our own breathing. Afterward, we talked, and she left, promising to come back later in the week, on Friday."

"Did she?" Sam asked.

Johns was listening with his mouth wide open.

"Yes, on Friday. After that, we started seeing each other twice a week.

"What did you talk about?" Sam asked.

"Mostly about our unhappy marriages. She told me that she was going to divorce her husband."

"Did she tell you that she loved you?"

Milz hesitated and hung his head. "No."

"How did that make you feel?"

"I told her that I had fallen in love with her."

"How did she respond?"

"She kissed me on the cheek and told me that Linda was an idiot. Look, I hated my wife, but I would never leave her, a religious thing, my Catholic upbringing, if you know what I mean. It's a terrible thing to love someone and you can't do anything about it."

"So why was she shagging you?"

"I asked myself that same question. I think she was at her wits' end, and I was safe. She could talk to me in confidence."

"Did you tell anyone about the affair?"

"No."

"Do you think your wife knew?"

"Hell no. And if she did, she wouldn't have given a shit!"

"Why was that?"

"The old bitch only wanted someone to snuggle up against at night. You know, something about having to sleep with a man. Shortly after our marriage, we got twin beds. Anyway, she didn't love me. I think a stuffed animal would have done the trick for her. She also reeked of alcohol and cigarette smoke, not to mention that she snored like eighty-year-old toothless man. I can't remember the last time we had sex."

Johns chuckled.

"So she didn't know about the affair as far as you were concerned?"

"If she knew, she never mentioned it."

"How about Mr. Leonard? Did he know?"

"Stacy said he only suspected it."

"So your affair was pretty much a secret?"

"I suppose so. If anyone knew, they never mentioned it to me."

Sam paused and thought about her next question. "Was Stacy on the pill?"

"She told me she was. We had unprotected sex."

"Let's talk about the day of the murder."

The color drained out of Herbert's face. He slumped down in his chair. "What do you want to know?"

"Tell us your movements."

Herbert shifted in his chair and looked out the window. "About two weeks before her death, things began to cool off between us. Instead of coming here two times a week, she only came once a week. She was changed. Something was on her mind."

"Did she talk about it?"

"No, but I knew something was wrong. My worst fear was that she was thinking about ending the affair."

"Did you see her the week of her death?"

"She called and said she was very busy that week and that her husband was going to Milwaukee for the weekend. He was leaving Friday afternoon, so she wouldn't be able to see me. I was devastated."

"So you didn't see her?"

"Friday afternoon, she called me and wanted to meet at the cabin. I was overjoyed. After she arrived, we shared a drink and had sex. I was beside myself with excitement. Then the shoe dropped. She told me that she was very sorry, but we couldn't see each other again. I asked her why, but she said it was personal. She told me I was a great guy and thanked me for being there when she needed someone. She kissed me on the cheek and drove away."

Sam's mind was spinning. Dr. Ken's report stated that Stacy had recently had sex. "So what happened next?"

Herbert sat silent, looking down at his hands. After Stacy left, he collapsed into a chair, staring out the window. He felt like a huge wild beast had landed on his chest, tearing his heart to shreds. He could barely breathe. When Stacy closed the door behind her, it was like slamming the door shut on his heart and their special relationship.

"I was crushed. I cleaned up the cabin and went to work. I arrived there around 5:30 p.m. I have a bottle of Wild Turkey whiskey in my desk drawer and sipped on that after the employees left for the day. I felt terrible, like suddenly losing someone that I passionately loved. I was consumed with sadness and loss. I could hardly breathe. I was in a state of shock and despondency, a living hell."

"What time did you go home?"

"Sometime between 9:30 p.m. and 10:00 p.m."

"Can you be more specific than that?"

"I wasn't paying attention to the time."

"Was your wife at home?"

"She was passed out on the living room sofa when I arrived, snoring heavily. I helped her into bed, and I had a fitful night's sleep. I probably only got about an hour of sleep."

"When did you hear that Stacy had been murdered?"

"The next day at work. Donna told me. She is my secretary. I couldn't believe it. I was sick."

"Did it occur to you to come forward and contact the police?"

"No."

A silence fell between them as Milz wrung his hands. This interview was taking its toll. "Can you think of anyone who wanted to harm Stacy?"

Milz shook his head. "No. Everyone loved her."

"Do you own a handgun?"

"No. I have two shotguns and a deer-hunting rifle."

"Does your wife own a handgun?"

"No, I don't think so. If she does, I have never seen it."

"I didn't see you at the funeral. Why was that?"

"I couldn't face it without breaking down. I truly loved her. I have also decided to drop out of the choir. It would be too painful for me to remain."

"Have you ever been to Stacy's house?"

"Yes, once. I was in New Glarus and stopped by to see her on the way home."

"Was she expecting you?"

"No. In fact, she wasn't happy to see me, so I immediately left. I cursed myself on the way home for my stupidity."

Sam smiled to herself. Mrs. Keel had recorded seeing a yellow Pontiac Firebird at the house in her notebook. A long silence passed between them. Sam glanced at the chief who shook his head.

"Is there anything else that you can think of that could help our investigation?'

"Does my wife need to know?" Herbert asked. He had an odd mysterious look on his face, like he was reflecting on his fate.

"Not at this time. However, we may need to interview her, given your affair with Stacy. But for now, what we talked about today will stay between Chief Johns and myself. By the way, what was the last thing you said to Stacy before she left?"

"I told her that I loved her," Herbert said in a low voice.

"Is there anything special about your wife that we need to know that you haven't told us?"

"Like what?"

"Anything that comes to mind."

Herbert raised his eyes to the ceiling. "One thing that is very strange, unnerving in a way, she has a spiritual advisor who lives in Madison named Madame Lulu. She specializes in tarot card reading, and Linda is besotted with her."

"Why is that?"

"Years ago, when Linda was in Madison, drinking with her friends one weekend, just for laughs, they all went to see Madame Lulu for a reading. She read Linda's cards and predicted that someone close to her was going to die. And sure enough, shortly afterward, her parents were killed in airplane crash. Spooky, if you ask me. Linda was convinced that the old hag could predict the future and has paid her an outrageous amount of money over the years. I tried to point out to Linda that she made all of Madame Lulu's predictions come true through her own volition. I told her that her shady fortune-teller was evil and a fraud. She promoted the devil's work."

"How did Linda react?"

"She cursed me and threw a glass of brandy at me. End of story. Full stop."

"Did Linda consult Madame Lulu before she married you?"

"Of course, she did. What a hack!"

Johns laughed out loud. Herbert looked relieved that the interview was over. They all stood up. Sam thanked him for the coffee and told Herbert that they would stay in touch and if he thought of anything else, to be sure to contact them.

* * *

"So what do you think?" Johns asked Sam as he backed out of the driveway, turned his car around, and drove to Monroe.

"I think he is holding something back. It seems to me that he truly loved Stacy. And I believe he did. The passion he felt for her could have driven him to do something terrible after Stacy ended the affair. I once heard that a love obsession can cause a man to fall madly, illogically, miserably, passionately, and all-consuming in love. Maybe he drank himself into a stupor when he returned to work and snapped. Just think about it for a moment. Stacy—the one person he truly loved—jilted him by ending the relationship. The rejection had to be an enormous blow to his ego. When he got back to the office, did the dam burst with an aching heart and a flood of tears? What was he to do? Was he angry, confused, or revengeful? Did he become irrational? Did he go to her house and murder her? Revenge can be a strong and overwhelming emotion. He probably felt betrayed. It can quickly turn into a misguided response to anger, injury, or humiliation. When does love become an obsession? Could that have been a motive for murder?"

Johns didn't respond for a long minute. "I can see your logic. You have a very good point, and it could have happened that way. But first, we need the facts to thoroughly check out his alibi. Was he telling us the truth or not? And remember, he was the last person to see her alive . . ." He paused again, thinking about what Sam had said. "By the way, I thought your interview was superb."

Sam blushed. "All that I know I learned from you!"

Johns chuckled at her tongue-in-cheek sense of humor. They agreed to break for lunch to mull over the interview and to meet again in the afternoon at one thirty. When they reconvened, they rehashed the interview with Milz and decided to thoroughly investigate his movements on the night Stacy was murdered. They both agreed that he was the prime suspect for now.

CHAPTER 9

After the interview with Herbert Milz Saturday morning and meeting with the chief in the early afternoon, Sam spent the rest of the day with Drew and Karin. On Sunday, they went to church, and the choir was in full voice singing the uplifting anthem "The Lord Is My Shepherd" with heartfelt passion and strong feelings. There was little doubt that Stacy Leonard was on their minds and in their hearts. After church services, Sam and Drew had lunch at home and went to Twining Park to enjoy the warm, sun-drenched afternoon. Sam was wearing a kangaroo-style baby wrap around her shoulder. Karin was nestled in the tight space fast asleep as they casually walked and talked while walking around the park. The robins were bouncing around, looking for worms, and the squirrels were chasing one another. The tennis courts were active, a softball game was in progress, and a shelter house was hosting a family gathering. This was a picture-perfect, relaxing day to be outside and to get lost in the wonderment of it all among the laughter and merriment in the park, a day where the people of Monroe were thoroughly enjoying themselves.

Drew was interested in the case, asking questions, so Sam felt comfortable filling him in by giving a brief summary. Drew wasn't shy about stating his opinions and his theories of the murder. Sam found this quite amusing, but she gave him all the rope he needed to hang himself on the intertwined threads he was trying to pull together. At first, he was convinced that Paul Leonard faked his stomach illness, drove home from Milwaukee, murdered his wife, and drove back to

Milwaukee. His motive was jealously and a $10,000 life insurance policy. It had to be him. But on the other hand, Herbert Milz could also be the killer. He was in love with Stacy, and she dumped him. "Unrequited love," Drew speculated, a crime of passion.

After spinning all this out for about a half an hour, Drew gave up. He assured Sam that her job was secure, admitting he didn't have a clue as to what he was talking about. Sam laughed, hugged him, and thanked him for his ideas. She told him that she would certainly follow-up on his suggestions.

Drew smirked. "Go ahead, make fool of me. I deserve it!"

Sam got a good belly laugh from his sarcasm, waking Karin. Drew also chuckled as Karin struggled to wake up. They went home, popped some corn for supper, put Karin to bed, and made love. They both slept very soundly and got a good night's sleep. The next day, Sam was going to visit Agnes Keel and return her spiral notebook.

Monday morning, Sam and the chief briefly discussed reinterviewing Paul Leonard. The chief suggested Wednesday morning would be a good time, and Sam agreed. The interview would take place at the station at nine o'clock.

Sam left the PD and drove north toward New Glarus to Exeter Crossing Road to the home of Agnes Keel. She was concerned about Mrs. Keel's well-being and state of mind. After arriving at the house, she knocked two times. She noticed Agnes peeking out the picture window. She unbolted the front door and ushered Sam in. Once inside the house, Agnes slammed the bolts back into place. While she was doing this, Sam heard the grandfather clock chime. The pendulum was merrily swinging back and forth.

"Can I get you a cup of coffee? I made it for myself a little while ago, but since you are here, I can spare a cup for you," Agnes said, staring at Sam, looking at the familiar spiral notebook in her hand. She was dressed in her pink bathrobe and wearing her pink Dearfoam bedroom slippers.

"That would be nice."

"Go ahead and sit by the window. I have started another notebook since you took my other one."

"I am returning your notebook as I promised," Sam said.

"I am not blind. I can see you are holding it in your hand. Put it on the table."

With that, Agnes went into the kitchen to fetch the coffee. Sam sat down and looked out over the cornfield at the Leonard house. The sun was shining brilliantly in cloudless blue skies, and the birds were gliding across the cornfield. She noticed a red-tailed hawk circling lazily in the sky. Agnes returned and set Sam's coffee cup down. She then sat down opposite Sam. Agnes picked up her own cup and took a sip.

"Did you find anything useful in my notebook?" Agnes asked.

"Yes. And thank you again for loaning it to me."

"Well, as I recall, I didn't have much of a choice, did I?"

Sam took a sip of coffee and nearly gaged. Agnes must have put three tablespoons of sugar in it. Sam hurriedly set the cup down.

"What, you don't like coffee?" Agnes asked, closely eyeing her.

"I love coffee, but I have already had four cups today."

"So why didn't you say so?"

Changing the subject, Sam pointed to the grandfather clock. "By the way, I noticed that your clock is up and running. Did you wind it?"

"Heaven's no. Jeffery came back from the grave and visited me last night. I talked to him for an hour, causing me to oversleep this morning."

Sam's jaw dropped in disbelief. "Can you say that again?"

"What's the matter with you? Weren't you listening? Are you deaf?"

"Yes, I was listening, but I was surprised. Can you tell me what happened last night?"

Agnes took a big gulp of coffee. "If you really want to know, I woke up at 3:00 a.m. The chimes going off woke me up. After all, they have been silent for two years. I immediately knew that Jeffery was in the house. I leapt out of bed, threw on my bathrobe and slippers, rushed into the living room, and turned on the lights."

"What did you see?"

"The pendulum of the grandfather clock was swinging back and forth, and the time was correct. Jeffery must have set it."

"Did you see him?"

"Yes. I mean, I saw his figure, which was barely visible, like a mist, sitting in the armchair across from the clock. It was him, and he looked good."

He is dead, Sam thought, shaking her head. "What did you talk about?"

"We didn't exactly talk like you and me, but I knew what he was saying. I told him that I dearly missed him and was keeping up his car log. He was happy to hear that. I told him about the murder at the Leonard house, and he said he wasn't surprised. Too many deaths haunted that place."

"What else did he say?"

"Well, he told me not to be afraid of death, it isn't so bad."

Sam had a hard time trying not to laugh. Agnes probably wound up the clock herself and set the time. Her seeing Jeffery was probably a dream or a hallucination, something that she desperately yearned for. Old age can play tricks on the mind as well as memories.

"So do you think he will return for another visit?"

"I hope so. After he faded away, I went over to the chair and felt the cool air where he had been sitting, a sure sign that he was really there and I wasn't having illusions."

Sam shook her head. She really needed to contact Social Services. "Have you seen anything interesting at the Leonard house?"

"Like what?"

"Like Mr. Leonard coming and going . . . ?"

"He is like clockwork and very predictable. He parks his car in the garage in the same place Stacy used to park her car. He leaves the house every morning at seven thirty in his white Plymouth Valiant. He returns home about five thirty and is in for the night."

"Where is Stacy's car?"

"How should I know? He probably sold it."

"Do any other cars visit the house?"

"Not that I have seen, but I am spending more and more time in the bathroom these days, GI tract problems."

Sam let the comment go without any further comment. She didn't want to go down the road of personal health issues with an elderly woman.

"How about Stacy's car? How long has it been gone?"

Agnes chuckled. "Like I said, he sold it."

"Sold it?" Sam asked.

"Yes. The day after the funeral, he parked it by the road with a 'For Sale' sign on it with his phone number. That was Friday morning."

"Why do you think he sold it?"

"That same day, two older gentlemen met him at 6:00 p.m. in his driveway. One of them handed him an envelope, cash I presume, and Mr. Leonard gave him the keys, title, and registration."

"How do you know that?"

"I was watching through my binoculars. Obviously, you have never sold a car."

Sam groaned. "So what happened next?"

"One of the old guys drove Stacy's car away, and the other guy followed him in his own car."

"Did you find that strange? By that, I mean, putting the car up for sale in the morning and selling it that same day?"

Agnes laughed. "Look, everyone around here knows the farmplace is haunted, surrounded by death and mystery. Stacy is just the latest in a long line of horrific deaths. Those old farts weren't just buying a car but a piece of the macabre history of Burr Oak Farm."

Sam didn't respond for several minutes. Agnes was right. Some people believe in ghosts, superstition, and cultlike beliefs, so buying the car probably made perfectly good sense to them, something that gave them bragging rights into the darker side of the psyche of their fellow human beings.

"So how about the traffic along Exeter Crossing Road? Any changes there?"

"Good heavens, yes. Since the murder, the traffic driving slowly past the Leonard house is amazing. Even at night, the cars are there.

Sometimes they stop and wait, hoping to see a ghost or something like that. I told all this to Jeffery."

Sam rolled her eyes. She opened the spiral notebook and pointed to the entry of a yellow Pontiac Firebird. "Do you remember seeing this car?"

Agnes looked at the entry and shrugged. "It's my handwriting. I don't remember the car. Is it recorded in the notebook only one time?"

"Yes," replied Sam.

"Whose car is it?" Agnes asked.

"It's part of our investigation, so I can't tell you."

"Does it belong to the killer?"

"Look, I am not saying that. The owner of that car is merely a person of interest."

Agnes clasped her hands together. "The next time I talk to Jeffery, I will ask him. He will know."

Sam let out a big sigh. "How much of your day is spent here at the table looking out the window?"

"Pretty much my whole day. I enjoy it. Watching the cars drive by and keeping an eye on the Leonard house. I told Jeffery years ago there would be another murder at that house someday, and I was right."

Suddenly, and without warning, a purple finch appeared at the window, madly flapping its wings, staring in at Agnes and Sam. It hovered there for about ten seconds and quickly flew away. Agnes screamed. A look of fear and terror on her face was a quick reflex. She turned pale. Sam thought she was going to faint.

"Are you all right?" Sam asked.

"It's a sign!" Agnes said, barely above a whisper. She was shaking uncontrollably.

Sam wanted to get up and put a reassuring arm around her but hesitated. Agnes stared past Sam as if in a trance. Sam remained silent. Agnes looked terrified. A long moment of silence passed. Finally, Agnes's shoulders slumped, and she looked at Sam.

"It's a sign," she said again. "I am going to die within three days. Mr. Death is coming to take me away."

"How do you know that?"

"My mother and grandmother told me all about the birds and the telltale signs to look for. The signs were a predictor of life and death, good times and bad times, and the weather. Was a marriage going to be a good one or full of sorrow? I immediately knew there was going to be a death in the Leonard house when I saw that owl sitting on the roof. And what happened? Stacy Leonard was murdered. The bird appearing today is a messenger. The finch came to tell me of my impending death."

"How do you know it's your death? Maybe it could be someone else's," Sam said as compassionately as possible.

Agnes looked out the window and back to Sam. She was thinking.

"When you spoke to Jeffery, did he tell you that Mr. Death was coming to fetch you?"

"No."

"Well then, don't you think if it was your time to die, he would have told you?"

Agnes had to mull over Sam's question. She had a good point. "I suppose so."

"There you have it, if the little bird came here today to tell you that someone was going to die within the next three days, you shouldn't assume it is going to be you."

Agnes felt relieved hearing her words and settled back into her chair. "Perhaps you are right. Can I get you another cup of coffee?"

Sam declined and looked at her watch. It was time to go. She thanked Agnes for the loan of the spiral notebook, the coffee, and seeing her. As they passed through the living room, Sam paused and looked at the grandfather clock. "Are you going to wind the clock and keeping it going?"

"Of course," Agnes said with authority. "Jeffery would want me to do that."

Before Sam left the living room, she went to the chair where Jeffery supposedly sat and casually extended her hand over the chair. No cool or cold air surrounded the chair. She felt a little foolish, but just to be sure, she had to do it. Sam felt sorry for Agnes. In her isolated lonely world, reality and imagination collided. After Sam left the house, she could hear the sound of the dead bolts being shoved noisily back into place. During her drive back to Monroe, Sam was resolved that she was going to contact Social Services to intervene in the life of a lonely, isolated, and paranoid old woman, a woman falling prey to her own imagination.

CHAPTER 10

On Wednesday morning, May 29, Sam and the chief were waiting for Paul Leonard at the station to be interviewed. The appointment was set for nine o'clock. After Sam visited Agnes Keel on Monday, she contacted Social Services when she returned to Monroe. She filed a formal report stating her observations and concerns for the safety and welfare of Mrs. Keel. The woman who took the report told Sam that they would get on it right away. Sam felt better now that an intervention was going to take place. She wished the best for Agnes.

As they waited for Leonard, Johns filled her in on a couple of details he had recently found out. They were sitting in the chief's office with the door closed. The first was that Johns had a meeting at the law firm of Newcomer, Pahnke and Fouts located on the east side of the square. The meeting concerned a legal issue with the city and the police department, but during a coffee break, the murder of Stacy Leonard came up. One of the lawyers mentioned that Paul Leonard had visited the firm and inquired about representation in a divorce proceeding. The inquiry was made about three weeks before Stacy's death. The meeting was a one-off, and they didn't hear from him again.

Sam leaned back in her chair, staring at the chief. "Well, that certainly changes the calculus."

"I agree. To my mind, it does strengthen the case for a motive for the murder. Her death certainly solved one problem for him as well as collecting $10,000 in life insurance. When we first interviewed him, he didn't tell us he had been to see a lawyer about a divorce."

Sam shifted in her seat. This piece of new information certainly sheds a new light on the upcoming interview. What else was he holding back?

The chief continued. "I called Brian Hoffman, the bowler who checked in on Leonard Saturday morning in his hotel room."

"What did he have to say?"

"He verified that Leonard complained about stomach cramps after the team's Friday night buffet supper. They were scheduled to roll three games starting again at seven o'clock. Into the first game, Leonard told the team he couldn't continue and left them around seven thirty. He told Hoffman that he was going to his room and to find him a sub."

"Did anyone check in on him after they finished bowling?"

"Hoffman said he went to his room about eleven o'clock, after leaving the bar in the hotel, and knocked on the door. When Leonard didn't answer, he assumed that he was sleeping and rejoined the team. They drank until midnight. The next morning, at eight thirty, he returned again to Leonard's room. Leonard answered the door and told him that he was sick all night and didn't sleep very well. That was the last time Hoffman or any of the other team members saw him . . ." The chief paused.

"Did any of the other team members get sick after eating at the buffet bar?" Sam asked.

"A very good question. Hoffman said it was only Leonard who became ill. He also said that the buffet table wasn't very big, so the other members of the team must have eaten some of the same food as Leonard."

"That raises the obvious question of whether or not Leonard was lying about being sick. Was he setting up his alibi for the time of the murder?"

"I thought about that as well. No one can verify his whereabouts from seven thirty Friday night until eight thirty Saturday morning, a span of thirteen hours. He could have left Milwaukee at seven thirty Friday night, drove to his home, murdered Stacy, and returned to Milwaukee. Going with that theory, he had the motive and the opportunity. And remember, he was the last one to see her alive, except for Herbert Milz whom she had sex with before her murder. But how about the gun? We need to find the gun or a witness that puts him at the farmplace at the time of the murder."

Sam raised her eyebrows, looking up at the ceiling. "We may have a witness. Remember me telling you that Agnes Keel saw a car pull up and park across the house on the night of the murder. After the killer left, the mystery car turned on its headlights and followed the car down the road. It was dark, so she couldn't identify the make or model of the car. But it seems more than a coincidence to me that the car was parked there at all. One of those two cars could have been Leonard's. By the way, any responses to your ad in the paper for any information at the time of the murder along Exeter Crossing Road?"

"As of yet, not a single response. I will run the ad again to see if anyone answers it."

There was a knock on the door, and Shirley opened it, telling Sam and the chief that Paul Leonard was waiting for them in the foyer. They immediately stood up and went to fetch Leonard. After greeting him, they took him into the windowless interview room. He sat down on one side of a gray metal table and the chief and Sam on the other. Sam asked him if he wanted a cup of coffee or a glass of water. He declined. From his body language, he looked very nervous. His hands were shaking.

"Thank you for coming in to see us today," the chief began.

Leonard nodded, looking at the chief and then to Sam.

"How are you doing?"

"Okay. But I think I am still in a state of shock. I am not sleeping well, and getting my affairs in order after Stacy's death has been a challenge for me."

Was "affair" a Freudian slip? Sam wondered.

"If you feel unwell, we can postpone our interview to another time," Johns offered.

"Thanks for the offer, but I would rather get this over with today."

"Any investigation of a murder is a methodical, tedious process for the police. We generally start with family members because they would know the victim best. Eliminating family members as suspects is standard police procedure so we can move on and find the killer. Any questions?" Johns asked.

Leonard tensed up. "How can I be of help?"

"For starters, you told us during our last interview that your marriage to Stacy wasn't a happy one. Would you care to elaborate more on that?"

"Must I?"

"Take your time, we are listening."

Sam had her notebook out, ready to take notes.

"I made a mistake when I married Stacy. After Alice, my first wife, died, I was beside myself with grief and loneliness. When I met Stacy, she resembled my wife in appearance and personality, even though she was twelve years younger than me. I was desperate and smitten at the same time. Two years had passed, and living alone in my house was maddening. I pursued Stacy with all my heart. I knew she didn't love me when we married, but I hoped that, in time, she would . . ." Leonard paused. Hearing his own words seemed to unsettle him.

"When did you know that you had made a mistake?"

"The realization came to me shortly after our marriage. The differences in our ages, our friends, and the expectations of the marriage became very apparent. She constantly reminded me that I was too old for her."

"How did that make you feel?"

"Angry and sad at my own stupidity."

"But you hung in there with her?"

"Yes, until recently. After the bowling tournament in Milwaukee, I was going to divorce her."

"Had you seen an attorney?"

The question caught Leonard by surprise. "So you know that I did. Monroe is really a small town."

"Did you tell Stacy about your visit to see a lawyer?"

"No. I didn't tell her."

"Why?"

"I needed to get it sorted first in my own mind. The meeting with the lawyer was the first step for me."

A moment of silence passed. Johns looked at Sam who shook her head. Leonard was fidgeting in his chair.

"Okay, moving on, you stated previously that Stacy's behavior changed prior to you going to Milwaukee. She seemed happier. And you suspected that she was having an affair. Is that correct?"

"Yes."

"Did you ask her?"

"No. But in my gut, I knew she was having an affair. I also realized that there was no turning back. I needed to go through with the divorce to keep my sanity. I am a respected pharmacist in a small town, and this kind of scandal could hurt my reputation and business."

"Any thoughts or names come to you as to who she was having the affair with?"

Leonard hesitated. "Maybe someone at the high school or the church choir. I just don't know."

"Did anyone or someone intimate to you or tell you that your wife was being unfaithful?"

"Some people probably knew, small town gossip, you know, but no one told me. I only had my suspicions."

"Do you know now?"

Leonard gulped. He turned pale. "My sister told me. It was Herbert Milz."

"Did you know it was him before your wife was murdered?"

"No."

"Do you think he killed her?"

Leonard's face looked ashen. "Can I have a glass of water?" he asked.

Sam jumped up and fetched a cold glass of water. After she returned and handed it to him, he drained the whole glass in one gulp. He stared into the empty glass on the table.

"I will ask you again. Do you think Herbert Milz killed your wife?"

Leonard stared at his hands and slowly shook his head. "Honestly, I don't know."

"Okay. Let's go back through the timeline again. Tell us about you leaving for Milwaukee and returning again."

Leonard looked up from the table and stared at the chief.

"Tell us again what you did after you got home that Friday afternoon."

"Do I have to? I already told you all I know."

"Just go through your movements again. Perhaps you forgot something important that you will remember."

Leonard sighed. "Okay. Like I said, I got home about 3:30 p.m. from work to gather my stuff and drive to Milwaukee for the bowling tournament. Stacy was home and wished me well."

"Did your wife kiss or hug or show any affection?" Johns asked.

"No. She waved at me as I drove down the driveway. That was all . . ." Leonard paused, trying to remember.

"Continue," Johns said.

"I drove to Milwaukee and found the hotel. I had supper with my teammates. It was a buffet line in the hotel dining room. I ate something that didn't agree with me, and I fell ill. I tried to bowl after supper, but I was so sick that I couldn't finish the first game. I told the team to find a sub, and I returned to my room."

"Did any of your teammates get sick?"

"Not that I am aware of. Well, anyway, I went to bed. I didn't sleep very well, making multiple trips to the bathroom."

"I spoke to Brian Hoffman. He said he went to your room at 11:00 p.m. to check on you, but you didn't answer his knocking on your door, so he left," Johns said, looking for any facial indicators that Leonard was lying.

"I must have been sleeping."

"Brian said he saw you again at 8:30 a.m. Saturday to inquire about your health."

"Yes, he came by to see me. I told him I was still unwell."

"What did you do after he left?"

"I went back to bed."

"What did you think was wrong with you?"

"Food poisoning, of course. I was registered for two nights, and I was hoping that I would feel better and rejoin the team. I hadn't eaten since supper the night before, and I was feeling weak. I must have fallen back to sleep because when the phone rang, it woke me up. It was the sheriff telling me that Stacy had been murdered and to hurry home."

"Did you tell your teammates that you were leaving?"

"No. I was in shock. I got dressed, checked out of the hotel, and drove straight home. I hardly remember the drive. My mind was a total mess. I just couldn't believe it."

"So when you departed Friday afternoon, Stacy didn't seem upset, nervous, or anxious about anything?"

Leonard was getting a little irritated with the repeat questions. "Like I said, we were having marital problems, and my leaving for the weekend didn't seem to bother her. I will admit that I was somewhat depressed knowing that the marriage was over and I wasn't looking forward to a divorce."

"But you hadn't told Stacy that you had been to see a lawyer?"

"No."

"So she wasn't aware that you went to see a lawyer?"

"If she knew, she didn't mention it to me."

"Okay. Moving on, now that some time has passed, can you think of anyone who would have wanted to harm your wife?"

"You mean apart from her lover?"

"Do you think he killed her?" Johns asked.

Leonard hung his head. "Not really. Why should he? Herbert probably loved her."

Johns paused in the questioning and looked at Sam. She was staring at Leonard.

"Do you own a handgun?" Johns asked.

"No."

"Did Stacy own a handgun?"

"No."

"Are you sure?"

"If she did, I have never seen it. Am I a suspect?"

Johns leaned back in his chair. "You must look at this investigation from our point of view. I am not saying you are guilty, but we need to eliminate you from our inquires. The sticking point here is that you have no alibi for the time of the murder other than that you were alone in your hotel room in Milwaukee. With no witnesses to collaborate your story, it is only reasonable to assume that you had the time to leave Milwaukee, drive to your home, murder your wife, and drive back to Milwaukee. Does that sound plausible to you?"

Leonard suddenly jumped up, bumping his knee on the table. Staring directly at Johns, he exploded, "Look, I did not murder my wife! I was going to divorce her, I admit that, but to murder her, absolutely not!"

The outburst caught Johns and Sam by surprise. "We are not accusing or arresting you at this time," Johns shot back. "Please sit down."

Leonard was shaking. He sat down again and looked forlorn. "Are we finished here?" he asked in a weak voice.

Johns nodded. "Yes, we are finished for now. You are free to go. But don't leave Monroe without telling us."

Without another word, Leonard stood up and walked out of the room.

"So what do you think?" Johns asked Sam.

"I think either Leonard or Milz could have killed her. They are both hiding something and lying to us about it. We need to get three search warrants for each of their homes and the cabin. The gun is a crucial piece of evidence, and it needs to be found. For the time being, these are our only two suspects."

"I agree. We can serve the warrants at the same time. I will go to the Milz home and cabin. You go to the Leonard home. Hopefully, we can locate the smoking gun."

CHAPTER 11

After the interview with Paul Leonard, Sam reviewed all her case notes and tried to puzzle out the two suspects and the murder. Was it a case of a jealous husband who snapped and committed murder for the insurance money, or a case of a jilted lover seeking revenge? Jealousy is a powerful psychological disorder where a sexual partner is involved. Was there any proof of an infidelity? The grieved partner can become preoccupied or obsessed by it. The rejection and loss of said partner can lead to madness. In the throes of mental anguish, people act irrationally and impulsively. It seems that they are incapable of stepping back from a flood of tormenting emotions consuming them, only to regret it later. The key she needed to unlock this murder was finding the gun or an eyewitness. The chief should have the search warrants ready to go either tomorrow or Friday. Until then, she needed to wait in the hopes of finding the gun.

When Sam got home from work, Drew had a surprise for her. Marco's Supper Club, located in the 1700 block of 11th Street, was having a prime-rib special dinner, and he had made reservations. The restaurant had a complimentary high chair for Karin. Sam was delighted. She took a quick shower and dressed in a cotton print dress and sandals. After her shower, she felt like a new woman. Going out with Drew and Karin was just what she needed to get her mind off the case. The supper was delightful, and Karin was happy. The waitress paid special attention to her and didn't mind picking up the small toys that Karin pitched off her tray to the floor. Karin thoroughly enjoyed herself, making a mess of eating mac and cheese and crackers with her tiny fingers. Sam brought along a sippy drinking cup for her. The other patrons stopped eating, watched, and smiled at Karin's antics with parental amusement. The whole evening was a huge and relaxing success.

Sam and Drew had a glass of wine and retired to bed after the ten-o'clock news. Sam was into a deep sleep when the telephone began ringing off the hook. The irritating sound jolted her out of a dream. It took her a few moments to come to, orient herself, and realize where she was and what was happening. Drew was fast asleep, softly snoring. He could peacefully sleep through a loud, booming thunderstorm with flashing bright lightning bolts over his head without breaking a sweat. She looked at the alarm clock: 1:30 a.m. She drowsily answered the telephone on the bedstand.

Chief Johns was on the other end of the line. He quickly told her that the body of a murdered man had been discovered by a Green County sheriff's deputy in the parking lot of the New Glarus Woods State Park. He would be there in fifteen minutes to pick her up. Sam immediately snapped out of her sleepy fog and was wide awake. She leapt out of bed, washed her face, brushed her teeth, and hastily dressed. Finding a notepad near the telephone in the living room, she quickly jotted down a note for Drew, explaining where she was. She saw the headlights of the chief's car approaching through the picture window in her living room and went outside. He pulled up to the curb, and she jumped into his car.

"We have to stop meeting like this," Sam said.

Johns laughed as he sped through the deserted streets of Monroe.

"I will tell you what I know. A sheriff's deputy was making his routine rounds when he spotted the parked car, lights off, in the parking lot of the wooded trail head at approximately 12:30 a.m. He pulled up alongside the car to investigate. He thought someone had parked there to sleep for the night. He was surprised when he discovered the body of a man slumped over the steering wheel with blood trickling down the side of his head from an apparent gunshot wound. He felt for a pulse. The man was dead. He called it in, and I was called to investigate. Other than that, I don't know anything else. We will get more information once we arrive on the scene."

"Was the gunshot self-inflicted?"

"I don't know."

"Has the identity of the victim been revealed?"

"We will know more once we arrive at the scene."

They drove in silence toward New Glarus. Sam's thoughts drifted to Agnes Keel. What did she say when the purple finch looked at her through the picture window? Within three days, a death will occur. Sam shook her head. Impossible! After they arrived, Sam saw two sheriff's cars and an ambulance. The victim's car was a copper-tone Chevy Camaro. Dr. Ken's car followed them into the parking lot.

"Hello, Chief," Dr. Ken said, exiting his car. "I can see that you don't punch a time clock either."

Johns grinned at his little joke and followed him to the victim's car, where the two deputies were standing. Dr. Ken examined the body and confirmed that the man was, indeed, dead and estimated the time of death as recent, maybe two or three hours earlier. Johns, looking at the corpse, guessed that the young man in the car was in his mid- to late twenties. Dr. Ken surmised the cause of death to be a single gunshot wound to the left temple. He would know more after the autopsy. Albert Swenson arrived and took the crime-scene photos; after which, the ambulance drivers removed the body from the car and left for the morgue in Monroe. Swenson told the chief he would have the photos ready Friday afternoon. The deputies and Johns watched the vehicles leave.

"What do we know?" Johns asked, looking at the deputies.

"I discovered the body at 12:30 a.m.," one of the deputies replied.

"Tell me want you saw."

"I was making my usual rounds when I spotted the car parked here with the highlights turned off. At first, I assumed that someone was parked here to spend the night, sleeping in his car. It has happened before. I pulled up beside the car, and I could see a body slumped over the steering wheel."

"Were there any other vehicles in the area?" Johns asked.

"No. My first thought was that it may be a heart attack. I jumped out of my car with a flashlight. The driver side window was down, and I could see blood on the side of the victim's face. I reached in through the open window and felt for a pulse. The body was cool to the touch and no pulse. By all appearances, I determined that he was shot in the head. I immediately called it in to dispatch."

"Did you open the driver's side door or touch anything other than the body?"

"No. I immediately knew this was going to be a crime scene."

"Did you see a gun?"

"Not outside the car. I haven't looked inside."

"Do you know who owns the car?"

"I ran the license plate. The car is registered to a Norman Stafford of New Glarus. He lives in the 600 block of 1st Street, the residential block just south of all the shops in the downtown area."

Johns wrote down the name and address. "Do you think he is the man in the car?" Johns asked.

"I personally don't know him, but I would think so."

Johns excused himself and went to his car and radioed the Monroe PD and instructed the night dispatcher to call Scott Brady in Madison to send his forensics team to New Glarus. He rejoined Sam and the sheriff's deputies and told them that the forensics team was on the way.

"Anything else for us?" the deputy asked.

"Yes. I want your report on my desk by tomorrow afternoon. Can you do that?"

"Not a problem."

"Also, could you stay a while longer and put up some crime-scene tape. I want to discuss this incident with Detective Gates, and then could you give her a ride home?"

"Absolutely."

The second deputy left them to continue his rounds. Sam and Johns approached the victim's car with their flashlights and stared at it.

"So what do you think?" Johns asked.

"Let us assume for the moment that the driver of the car is Norman Stafford. Unless he is left-handed, and the gun is found in the car, we can theorize that he was murdered. Two murders, two weeks apart? I think it's too much of a coincidence."

"So you think there is a nexus between the two murders?" Johns replied.

"Too early to tell, but I just have that feeling. I am wondering if the same gun was used for both murders."

"Okay. So after Dr. Ken's autopsy, if Mr. Stafford was killed by the same gun that killed Stacy Leonard, we have a second murder by the same killer."

"That's my first impression, a gut feeling, of what I see here tonight."

"But why? That's the question. We have a long way to go to find an answer to answer that one and a motive," Johns mused.

"I agree. When I get home tonight, I will review my case notes and find the car log Agnes Keel recorded in her spiral notebook. I will be looking for a copper-tone Chevy Camaro. If I can find one, eureka! We will have a link between the Leonard's house and Norman Stafford."

"Good point. You do that, and try to get some sleep. I am going to wait for the forensics team. After they arrive, I am going to Mr. Stafford's home address. I will have to break the horrific news to whoever is living there and ask someone to ID the body."

"One other thing," Sam said, "do you see any bullet casings?"

Johns searched the area outside the car with his flashlight. Then he opened the car door. No casings. "Murder!" he muttered to himself.

Sam nodded and turned to rejoin the deputy waiting to take her home. But she abruptly stopped, turned around, and looked at the chief.

"Do you believe in ghosts?"

"What? Why did you ask me that?"

"Mrs. Keel believes in them. Do you?"

"No, and why do you ask?"

"Just curious," Sam said.

"Well, first of all, I have never seen one, and second, I think that people who believe in them have an intense interest in the afterlife. By that, I mean believing that they see the ghost of a deceased person gives them the hope of the afterlife."

"How about superstitions?"

"Like what?"

"For instance, seeing a bird looking into your house through a glass window means that a death will occur within three days."

"Now I have heard that one. But I don't believe it. A fortune-telling bird? Give me a break. My mother believed in that nonsense, a broken mirror or throwing salt over your shoulder, a waste of salt in my opinion," Johns replied.

"So you don't believe in any of that?"

"I only believe in data and the facts, more down-to-earth analysis than interpreting shooting stars or tea leaves for me. Don't let Agnes Keel get into your head. Just follow the facts."

Sam laughed. "Okay. If I need some spiritual intervention solving this case, I guess I will need to see a medium with supernatural powers."

"What you need is some sleep!"

Johns watched as Sam got into the sheriff's car and departed for Monroe. He climbed into his own car and waited for the forensics team to arrive. All this talk about the curse of Burr Oak Farm, ghosts, and superstitious beliefs was silly. He was convinced that these two murders were somehow tied together. Did either of his two suspects have a direct link to Norman Stafford? If so, which one? Stacy Leonard and Norman Stafford lived fairly close to each other, less than 10 miles. Was there a connection there? Johns knew that maybe he was assuming too much at this stage of the investigation, but the idea was intriguing. The three search warrants he applied for should be ready to go by Saturday. If the ballistics report confirmed that both murders were committed by the same gun, that would open up a whole new line of inquiry. He made a mental note of people who still needed to be interviewed: Mrs. Linda Milz, the bartender at the country club, the employees at Milz Auto Sales and Repair Shop, the employees at Paul Leonard's pharmacy, and anyone in New Glarus who knew Norman Stafford. These thoughts rolled around in the chief's head. He laid his head back on his head rest, closed his sleepy eyes, and fell fast asleep.

Suddenly, there was a loud banging on his car window. "Johns, wake up! You are in dereliction of your duty. A court-martial offense if I ever saw one!"

Johns jumped. He saw Scott Brady grinning at him through the window. He rubbed his eyes and opened his car door. "What took you so long?" he asked, trying to wake up.

"You have some nerve calling me out in the middle of the night. My wife will never forgive you."

"Why?"

"Sex, of course! This is our date night."

Johns laughed. "You are in desperate need of a therapist if you ask me. Who, in their right mind, would want to have sex with you?" Johns climbed out of his car and showed Brady the crime scene.

"So what do we have here?"

Johns filled him in on the murder and told him that he needed to contact Dr. Ken to do a ballistics test on the bullet. He wanted to know if it came from the same gun that killed Stacy Leonard. Also, fingerprints or anything else useful in the investigation would be helpful. Johns looked at his watch. The time was 5:00 a.m. He left Brady and his team at the scene and drove to New Glarus to face whoever lived at Norman Stafford's home address.

CHAPTER 12

C hief Johns called Sam at home Thursday morning, and they agreed to meet at eleven o'clock at the PD. They were both tired, getting very little sleep the night before. After Sam was dropped off by the Green County sheriff's deputy, she couldn't get to sleep. She tossed and turned and finally got up, not wanting to wake Drew. She went to the kitchen, poured herself a glass of cold milk, and sat on the sofa in the living room in the dark. Her mind was whirring with this new development in the case. She was convinced that the two murders were somehow connected. The unanswered questions were maddening. Could Stacy and the murdered man have been involved? Did either of the two suspects implicated in Stacy's murder know the murdered man? Was this a case of jealousy and revenge gone amok? She finished her milk and lay her head back on the sofa.

Drew woke her, holding the note she had written to him before Johns picked her up. "My, my, you have had a busy night," he said, grinning at her.

"I see you got my note," she drowsily replied.

"I found it and you at the same time. What's going on?"

Sam was very groggy, trying to wake up and get her bearings. Drew gave her the time she needed and went to the kitchen to brew them a cup of coffee. Sam went into the bathroom and washed her face with cold water. As they sat at the kitchen table enjoying their coffees, Sam filled him in on the details of finding the body at the New Glarus Woods State Park and her suspicions that the two murders were somehow linked together. Too much of a coincidence. As Drew poured her a second cup, the sound of Karin waking up and whimpering in her crib demanded immediate attention. Drew jumped up and went to fetch her. The routine of another day had begun. Sam took a shower as Drew changed and dressed Karin. He seated her in her high chair and gave her a sippy cup filled with orange juice. Karin loved orange juice. Sam shortly joined them and fed Karin some rice cereal, cut-up bananas, and toast. Karin was delighted and happily tucked in, making a mess of her high chair tray. While this was going on, Drew showered and got ready for work.

After Drew dropped off Karin at Mrs. Sturzenegger's house, he went to work. Sam lay down on the living room sofa and closed her eyes. Her need for sleep was overwhelming, and her eyelids slowly lowered and slammed shut. The telephone rang at ten o'clock, waking her up. It was Chief Johns, wanting to confirm their meeting at eleven o'clock to debrief. She went to the bathroom and washed her face and brushed her teeth. Her brain started to engage, once again thinking about the night before and the murder case. She arrived at the PD at ten forty-five, and Johns wasn't there, so she went to her desk, opened her notebook, and wrote down some of her thoughts. Johns arrived at eleven fifteen and apologized for being late. They each grabbed a cup of coffee from the break room and went into the chief's office.

"You look like hell," Johns said.

"You don't look so good yourself," Sam replied.

Johns laughed. "There you have it. Two police officers in need of a long summer's nap."

Sam grinned at him and took a sip of her coffee and grimaced.

"Bitter!" Johns began. "I went to the Stafford home shortly after five o'clock this morning."

Sam was totally focused on the chief as he spoke.

"I got his parents out of bed. As you can imagine, they were in shock upon hearing the news. I asked them to come to the morgue to identify the body. They asked me if I was sure it was Norman. I described his physical characteristics and his car. His mother wept. They dressed and followed me to the hospital. After they identified the body of their son,

I asked them if they were up to answering a few questions. They agreed, and we went to the hospital cafeteria, grabbed coffees, and sat alone at the east end of the dining room."

"How horribly sad. It must have been quite a shock for them," Sam said softly.

"Yes. They were devastated and in a state of shock, disbelief." Johns opened his notebook and started to narrate his handwritten notes. "Norman was twenty-seven years old. He attended the University of Wisconsin in Platteville and worked for the Tschanz Insurance Agency in New Glarus, selling car, home, and life insurance policies. He lived at his parents' house, saving his money to eventually buy his own home. He was single and dated several girls, looking for 'Miss Right.'"

"Did he know Stacy Leonard?" Sam wanted to know.

"If he knew her, his parents weren't aware of it. Anyway, he never mentioned her name to them."

"If he was having an affair with a married woman, that would demand some secrecy, I would think," Sam suggested.

"Let's not get out in front of ourselves. Well, anyway, not coming home at night wasn't that unusual for him and was apparently part of his social life. Sleepovers, I would assume."

Sam smiled. "Whatever."

"I asked them if they knew of anyone who would want to harm Norman. 'Everybody loved him' was the response. I asked them if he complained about anyone recently, someone who irritated him or had any hard feelings against him. Again, no one came to mind. I ended the interview not wanting to distress them any more than necessary."

"Well, someone had a grudge against him."

"We will need to interview his colleagues at the Tschanz Insurance Agency. Maybe one of them could shed some light on his murder."

There was a knock on the door. Shirley looked in and told the chief he had a call from a member of Scott Brady's forensics team on line 2. Johns immediately picked up the telephone, and the call was put through. He listened patiently and thanked the caller. He also told the caller to thank Brady for the timely information. Sam sat silently as the chief took the call. After he hung up, Johns looked at Sam.

"How interesting," he said. "Do you remember the mystery fingerprint that the forensics team found in Stacy Leonard's house on the liquor bottle?"

Sam nodded. "Don't tell me the fingerprint belonged to Norman Stafford."

"Bingo, you are correct. Brady's team lifted the fingerprint from Norman's car and made the match. Also, no gun or gun casings were found at the scene. So the killer obviously took them with him." Johns settled back in his chair and steepled his fingers. His mind was spinning.

"What are you thinking?" Sam asked.

"Remember when we asked Leonard about the life insurance policy?"

Sam nodded.

"I would bet that he got it through the Tschanz Insurance Agency."

"That would be an interesting connection."

"I am going to call Paul Leonard at the pharmacy!" Johns exclaimed.

He reached for a telephone directory from his desk drawer, looked up the number he was looking for, and made the call. He held the receiver out so that Sam could listen in on the conversation.

"Hello," Paul Leonard said, answering the telephone on the second ring.

"This is Chief Johns calling, and I have a question for you. Is this a good time?"

"Yes, of course. What is your question?"

"Do you remember telling us that you and your wife had a life insurance policy?"

"Yes."

"Do you remember when you took the policy out and the agency who issued it?"

"Of course. About a year ago, Stacy insisted that we have the policy. She handled all the details through the Tschanz Insurance Agency in New Glarus."

"Were you involved?"

"Not really. I thought it was a good idea, and I wrote the check."

"Do you remember the name of the agent who wrote up the policy for you?"

There was a long pause. "Forgive me. As a matter of fact, I was just thinking about them, and I was going to look for the policy. After I get all the paperwork completed concerning Stacy's death, I will be contacting the agency, but for the moment, I can't recall the name of the agent. I only met him once, and that was when we signed the policy papers in New Glarus."

"Why did you get the policy in New Glarus and not Monroe?"

"Good question. I guess I never gave it a second thought. Stacy handled all the details, and I was good with that."

"Did you ever see the agent at your home? Either for business or of a personal nature?"

"No. I don't think so. I would have remembered that."

"Does the name Norman Stafford mean anything to you?"

"No, I don't think so. Why?"

"He was found murdered early this morning, and he worked for the Tschanz Insurance Agency."

"Oh my god!"

"We are only making inquiries at this time . . ." Johns paused, giving Leonard a moment. "If we have any further questions, we will contact you. And in the meantime, when you come across the agent who issued the policy, please contact us."

"Okay," Leonard replied in a concerned tone of voice.

"Thank you again for taking the time to speak with me."

There was only silence on the other end of the line.

"Is that all?" Leonard finally asked in a very nervous voice. His mind was spinning.

"That's all for now. And thanks again for taking the call."

Johns hung up the telephone and looked at Sam. She was thinking.

"Can it be true?" she asked.

"What?"

"That Stacy was having an affair with two men at the same time?"

Johns glanced at the ceiling. "We haven't established that, but if what you are thinking is correct, are you suggesting that she dumped Herbert to be with Norman Stafford? Interesting thought. In any case, her marriage to her husband was definitely over."

"Reminds me of a four-legged love triangle," Sam mused.

Johns laughed. "Something like that if, in fact, she was shagging Stafford and Herbert at the same time."

Sam settled back into her chair and waxed philosophically. "What a farcical melodrama. Here we have an unhappily married woman who is looking for an escape strategy. Her husband is also unhappy, but they don't talk about their doomed marriage. The best option for her would be to simply tell her husband that she no longer loved him and file for divorce. In doing that, only two people are involved. But instead, for whatever reason, she starts an affair with Herbert Milz, another unhappily married spouse. And if that wasn't enough, at the same time she starts a second affair with Norman Stafford, a single man. We haven't established that fact yet, but I wouldn't be surprised. What an entanglement of unsuspecting players. So what are the unforeseen consequences of this Greek tragedy? Two people are dead. And for now, we have two prime suspects, maybe more later, and anyone of them could be the killer."

Johns nodded. "You are certainly up on your Greek mythology. I agree. If you look at this case from 30,000 feet, it does look ridiculous. After all, human behavior can be very complicated, unpredictable, and irrational, with tragic results. We can't stop people from acting out. We can only arrest them and bring them to justice."

A comfortable silence fell across the room, like two old friends visiting each other and enjoying a quiet moment without speaking to each other.

Sam abruptly sat up and exclaimed, "Wait! I haven't checked Agnes Keel's log for the copper-tone Camaro!" Rustling her notes and papers, Sam muttered to herself as she began searching, "I have my copy of the log entries here. Let's see . . . Yes! Here it is! Starting at noon on Friday, the day of Stacy's murder, Agnes saw Stacy's blue Nova at the house and the arrival of the copper-tone Camaro! That had to be Norman Stafford!" She paused, letting that confirmation sink in. Her eyes widened as she offered, "This is just a thought, but maybe Stafford and Stacy were plotting to get Herbert out of the picture by breaking up with him."

"But why?" Johns asked. "If you were shagging one guy, would you really want to tell the other guy? Wouldn't that admission put your own life at risk or at the very minimum end a relationship?"

"Good point. So why was he at the house?"

"Something that we may never know."

"Moving on, could Herbert have somehow found out and killed them both?"

Johns was intently listening to Sam.

"So Stacy ditches Herbert, and he kills her in a jealous rage. Then he finds out about Stafford and kills him as well, blaming him for the breakup. Is that plausible?" Sam asked.

"Whoa, Detective, let's not get out in front of our skis. How about Leonard? Couldn't we make the same argument and case against him?"

Sam smiled. "I suppose so. Like you said, emotional entanglements can be tricky and complicated. So what is our next step?"

"I think we should interview the employees at the Tschanz Insurance Agency. By now, they have heard the news about their colleague. Perhaps they can shed some light on Norman's murder."

"I can call and make the appointment for Monday. That will give them time to get over the shock. Do we need to interview his parents again?" Sam asked.

"Not at this time. I think his coworkers in the office would probably have more information than his parents, if you know what I mean."

"Kids can be very secretive where parents are concerned, right?"

"Yes, and I speak from experience," Johns lamented.

Sam smiled. "Who else should we interview?"

"I will interview the employees at Milz Auto Sales to check out Herbert's alibi. After that, I will interview Linda Milz. Herbert said he went home from work around the time of the murder, found his wife sleeping on the sofa, and put her to bed. I am also interested to know if his wife knew about the affair."

"Could she be a suspect?" Sam asked.

"I don't know. If their marriage was one of convenience and not of love, what would be her motive? Jealously? I think not. For the time being, I am more concerned about Herbert. If his alibi checks out, we can eliminate him from our inquires."

"Do you think his wife would lie to give him an alibi?"

"I don't know that either. I think my interview with her should be very interesting."

"Then what about Herbert's employees? Would they lie?"

"Good question. How far does loyalty extend? I guess I will find out."

"How about the employees at the pharmacy? Would they lie to protect Leonard?" Sam asked.

"I have been thinking about that. If they don't have any direct knowledge of the murders, maybe they could shed some light on Leonard's state of mind."

"Sounds good," Sam said. "I will call and set up the interview in New Glarus. The employees at the Tschanz Insurance Agency shouldn't be too surprised to hear from me. Then I will interview them."

Johns stood up. "By the way, Judge Dietmeire told me that he needed some time to think about my request for the search warrants for the gun at the homes of Paul Leonard and Herbert Milz. He has concerns about small town politics and very public professional reputations. He would let me know by Wednesday. So we will meet again after the interviews are completed. Also, all the final reports from Brady's team, the sheriff's department, and the autopsy will be available next week. But in the meantime, I will pick you up at noon tomorrow and drive to New Glarus Woods State Park. I want to take a second look at the crime scene with fresh eyes."

* * *

As promised, the chief picked Sam up at the PD on time, and they rode together to New Glarus. The chief looked irritated as he drove north along Highway 69. He had spent the morning answering questions from both the mayor and the chair of the police and fire commission Roger Nussbaum. After the news of the second murder became public, it quickly had a hair-on-fire effect for the citizens of Green County. Both of their offices received a flood of phone calls, wanting to know if it was safe to be outside and if the killer was arrested. The chief gave them his usual "no comment" on an ongoing investigation and assured them that if anything broke in the case, they would be the first to know. The newspaper also called him, wanting information, but they got the same response other than the victim's name and scene of the crime, which they already knew. The pressure was on to get results, and the chief was feeling it.

When they turned into the parking lot of New Glarus Woods State Park, they saw a bevy of cars parked there and people milling around and talking. The yellow crime-scene tape was fluttering in the breeze where the victim's car had been found, adding to the mystique of the parking lot. The car itself had been towed away.

"Oh shit," the chief muttered to himself.

After they parked and exited the car, the crowd merged on them, asking questions. The chief held up his hands for silence and told them that he had no information and to leave the area and to go home. Even though the crime scene had been cleared by the forensics team, the yellow tape remained behind, marking the area. About half the crowd dispersed, and the other half intently watched from a distance as the chief and Sam surveyed the scene. The officers felt very uncomfortable and had to whisper to keep their voices from prying ears. Eventually, the crowd got bored and left the parking lot one by one. Alone at last, they both exhaled a big sigh of relief.

"The chamber of commerce isn't going to be happy about this," the chief said in a flat voice.

Sam smiled at his sarcasm, looking at the crime-scene tape. "Well, it looks pretty straightforward to me. Norman Stafford was sitting in his car, waiting to meet his killer. For what purpose? We don't know yet. From what you told me, he must have been surprised. No sign of a struggle. The killer simply walked up to his open car window and shot him in the head, picked up the bullet casing, and drove away. Very cold, very calculated. Premeditated, to be sure."

Johns nodded. "I don't think it was the outcome he was expecting. Anyway, once all the forensics evidence is in, I wouldn't be surprised if the two murders are somehow linked. Too much of a coincidence with both murders occurring about a mile apart and a handgun being the murder weapon."

They spent approximately two hours at the crime scene, theorizing and imagining different scenarios for the murder, spinning out different theories of what-ifs but no facts. Both Johns and Sam felt their blood pumping wildly through their veins. The hunt was on to find the killer or killers. They were very much looking forward to the upcoming interviews, searching for possible suspects.

As the chief gathered up the yellow crime-scene tape and deposited it into the trunk of his car, Sam noticed the clear blue skies overhead and the relative peace of the park. The summer tree leaves were fluttering on a gentle breeze, and the song birds were singing in the branches. Gray squirrels were scampering around, chasing one another. A sweat bee buzzed around her arm, and Sam brushed it away. It was hard for her to imagine that this tranquil and beautiful place was witness to a brutal murder during a celestial starry night under the cover of darkness, a stark contrast between the two images.

CHAPTER 13

After an enjoyable weekend with Drew and Karin, Sam was driving north to New Glarus Monday morning, June 3. She was disappointed that the search warrants were being delayed until Wednesday. She felt a sense of urgency to find the murder weapon. The day was dark and cloudy with a threat of rain in the afternoon. She had called Friday and scheduled an interview with the owner and the employees of the Tschanz Insurance Agency located downtown in the 500 block of 1st Street. The appointment was set for eleven thirty. Chief Johns was going to interview the employees at Milz Auto Sales in the afternoon.

Sam's thoughts drifted a back to her weekend off. Spending quality time with Drew and Karin was renewing. The murder case faded into the back recesses of her mind. They visited Sharon at the nursing home on Saturday and had a delightful time. Karin was the center of attention, and she loved it. To their surprise, Sharon had taken up knitting and had knitted her granddaughter an ill-fitting pink cardigan. The old woman could certainly keep a secret. She thought it fit perfectly, and the little princess smiled as her small hands rubbed against the soft yarn. Never apologize, that was Sharon's mantra. They took Karin outside under the pergola to enjoy the sun-drenched day. Sharon behaved herself and doted on Karin, leaving her sarcasm and witty remarks behind in her room. Watching grandmother and granddaughter interacting was a sight to behold. The day was filled with laughter and love.

Sunday was another picture-perfect day, so they took a drive to Lake Le-Aqua-Na State Park in Lena, Illinois, for the afternoon. Sam packed a picnic lunch, and they dined on a wool blanket they brought along and sat on the grass near the lake. Karin and Drew took a nap after lunch under the warm afternoon sun. Sam took a photo of them sleeping together. It was a memory-making photo and day, to be sure.

Sunday night, after Karin went to bed, Sam switched mental gears. She reviewed her case notes again to get ready for her interview at the Tschanz Insurance Agency. She spent a restless night, tossing and turning, going over her list of suspects and possible motives for the murders in her head. She was hoping for that *aha* moment when the pieces would come together to solve the case, but that didn't happen. She was wide awake when the alarm sounded at 6:00 a.m.

At 11:15 a.m., Sam found an empty parking space and parked her car in front of the insurance agency. Howard Tschanz shook her hand and welcomed her as she entered the agency. A reception desk was located to her immediate right, and a number of agent desks were lined up toward the back of the room. Mr. Tschanz was an affable-looking, paunchy man with a ready smile and thinning hair. At fifty years old, Tschanz had a round face with perfect small teeth and stood 5 feet 9 inches tall. He was wearing a lightweight summer suit and a pair of wire-rimmed spectacles sitting comfortably on his long nose. He had a perpetual squint in his left eye. His employees had gathered at the back of the office area, seated on folding chairs. Tschanz turned the sign that hung on the front door over to "Closed" and led Sam to the back of the office area. He introduced her to his small staff. There were one woman and two men waiting in anticipation for the interview to begin. Tschanz introduced them to Sam. The woman was the receptionist, Betty Stauffacher. She was middle-aged with a warm smile. The other two were agents, Buddy Powell and Dan Woodman. Powell was in his thirties with a crew cut and a large nose. Woodman was older, sporting a short gruffy beard and wearing a short-sleeved shirt and tie that didn't match in color. Tschanz took the lead, telling Sam that his agency was small, having only himself and three associates. Norman Stafford was the newest employee and had only worked for him a couple of years.

Everyone liked him, and he got on well with the team. After his brief introductory remarks, Tschanz sat down and waited for Sam to begin. She looked at their anxious faces.

"I want to thank Mr. Tschanz for organizing this interview today. First, I want to give you my condolences for your loss. As you already know, your associate Norman Stafford was found brutally murdered last week in the parking lot of the New Glarus Woods State Park."

Betty gasped. Her right hand covered her mouth.

"During a police investigation, we try to get as much background information on the victim as possible to help us in our inquires. I have a few questions for you. But before I start, do you have any questions for me?"

They all looked at one another and shook their heads.

"Okay. Can any of you tell me Stafford's movements on the day of his death? That would have been last Wednesday. I am also interested in his recent behavior. Did he seem upset about anything? Or was he happy? Anything to indicate that he may have felt like his life was in danger?"

Betty hesitated and spoke up. "On Wednesday, he came to work at 9:00 a.m. as usual. He seemed to be in good spirits. He made a few phone calls and scheduled a couple of insurance visits with prospective clients. He had one client visit in the afternoon and left the office about 11:00 a.m. and returned to the office around 4:00 p.m. He was happy because his visit was successful, and he was going to write up a new homeowner insurance policy the following day for a signature. He left the office around 5:00 p.m."

"Did he say where he was going?"

Betty wrinkled her brow. "Not that I recall."

"How about the rest of you, can you add anything?"

"Not really," Woodman said. "It was a day like every other day. Nothing unusual that stood out."

"Do you know of anyone who would want to harm him?" Sam asked.

A moment of silence passed. "Like who?" Powell asked.

"Well, for instance, was there anything in his love life that comes to mind? An unhappy love affair or anything like that?"

They all shook their heads.

"Norman dated several girls," Betty said. "He would talk about them sometimes but nothing serious."

"So he didn't have a steady girlfriend?" Sam asked.

"Not that I know of. Some of his breakups were interesting from his point of view. Men!" Betty said in an exasperated voice.

Woodman smiled at her remark and fidgeted in his chair. "I had a couple of beers with Norman after work about two to three weeks ago, and he did say that he was seeing someone new."

Sam leaned in and stared at him.

Woodman continued. "He didn't say much about it, but it seemed to me that something was on his mind, you know, bothering him."

"Like what?"

"He was cryptic, you know, very mysterious."

"What did he say?" Sam asked, pressing him.

"He said that there was this girl that he liked very much, but the relationship with her was complicated. He said that the passion was there, but the circumstances were awkward."

"What did he mean by that?"

"When I asked him, he abruptly changed the subject."

"Did you speak to him about it again?"

"No. The subject never came up."

"What do you think he was referring to?"

"I don't know."

"Well, take a guess."

Woodman looked down at his shoes. "My immediate thought was that he was having an affair with a married woman."

Betty slumped down in her chair and sighed. "Well, I declare."

"Do you know the name of the woman?"

"No. He never said."

Sam looked at the others who were staring at Woodman. "How about any of you, any thoughts?"

They all shook their heads. "If he was having an affair, he never mentioned it to me," Tschanz said.

"Does the name Stacy Leonard mean anything to you?" Sam asked.

A collective gasp permeated the atmosphere in the room. They had all heard about her murder.

Tschanz spoke up. "After her death, Norman showed me the $10,000 life insurance policy on her. We were going to contact her husband after her funeral."

"Did he say anything about her death?"

"No. He just handed me the file and asked me to take care of the details for the payout."

"Did you find that unusual?"

"I thought it a little irregular since he wrote up the policy."

"Thinking back on it, could Mrs. Leonard have been the woman that he was having the affair with?" Sam bluntly asked.

His jaw dropped, and his mouth flew open. "I honestly don't know, I suppose so."

There was a real tension in the room. Sam could feel it.

"Are you suggesting that Norman could have killed Mrs. Leonard?" Woodman weakly asked, looking at Sam. All eyes were staring at Sam.

"I am not saying that. The facts are that we have two unexplained murders on our hands. Are they related? We think so. But as to who did it, that's what we are trying to puzzle out and determine. Did the same person kill them? I am not here to accuse anyone, just to get background information on Norman Stafford to help us with our inquires."

Sam's questions had the group off balance. How well did they really know Stafford, their colleague and friend? Was he capable of murder? And who murdered him? Was he correct when he told Woodman that his affair was complicated? Did that complication lead to his death?

"Did Norman's demeanor change after the death of Mrs. Leonard?" Sam asked.

"He did seem more withdrawn, quiet, like his mind was somewhere else," Betty offered.

"Was he surprised by her death?"

"I can't recall him commenting on it. I suppose he was like the rest of us, in shock. Murder is such an awful and frightening thing, especially in small town like New Glarus."

"Did you ever suspect there was a romantic relationship between the two of them?" Sam asked again.

"Never. He didn't even mention her name until after her death when he gave her file to Mr. Tschanz," Betty said.

The group was having difficulty processing the interview. Sam could clearly see that. She needed to change her line of questioning, take a chance.

"Was Norman in any kind of financial trouble?"

The tension in the room relaxed a little.

"Everyone knew that he lived with his parents, trying to save money to buy his own house. That was no secret. Other than that, he made enough money to pay his bills as far as I know. He never asked me for an advance on his wages or a raise," Tschanz said.

"Do the rest of you agree?" Sam asked.

Some nodded, some shrugged.

"If he was in desperate need money, I wasn't aware of it. Perhaps you should ask his parents," Woodman offered.

Sam looked at Howard Tschanz. "Did Norman have any clients from Monroe other than Mr. and Mrs. Leonard?"

"No, I don't think so."

"Mr. Tschanz is correct," Betty quickly said. "I record all the policies, and that was the only one Norman had from Monroe."

"Was that unusual?" Sam asked.

"Not really. All our policies are mostly local folks and businesses."

Sam was satisfied with her answer. Moving on, Sam knew she was pulling on a thread with her next question.

If Norman was in financial difficulties with someone, could his death be connected with that and the two murders weren't related, only coincidental?

It was a bit of a stretch, but the thought did occur to her. The answer to that question would have to wait. Maybe his parents could answer it. Nevertheless, today Sam learned that Norman was having an affair that he kept secret. Sam was convinced it was with Stacy Leonard. It didn't appear on the surface that Norman was having any financial troubles, so that led her thinking back to Stacy.

What was it that caused his death two weeks after her murder?

A silence fell on the room as Sam pondered her next question. She wanted the question to be intriguing enough to shake a memory loose that could help with the investigation. Would it work?

"Right, I want you all to think about this next question and take your time answering it. Assume for a moment that Norman Stafford and Stacy Leonard, a married woman, were having an affair. Norman was keeping the affair under wraps, only tipping his hand once to Dan Woodman, intimating that he was having an affair with a married woman and it was complicating his life. Then suddenly, Stacy is murdered by a person unknown. That news must have really shocked him. Please try to remember how Norman reacted to the news. His lover had just been killed. It must have hit him pretty hard. Then two weeks later, he himself is murdered only a couple of miles from Stacy's house. For what purpose? Are the two murders linked? Please think about what I am asking before you answer."

Sam watched them as they tried to puzzle out an answer. *Was it a fair question? Would they have the courage to speak? Speculate? Remember something?*

After about ten minutes, Buddy Powell spoke. He had remained fairly quiet during the interview. "Your question is very intimidating. The obvious answer is that Mr. Leonard must be the killer. I am sure you have already thought of that. But on the other hand, who was the last person to see her alive? Not her husband, he was in Milwaukee. In crime novels, isn't that person the killer—the last one to see her alive? I am out of my depth. I have no clue as how to answer your question. I will say this: If Norman was upset by her death, he didn't show it here at the office."

Woodman spoke up. "I don't know. Like Buddy said, I don't have an answer to your question or even an educated guess. I never suspected that Norman had any involvement with her."

The same answer was repeated by Betty and Mr. Tschanz. Sam was okay with that. She thanked them for seeing her and shook hands with all four of them before she departed. She told them to call her if they thought of anything later that would help in the investigation.

On her drive back to Monroe, the question of how the two murders were linked together tormented her. Sam was disappointed that the interview didn't move the case forward. However, the one interesting fact that came out was that Norman wasn't more upset by Stacy's murder. If he was in love with her, his response to the killing should have been more demonstrative, an outward showing of emotion or grief. The folks in the office would have certainly picked up on that. But apparently, that didn't happen. They were surprised when Stacy was suggested as his possible lover. So what was up with Norman? Did he kill Stacy, or did he know who did?

CHAPTER 14

A s Chief Johns was reviewing his case notes before going to the scheduled interviews at Milz Auto Sales at 1:00 p.m., Scott Brady called. The call was brief, giving Johns a summary account of the evidence found at the crime scene or, more accurately, what wasn't found. According to Brady, he theorized that the killer approached the victim's car and shot him though the open driver's side window. No latent fingerprints were found on or inside the car, only those of the victim. No gun was found, indicating that the killer took it with him. A ballistics test was run comparing the bullets from each murder—a match. The murder weapon was a small-caliber Smith and Wesson 9mm handgun. So the same gun killed both victims. Also, he reaffirmed that the mystery fingerprint on the whiskey bottle found in Stacy Leonard's house belonged to the deceased Norman Stafford. Other than that, nothing to indicate or identify who the killer was. A written report would be on Johns's desk in a couple of days. Johns thanked Brady for expediting the processing of the crime scene and offered that the drinks were on him the next time they got together.

After hanging up the telephone, Johns leaned back in his chair. He found it interesting that the killer left no traceable evidence at either crime scene. Apparently, the killer just walked up to the victims and shot them. There wasn't a struggle or altercation of any kind. The only assumption that Johns could ascertain was that each victim must have known the killer. But how was that possible? A music teacher in Monroe and an insurance agent in New Glarus? What was the connection? He hoped that Sam would be able to find the answer to that question at the Tschanz Insurance Agency.

*　　*　　*

Johns parked his car in front of Milz Auto Sales at precisely 1:00 p.m. under darkening cloudy skies. He noticed Herbert's yellow Pontiac Firebird parked next to the sales office. Looking around the car lot, he saw a salesman with a customer looking at a preowned classic dark green 1951 Deluxe Chevy Coupe with a large external sunshade. Herbert greeted him outside and showed him into his office as a couple of raindrops started to fall, splashing on the parking lot. Herbert told him that only two employees saw him return from Cadiz Springs on the night of the murder: Donna Crandall, the receptionist bookkeeper; and Jim Hull, a salesperson. The other employees had already left for the day. Both of them had agreed to meet with Johns for the interview. The chief thanked him and requested to meet with Ms. Crandall first. Herbert fetched her, made the introductions, and closed the door to his office behind him, leaving them alone.

Crandall was a neatly-dressed middle-aged woman. Her demeanor was one of self-assured confidence. She had never married and lived with her pet cat Pepper. Her auburn hair was permed, and her fingernails were perfectly trimmed and painted red. She reminded Johns of a no-nonsense woman who was very capable performing her duties. She didn't have a ready smile, but at the same time, he liked her. There were two cushioned armchairs located in front of Hebert's desk. She sat down in one, and Johns settled himself into the other. Crandall waited for Johns to begin. He skipped the small talk and got down to business.

"As you know, the police are investigating two murders. Your boss, Herbert Milz, knew the first victim, Stacy Leonard. In fact, he saw her on the day of her murder. In order to eliminate him from our inquires, we need to substantiate his alibi for the night of the murder."

Crandall gasped. Hearing the words caused her chest to tighten.

Johns noticed that she visibly tensed up. He continued. "On the night of the murder, Friday night, he told us that he returned to the office from Cadiz Springs around 5:30 p.m. Is that correct?"

"Yes. My regular weekly workday ends at 5:30 p.m., and I work a half day on Saturday. I saw Herbert arriving as I was getting ready to leave."

"How did he seem to you? Was he in a state, or did he look normal?"

Crandall was thinking. She loved and respected her boss and didn't want to cause him any harm. When Herbert told her about the interview, he instructed to her to tell the police the truth.

"I immediately knew that something was wrong. He rushed past me without saying a word and disappeared into his office, slamming the door. He was definitely out of sorts. I thought about going to him and ask if everything was okay, but I changed my mind."

"Why was that?"

"I heard him opening his desk drawer and the clink of a glass. I know that he keeps a bottle of whiskey in his desk drawer. I wanted to help him, but I didn't want to intrude at the same time, so I gathered up my things and went home."

"Was that the last time you saw him?"

Crandall hesitated. She did see him again later that evening. Driving home from her sister's house, she saw Herbert's car speeding north on 18th Avenue and then onto Highway 69. He was driving erratically. Her immediate thought was that he had too much to drink, and why was he heading north instead of going home? Johns noticed her hesitation.

"Yes, the next time I saw him was Saturday morning at the office," she lied.

"Did he often drink on the job?"

"It was only after he got married to Linda that he started drinking. Have you met his wife?"

"No."

"I don't understand it. How can a man with such a kind nature and pure soul marry such a woman? Shortly after he married her, he started spending more and more time at work. Jim, who works the sales floor until 8:00 p.m., tells me that Herbert sometimes doesn't leave work until he does. They close up the office together."

"So he doesn't go home for supper?"

"No. Jim tells me that he will leave the office and get a carryout supper for himself from a local restaurant. Jim told me that he is miserable and sometimes Herbert tells him that marrying that woman was the biggest mistake of his life. He suffers in silence."

"Does anything make him happy?"

"Well, yes. He has a wonderful singing voice and enjoys singing with the choir at the First Christian Church."

Johns leaned back in his chair. Crandall was more forthcoming and franker in her opinions than he expected.

"Did he change in the last couple of months? Like, for instance, was he in a better mood?"

Crandall hesitated. She was thinking, *Yes, he was happier. He had a bounce in his step.* She was happy for him. "You are correct. Jim and I immediately noticed it after his return from Florida. Something changed. Jim was convinced he was having an affair, and we were glad that he found some happiness. We didn't know who the woman was, and we didn't ask."

"You now know who that woman was?" Johns asked.

"Yes. Stacy Leonard, the pharmacist's wife," Crandall said, looking down at her hands. Her face was overcome with a certain sadness.

"When did you find out?"

"My brother-in-law is a Green County sheriff deputy, told my sister, who then called me early Saturday morning at work with the news of Stacy's death. I was shocked to say the least. I told Herbert when he came to work."

"How did he react?"

"He turned very pale, and I thought he was going to faint. I immediately knew it had to be her. He was in shock. Herbert went to his desk, sat down, and stared into space. I got him a cup of coffee. He started to cry. I didn't know what to do. I rushed out of the office and got Jim. We just stood there outside his office door, watching him. Jim whispered to me that Stacy Leonard must have been his lover. I agreed."

"What happened next?"

"Well, he got up without saying a word, went to his car, and left."

"Did you know where he went?"

"No. And we didn't see him again until Monday morning. He was changed. He had turned inward and wasn't his usual self. We felt sorry for him and gave him the space he needed."

"How does he seem to you now?"

"Remote and conflicted, like a man mourning a lost love for instance. It's hard to explain."

Her face suddenly welled up, and a tear escaped Crandall's eye. She brushed it away with her hand.

Was Donna Crandall in love with her boss? Johns wondered.

"Anything else to add?" Johns asked.

Crandall slowly shook her head. "Can I go?" she asked in a soft voice. The interview was taking its toll on her.

"One more question, did you know Norman Stafford, the man murdered in New Glarus?"

Donna shook her head. "No."

Johns nodded. Crandall stood up and left the room without another word. She was visibly upset. Johns answered his own question. She was obviously in love with her boss.

*   *   *

Jim Hull entered the office and shook hands with Johns. He was one of two car salesmen. Jim was full-time, and the other was part-time. He was in his fifties, average in height, had blue eyes, blondish short hair, and a ready smile. Being born and raised in Monroe, he knew almost everyone. He seemed a little nervous sitting across Johns. His hands were slightly shaking. Being interviewed by the police can be very intimidating.

"Thank you for seeing me today. As you know, we are investigating two murders."

Hull stared at Johns, listening intently.

"Your boss, Herbert Milz, had a personal relationship with the first victim, Stacy Leonard. Were you aware of that?"

Jim nodded. "I suspected that Mr. Milz was having an affair, but I didn't know who the woman was until after her death."

"How did that make you feel, the affair?"

"Jolly good for him. Every man deserves a little happiness in their life, don't you agree?"

"Why do you say that?"

"It is well known that his wife is a world-class bitch, a life sentence, like being in prison. Well, anyway, he never drank at the office until after he married her. Shortly after the marriage, he fought to keep the business open, and we really appreciated that. His new wife wanted him to sell it. He is a kind, caring man and has always treated us with respect and loyalty."

Johns rocked back in his chair. *Does loyalty go both ways?* he thought to himself. "So tell me about the night Stacy Leonard was murdered. Mr. Milz said he arrived at the office around 5:30 p.m. Is that correct?"

"Yes. He arrived in an obvious unsettled state, you know, not himself. He left earlier in the day in a good mood and returned later in a sour mood. It was apparent that something had happened. He immediately went into his office and shut the door. Donna came to me and told me about her concerns. Something was not right with him."

"What did you do?"

"Nothing. If he wanted to be alone, that was his business. After Donna went home, I worked the car lot until 8:00 p.m. and went home. I asked Mr. Milz through his closed door if I should lock up, but he said he would. So I left him there."

"So you didn't actually see him other than observing him when he arrived at the office at 5:30 p.m.?"

"Correct. I saw him drive into the lot and get out of his car."

"Did you know Stacy Leonard?"

"I knew of her, but that was all. I didn't have any contact with her. But her husband bought his Plymouth Valiant from us a number of years ago."

"What can you tell me about Linda Milz? You indicated that you didn't like her."

"Where do I start?" Hull asked himself, glancing to the ceiling. "Before Mr. Milz married her, he was an easy-going man with a good heart. He worked very hard building up the business. He joined the country club in order to boost sales. And it worked. We sold more cars to country club members than ever before. But every upside has a downside, and in this case, it was Linda. She had a reputation that extended beyond the confines of the country club. She was a drunken she-devil that used her wealth to make herself a name in the community. The merchants fawned all over her because she paid top dollar for their merchandise."

"Did she ever buy a car from you?"

Hull laughed. "She wanted a fancy Buick Riviera and touted the fact that only Madison car dealers could do her bidding. Truthfully, I am glad I didn't have to deal with her and pay her false compliments to get her business. After all, a man has his pride."

"So Mr. Milz didn't know her until he joined the country club?"

"As far as I know."

"So what happened, why did he marry her?"

"In my opinion, he was bullied into the marriage. In many ways, he was naive in the ways of the world when it came to women. He is a shy man, keeping mostly to himself. When he was building up the business, he worked very hard, putting in long hours. I started working here part-time, and I never saw a more dedicated man than him. He told me that Linda had a reputation at the country club, and he tried to avoid her. But Linda, an only child, was raised a spoiled brat who would do anything to get what she wanted. Power and control, that was her mantra. And she went all in after Mr. Milz."

"Why?"

"Honestly, I don't know. She had wealth, he didn't. He was a nice guy, she was a bitch and seemed to revel in it. She was pushy and aggressive, he was even-tempered and mild. Maybe she acted out of panic. She was getting older and not married. Who knows? So she marries a man whom she could totally dominate and control. Only God knows the answer to that!"

"Do you think that Mr. Milz is capable of harming anyone?"

Hull sat bolt upright in his chair and glared at Johns. "Absolutely not! He is incapable of swatting a fly!"

Johns gave Hull a moment to settle down. "Did Donna Crandall tell you about Mr. Milz and his reaction to the news of Stacy Leonard's death on Saturday?"

"Yes. She told me."

"What did you think?"

"I felt sorry for Mr. Milz. He must have truly loved Mrs. Leonard."

"Were you at work when he arrived Saturday morning?"

"Yes. But he left shortly after hearing the news."

"Any idea where he might have gone?"

"My guess would be to his cabin at Cadiz Springs. That's his refuge and retreat."

Johns straightened up in his chair. "Okay, let's recap our interview. Mr. Milz is in an unhappy marriage. He was bullied into a marriage to a woman he didn't love. He met and fell in love with a married woman and had an affair with her. That same woman is brutally murdered. Mr. Milz is heartbroken. He is a suspect, and we are trying to eliminate him from our inquires. Is there anything I have left out?"

"He isn't a killer."

"So after eight o'clock on that Friday night, you can't verify the movements of Mr. Milz?"

Hull shook his head. He looked sad. "No," he said in a weak voice.

"Did you know Norman Stafford, the man killed in New Glarus?"

"No."

"Okay then, if you can remember or think of anything to help our inquiries, please call."

Hull nodded. Johns stood up and shook hands with him. Hull left and Mr. Milz reentered the office.

"Anything else, Chief?" he asked.

Johns thanked him for his time and arranging the interviews. As Johns drove to the PD with his windshield wipers on, he shook his head. *Was this another dead end?*

CHAPTER 15

L inda Milz nervously paced around her living room floor with a brandy old-fashion in her hand. It took her an hour getting ready to see the chief. She decided to wear a light cotton dress with a plunging neckline and a black push-up bra. That should get his attention. Complimenting her dress, she wore a pearl necklace and open-toed sandals, showing off her pedicured red-painted toenails. If nothing else, the chief would have something to look at and admire during the interview.

She and Chief Johns had arranged to meet at her home at 4:00 p.m. She was annoyed because the chief wanted to interview her about Stacy Leonard's murder. Also, her bridge club met on Monday afternoons at three o'clock at the country club. She had to cancel and find a substitute. She was a good bridge player and hated to miss a game. She told the chief on the telephone that the meeting with him was a total waste of her time. All she remembered on the night Stacy was murdered was Herbert waking her up around nine thirty or so after she passed out on the living room sofa. He put her to bed. End of story. She told Johns the interview was meaningless and didn't see it as anything more than harassment. She insisted that she didn't know of anything of importance that could help him in his inquiries. Only after Johns told her that she could always come to the PD for the interview did she recant and agree to meet at her house.

Stopping in front of an oversized oval antique mirror hanging on the east wall of the living room, she took an inventory of herself. She was in her mid-thirties but looked older. She saw prominent bags under her brown eyes from a lifetime of boozing and too many late-night parties. The bags under her eyes and a couple of new wrinkles were visible evidence how she lived her life, the choices she had made. How did the lines between right and wrong choices get so blurred? What was she thinking when she married Herbert? What happened to her girlhood effervescence? Her painted face and the expensive French perfume that she used to trick and fool men into having sex? Nevertheless, her bleached blond hair and pageboy haircut still made her quite attractive to men. Her parents had her nose straightened and turned up at the end when she was sixteen to improve her looks. Years of dental braces and teeth-whitening worked its magic. She was in love with her looks, except for those annoying bags under her eyes. Surgery was needed to get rid of them.

This whole business with Hebert and his affair was embarrassing. Her drinking buddies at the country club teased her about it. Not that he was stepping out on her, but that it became public. For the country club members, a scandal like this was generally hushed up and buried. Now and again, a divorce would happen, but the steamy details were covered up and remained private. The reputation of the club was more important than silly affairs and the soap-opera dramas that played out around them.

The chiming pendulum antique clock on the fireplace mantel rang out four times. He was late! Linda was instantly upset. She finished her drink and made herself another one. This would be her third drink of the day, and she was just warming up. After the interview, she would drive to the club for supper and a night of drinking with her girlfriends. The drive from her house was about four minutes, but she liked parking her expensive Buick Riviera near the entrance to show it off. She scoffed at the Cadillac owners much to her amusement and enjoyment. When she confronted the witless owners, she told them that they had no taste in cars, just driving around in long gunboats looking for an ocean and a place to dock taking up two parking spots. She wasn't bashful and used her tongue as a sharp weapon. The wives of the other members loved her for her brash and abrasive wit when speaking to their husbands, something that they would never dare or dream of doing.

At 4:10 p.m., Johns pulled into the driveway of the 4,500-square-foot house and parked. The landscaping in front of the house was immaculate, and the grass was trimmed to perfection. Johns wondered how much money was spent on the lawn maintenance. He could see a golf course fairway when he looked past the corner of the house. Arriving at the front door, he pushed the doorbell and heard the Westminster chimes inside, announcing his arrival. The door flew open, and Linda Milz glared at him.

"You are late!" she said, slightly slurring her words.

Johns was taken aback. He just stared at her. Her painted face and sexy dress were too much for him. From the expression on her face, he could see a dark cloud hanging over her head. He instantly knew this was going to be a challenging interview.

"Can I come in?" he asked.

"If you must."

Linda led him into the living room and seated him on an expensive oversized light-blue stripped cushioned chair facing out a picture window overlooking the golf course. Johns could see two stopped golf carts and the players were drinking beer and talking.

"Can I get you something to drink?" Linda asked. "A beer perhaps?"

"Thank you, but no, I am on duty."

Linda raised her eyebrows in disgust. "Well, then I guess I must drink alone." She seated herself on a matching chair across from Johns. "This is a by-invitation-only private party, so start asking your mundane questions. I will give you only thirty minutes because I have an appointment at the club."

Johns felt his face redden and his blood pressure rise as Linda took a sip of her drink. She was trying to take over the interview and show her superiority by dictating the rules.

"I will be here for as long as it takes," he firmly responded.

She was who she was, and she didn't give a fig whether Johns liked her or not. A short pause of defiance followed.

"Fire away. I am all ears," Linda retorted.

Johns needed to control his emotions. The blatant arrogance of this woman was maddening. "As I told you on the telephone, we are investigating the murder of Stacy Leonard, the woman who was having an affair with your husband."

"So what of it? Why should I care about what Herbert does or doesn't do?"

The third drink was having its desired effect. The genie was out of the bottle. Linda was feeling emboldened and combative.

"Look, this is a murder inquiry, and I expect your full cooperation. If not, we can continue this interview at the PD."

"Ask away," Linda sarcastically said, slumping back in her chair. No police officer was going to intimidate her.

"Given your husband's relationship with Mrs. Leonard, we need to confirm his alibi for the night Mrs. Leonard was murdered."

Linda laughed. "You have got to be kidding! Herbert murder anyone? How absurd is that? He doesn't have the balls to harm a fly. Are you looking for something that isn't there?"

"Just answer the question," an exasperated Johns said.

"Like I told you on the telephone, I came home from the club, and I was very tired. I fell asleep on the sofa," she said, pointing to the sofa. "Herbert woke me up and put me to bed."

"Had you been drinking?"

"Who told you that?"

"Just answer the question."

"Well, I had been at the club, so draw your own conclusions."

"Herbert told us when he arrived home sometime between 9:30 p.m. and 10:00 p.m., he found you passed out on the sofa. He helped you to bed."

"If he told you that, it is probably true. But then again, he didn't tell me about his pedestrian tryst with that horrible woman. It's all a matter of trust when it comes to marriage, don't you agree?"

Johns didn't respond to her question. A wry smile suddenly crossed her painted lips. She shifted her position in her chair and casually crossed her legs in such a way that her dress rose above her tan line exposing the pale whiteness of her inner thighs and her black laced panties. She was intently watching Johns for a reaction. He remained stone-faced, stoic. She crossed her legs again, allowing her dress to drop back to her knee.

"Are you sure I can't get you a drink?" she asked.

Johns ignored her question. "When did you find out about the affair?"

Linda sighed. "One of my dearest friends called me Sunday afternoon, informing me that Hebert was having an affair with the murdered woman."

"Who called you?"

"Millie Chesebro."

"Was that the first time you heard about it?"

"The murder or Hebert's affair?"

"Both," Johns replied.

"I heard about the murder on Saturday. Town gossip travels fast. Then on Sunday, Millie told me about the affair."

"How did that make you feel? Did you ask Herbert about it?"

"He was at his Cadiz Springs cabin on Sunday, so I grilled him when he got home. In fact, he was at his cabin both Saturday and Sunday. He owned up to the affair right away. But he said he didn't kill Mrs. Leonard. He is such a wuss. Lying to me is such a total waste of time, and he knows it."

"Was it unusual that he was at the cabin both days?"

"He has done that in the past. He tells me that he needs the time alone because of the pressures of his job. It's a cock-and-bull story, of course, but that's what he says."

"What did you say to him?"

"I told him I didn't give a shit about the affair, but the humiliation and embarrassment for me was unforgivable. How was I going to face my friends? We all live in a small town, and everyone knows everybody's business. Any good news is temporary, but any bad news sticks to you for life, you know, like shit from an exploding toilet. How can I live with that? I will remind you, Chief Johns, that I have standing in this community. But of course, he never gave that a second thought. I was furious at his stupidity."

"I will ask you again, do you think your husband killed Stacy Leonard?"

"Are you deaf? Refer to my previous answer. He doesn't have the courage or the guts."

"Okay. Can you think of anyone who would want to harm her?"

"Are you kidding? I didn't even know the woman." Linda finished her drink and stood up. "Mind if get a refill?" She made herself another drink and sat down again, looking at her watch. "Is this almost over? I need to be at the club."

Johns grimaced. "Just a couple of more questions. Are you familiar with the cabin at Cadiz Springs?"

"I was at the cabin once, and that was enough for me. I can't imagine why Herbert spends so much time there."

Johns smiled. He knew. "Herbert told us when we interviewed him that he was at the office from 5:30 p.m. until around 9:30 p.m. Friday, after which, he went home. Did he tell you that he came straight home from the office?"

"I didn't ask him. Why should I?"

"So where were you that Friday night? And when did you get home?"

Linda sniggered. "So now I am a suspect?"

"No. I am not saying that. We are only concerned with everyone's movements and a time line to get the complete picture."

"The bartender's name at the club is Brian something or other. If anyone can tell you, he is the man. He probably knows more about the members than they know about themselves. You should ask him. I don't remember the exact time I left."

"Did you drive straight home?"

"Of course. I wasn't going to leave my car there and walk home."

"Okay, one more question, do you or Herbert own a handgun?"

"Why?"

"To protect yourself or for target practice, for instance."

Linda sat straight up in her chair. "Are you saying that my life is in danger?" she said in a snarky tone of voice.

"Not at all. I only want to know if you own a handgun."

"No. We don't. If Herbert owns one, I have never seen it. But if you think my life is in danger, I can always buy one."

Johns was getting really annoyed and exasperated, given all the caustic comments and attitude being thrown at him by this self-centered egotistical woman. He had had enough for one day. A long silence passed between them, making Linda nervous. What was she thinking? He stood up and thanked her for her time. He would be contacting her if he had any more questions. Linda jumped to her feet and ushered him to the front door, slamming it shut behind him.

Johns shook his head as he made his way back to his car. "That woman is as twisty as a cork screw," he said to himself. Herbert was right. His wife was a first-class bitch and how he stays married to her is mind-boggling. A brief thought suddenly occurred to him. *If Herbert was the killer, he chose the wrong victim!* Johns immediately laughed at himself as backed out of the driveway.

As he stopped at the end of the street for a stop sign, he suddenly had an idea. He turned east toward the country club, parked, and went inside. He asked to see Brian, the bartender. Brian Gullickson shortly appeared. He was tall, 6 feet 2 inches, with sandy blond crew cut hair, blue eyes, and a broad toothy smile. He gave Johns a firm handshake. They went outside to the parking lot to talk. Johns told him about the investigation and wanted to speak to him in the morning. Brian quickly agreed and said he would be at the PD at eleven o'clock.

On his drive back to the PD, Johns's mind kicked into gear. What if Herbert left the office at 9:00 p.m., not around 9:30 p.m. like he said? He would have plenty of time to drive to Stacy's house, kill her, and be home again to put his wife to bed at, say, 10:00 p.m. The sun setting on Friday was approximately 9:30 p.m., so the possibility that Agnes Keel couldn't identify the car because the sky was darkening and the shadows were getting longer was reasonable. And also, her eyesight probably wasn't that good. He decided to make the drive himself to record the time from Milz Auto Sales to Stacy's house and back to Monroe just to satisfy his own curiosity. Also, could Herbert have done this under the influence of alcohol, after drinking heavily at the sales office?

CHAPTER 16

The next morning, Tuesday, Johns and Sam agreed to debrief at ten o'clock in Johns's office. That would give them an hour before the Brian Gullickson interview. Sam was feeling perplexed. She reviewed her notes again regarding the interviews at the Tschanz Insurance Agency. On a sheet of paper, she had written down the victims' names, Stacy Leonard and Norman Stafford, with doodling circles around them. Then she wrote down the names Paul Leonard and Hebert Milz. Next to their names, she had penciled in a bold underlined question mark for a possible third suspect who hadn't surfaced in the investigation. Her diagram looked like a pyramid with the two victims at the top and the three suspects at base. She connected the names and the question mark with dotted lines. The visual representation was helpful, but nothing new jumped out at her from the simple diagram. It was frustrating. Either Paul Leonard or Herbert Milz or the question mark could have killed Stacy and Norman. The motive was certainly there for the two prime suspects, but what about the question mark? In the meantime, the death of Norman Stafford niggled her and remained a mystery. Why him? Other than Stacy, who even knew he existed or had any contact with him? Neither Leonard nor Milz mentioned him during their interviews. So why was Norman Stafford killed? Sam drew three circles around the question mark. "Who are you?" she asked herself.

At 10:00 a.m., Sam and Johns convened in his office. Each of them brought a mug of coffee. After Sam was settled in her chair, she began reading from her notes concerning the interviews at the Tschanz Insurance Agency. She concluded that nothing helpful came out the meeting, other than Norman keeping his affair with Stacy a secret. Sam showed her hand-sketched diagram to the chief. Johns smiled at the drawing and agreed. *Who, indeed, was the mystery question mark? What was his involvement in the two deaths?*

"So how did it go with you?" Sam asked, sipping her hot coffee.

"Not much to report with the interviews at Milz Auto Sales. Yes, the employees guessed that Hebert was having an affair, but they didn't know with whom. They verified Herbert's story about returning to work at 5:30 p.m. on the night of the murder. However, neither one of them had any firsthand knowledge of where he went after leaving work that night."

"Do you think that they were telling you the truth?"

"I don't think they would have any reason to lie. They weren't connected to the murder in any way that makes any sense."

"So what are we left with?" Sam asked.

"A timeline."

"Explain."

"Okay. Herbert said he left the office at approximately 9:30 p.m. and went home. He had been drinking. We only have his word that he went straight home. But what if he left before 9:30 p.m. and instead drove to Stacy's house? He was intoxicated, lost his temper, and shot her. Then he picked up the spent bullet casing and drove home to find his wife passed out on the sofa. I will make the drive myself to test out my theory that he would have had plenty of time to commit the murder."

"That sounds plausible. He would have plenty of time to make the round trip. But how about Norman Stafford? Why kill him?"

"Good question. How about this: Remember Agnes Keel saying it was too dark to clearly see the driver or the make of car that night pulling up in front of Stacy's house? It was getting dark, and the eyesight of an elderly woman looking through a pair of binoculars probably wasn't too good. But—and I find this interesting—she said that a second car stopped and parked on the shoulder of the road, turning off its headlights at the same time the mystery car was at the house and Stacy was being murdered."

Sam sat straight up in her chair. "Oh my god!"

"Yes. The driver of the second car could have been Norman Stafford. He was there to see Stacy, but seeing the other car, he stopped and waited. Then he saw Herbert or whoever leaving the house and speeding down the driveway."

"Why didn't he go to the house to check on Stacy?" Sam asked.

"Honestly, I don't know. Did he follow the driver home to see who he was? Did he return to the house and find Stacy dead? Did he leave and not report the murder to implicate himself? Too many unanswered questions."

"If your theory is correct, that eliminates Paul Leonard as a suspect."

"Remember, it's only conjecture."

"Okay, then why would Herbert kill Stafford?"

"Maybe Norman threatened Herbert or was trying to blackmail him if he was, in fact, the killer."

Sam slumped back in her chair and stared at the ceiling. She was thinking. Johns gave her the time to finish her thought.

"What do you think of this hypothesis?" she asked. "Norman followed Herbert back to Monroe. Then he returned to Stacy's house and confronted her about her relationship with Herbert. Agnes Keel, by this time, was probably asleep and didn't see him return to the house. They had an argument, and Norman shot her in a jealous rage. If it went down that way, then the question remains— who shot Norman?"

Johns wrinkled his eyebrows. "Why do you always do this to me? I have solved the murders, and then you pour cold water on my theory."

Sam chuckled. "We need facts and data. However, your theory is very thought-provoking and interesting."

Johns wrinkled his nose. They remained silent for a moment, thinking about Johns's theory and Sam's rebuttal. Was any of it plausible?

"So how did it go with Linda Milz?" Sam finally asked, breaking the silence.

Johns exhaled and sighed. "What a piece of work."

"I have never met her. Is she as bad or worse than Herbert indicated?"

"I can tell you this: In my opinion, she is vain, self-indulgent, insecure, and a snob of a woman. I think controlling and manipulative would best describe her."

"Whoa. What are your true feelings?"

Johns laughed. "Am I that transparent?"

"Like a looking glass. Did you learn anything useful?"

"Putting aside the fact that she loathes her husband, not really. She does confirm that Herbert woke her up sometime around 10:00 p.m. and tucked her into bed. She admits she was passed out on the sofa."

"When did she learn about the murder?"

"Saturday. Local town gossip made its way into her house. And on Sunday, a friend of hers, Millie Chesebro, called and told her that Stacy and Herbert were having an affair. The news about Herbert's infidelity really pissed her off."

"Do you think she was telling you the truth?"

Johns shrugged. "Who knows? Well, anyway, she gave Herbert the riot act for belittling her and her precious reputation."

"Doesn't sound like much of a marriage to me," Sam said.

"For some reason, that woman really got under my skin. I just didn't like her. Is evil the right word?" Johns paused and then continued. "What was she thinking when she married Herbert? What did she expect to accomplish? She sorely lacks any kind of human empathy when it comes to relationships."

Sam slumped back in her chair. "Only a shrink can answer your questions. With that being said, Herbert's remorse must be great," Sam offered.

"On that point, I fully concur."

"Does she own a handgun?"

"She says she doesn't."

"Do you believe her? Or more importantly, do you consider her a suspect?"

"Not at this time. She reminds me of one of those people not destined for greatness, a person who bumbles and stumbles their way through life lost in an alcoholic haze of self-pity. Hopefully, Brian

Gullickson can help us untangle this enigma of a woman." Johns looked at his watch. "It's almost 11:00 a.m. I will go to the front desk to wait for him. We will do the interview together."

Sam nodded. She stood up and went to the restroom and back to her desk. She felt frustrated. Too many theories, not enough facts.

Brian arrived on time, and Johns took him to the interview room. Sam joined them. Brian refused a cup of coffee or a glass of water. He sat down across the gray metal table, looking at the chief and Sam.

"Thank you for coming in to see us on short notice," Johns began. "How can I help you?"

"As you know, we are investigating the deaths of Stacy Leonard and Norman Stafford. Herbert Milz was having an affair with Stacy Leonard, and we are trying to piece together their relationship. Both Linda Milz and Herbert are members of the country club. I interviewed Linda yesterday, and she told me that you could vouch for her movements on the night Stacy Leonard was murdered." Johns stopped and looked at Brian squarely in the eye. "Any questions?"

Brian grinned at Johns. "It must have been quite the interview, knowing what I do about Linda Milz. Well, anyway, Mrs. Milz came to the club shortly after I spoke to you in the parking lot yesterday, and she was all fired up. She was already in her cups, if you know what I mean. She told me that you were accusing her of murder and she wanted to confirm with me that I remembered her being at the club that Friday night and what time she left. She was in a state of panic, confusion, or whatever, not her usual bossy self."

"Did she ask you to lie?"

"Heavens no. I think she was trying to remember what happened and her own movements. You must have really shaken her up."

"That's the reason for this meeting. What do you remember from Friday night?"

Brian slumped back in his chair, gathering his thoughts. "Well, to be honest, nothing unusual stands out. Just another Friday night of drinking, dinner, playing cards in the lounge, and of course, more drinking."

"Did Linda play cards?"

"By card playing, I mean, high-stakes poker and other games of chance, men only. Mrs. Milz plays bridge with her friends in the afternoon. She mentioned to me that your visit yesterday was very inconvenient, causing her to miss one of her precious card games. She is an excellent player."

"Okay. So what do you remember about that night?"

"Mrs. Milz came to the club around 5:00 p.m. Her friends had bemoaned that fact that she was late and wasn't there when I was serving them drinks. Well, anyway, after she arrived, she and a couple of other women sat in the lounge, drinking and laughing before dinner."

"How many drinks did she have before dinner?"

"Three to four brandy old-fashions was the usual norm. She has a high tolerance for liquor. Well, anyway, the trio went to dinner and returned to the lounge for a night cap, which usually meant more drinking until nine or ten o'clock."

"So how many drinks do you think she had in total before she left?"

"Let's see. Three drinks before dinner, two with dinner, and three or four after dinner. Between nine and ten would do it."

"That's a lot of alcohol," Sam said.

Brian shrugged. "You should see her weekly bar tab. We refer to it as occupational drinking."

"Did you see her leave? Do you remember the time?"

"I didn't exactly see what time she left. I would guess sometime after 9:00 p.m."

"Could she have left before then?"

"It's possible. I didn't have any reason to keep tabs on her."

"After a night of drinking, did she normally go home?"

Sam was interested in the direction Johns was taking with his questioning. Brian paused. He was thinking.

"I suppose so. I can't think of anywhere else she would go."

"So she wasn't impaired to the point of not driving safely?"

"I wouldn't say that. As far as I know, she always made it home without incident."

"Did her husband ever meet or join her at the club?"

"No, never. After they got married, he came in a few times. Mrs. Milz got so wasted I think Herbert was totally humiliated and embarrassed. I haven't seen him for a year or more."

"How would you describe their marriage?"

Brian smiled. He seemed too relaxed, a man with secrets. "Over the years, I have seen many things at the club that are repulsive and disgusting. The pay is good, and I consider the generous tips I receive as hush money. It's a culture—a cult, if you like—of people with personal problems. I turn a blind eye to it, and we coexist. I have earned their trust through my discretion as a bartender. To answer your question, though, Mrs. Milz rarely talked about her husband, you know, like he didn't exist."

"So from the amount of time Mrs. Milz spends at the club, would you say that they lead separate lives?"

"Marriages are complex things. Did they live separate lives, you ask? I think they had worked it out."

Sam thought Brian was a smart and clever guy. He was answering questions without answering them.

"Did you know either Stacy Leonard or Norman Stafford?" Johns asked.

"I knew that Stacy Leonard was married to the town pharmacist. That's about all I know about her. They weren't club members. As for Norman Stafford, I never heard of him until his death."

"One more question, does either Mr. or Mrs. Milz own a handgun?"

Brian shook his head. "Not that I am aware of."

A moment of silence passed. Brian looked comfortable, in that he didn't seem nervous or anxious. He had done his job. Johns looked at Sam who shook her head. Johns stood up.

"We don't have any more questions for you at this time. I will contact you if anything else comes up. If you can think of anything that might help us in the investigation, please feel free to contact me."

Sam and Brian stood up. Brian shook hands with the chief. "Glad to help."

Brian exited the interview room, and Sam escorted him to the front door and rejoined the chief. This time they sat across each other at the table.

"Did we learn anything new?" Sam asked.

"I was wondering if Linda could have left the country club before 9:00 p.m., driven to Stacy's house, killed her, driven home, and passed out on her living room sofa. That's why I was interested in the amount of booze she normally drank at the club."

"I can help you there. A brandy old-fashion has approximately two ounces of brandy in it. Brian said that Linda could consume as many as ten drinks in a day. If she started drinking at three o'clock Friday afternoon and quit at nine o'clock that night, that would be twenty ounces or a little shy of a fifth of Brandy. She would have consumed all that alcohol in the space of six hours. Unless she has the tolerance and body weight of an African elephant, there is no way she could have done what you are thinking."

"So you don't think it possible?"

Sam laughed. "I pass out after two drinks. Once, at a party during my college days, I had five drinks and spent the night praying to the porcelain god while my head was spinning in circles. I was never so sick in my life."

"One of your better nights, Detective?"

Sam ignored him.

Johns looked at the ceiling. "I heard once that the drinks at the club were watered down as the boozing got later into the evening. Maybe Linda wasn't as drunk as Brian intimated."

Sam didn't say anything and reflected on the chief's comment. "That's a good point. Okay, so what's our next step?" she asked.

"I think we are getting a clearer picture of events. The way I see this case unfolding is that Herbert and Stacy started having an affair. All seemed to be going well for the two of them for a while. Then Stacy found another lover and ditched Herbert for Norman Stafford. Pretty straightforward, I would think. A daytime soap opera with lots of melodrama, sentimentality, passion, and anxiety. Then enters a third person, someone who has been betrayed, enraged, or something else that made him so angry that he kills two people. He may even be the question mark on your diagram. One thing is for sure, the killer is either very clever or very lucky. But he has made a mistake somewhere, and we need to discover it and bring him to justice. Every murderer screws up somewhere, and we need to find the mistake. Sound good so far?"

Sam nodded. "So what's missing?"

Johns continued. "The gun, the murder weapon. Where is it? Find the gun, find the killer," Johns said, answering her question. He sat back in his chair and stared at Sam.

"Where do we look?" she asked.

"As soon as I get search warrants for Paul Leonard's house, Herbert Milz's house, and the cabin at Cadiz Springs, we will make a thorough search of the houses and surrounding grounds. An unannounced search warrant should shake everybody up. Even if we don't find the gun, the search may cause the killer to panic and make a mistake."

With that being said, the meeting ended. Sam was anxious to start the searches, something to get them going and solve the case. In the meantime, she was going to interview the employees at the pharmacy.

CHAPTER 17

Paul Leonard was very accommodating when he scheduled the meeting with Detective Gates and his employees. He would manage the cash register while the interviews took place in his office at the back of the store. The pharmacy was located on the northside of the courthouse square, just two blocks from the PD. The interview was set for four thirty Wednesday afternoon. There were three full-time employees, all women, at the store. One woman, Joan Grenzow, was on vacation with her family to their cabin in Northern Wisconsin. The other two women, Rhonda Hasse and Joy Holcomb, were middle-aged and had worked at the pharmacy for years. Hasse was married to a local farmer and worked there to supplement their farm income. She was of average height and looks with shoulder-length auburn hair. She had calloused hands, representing the hard work of working on a farm. Holcomb, by contrast, was a spinster. She was very tall and thin with short brown hair and wore black rimmed spectacles. She was the bookkeeper and helped out in the store when needed, stocking shelves or working the cash register. She was in an unrequited-love relationship with Paul Leonard. Why couldn't Mr. Leonard see her feelings for him? Or if he did, why did he choose to ignore them? All three women were well known in Monroe and were part of the grapevine of local gossip and rumor that sustained the city. Hasse and Holcomb talked between themselves as they waited for Detective Gates to arrive. They were seated in front of Leonard's desk on high-backed oak chairs.

"So what do you think?" Hasse asked.

Holcomb shifted in her chair. She didn't know what to think. The shock of Stacy's death was very unnerving for her. In her heart of hearts, she secretly hoped that Leonard would take notice of her and think of her in more personal terms, not just another employee and a bookkeeper. She tried to convey her sincere condolences to him after Stacy's death, but his mind seemed to be elsewhere. Something much deeper was bothering him. If he would only confide in her, she would go to the ends of the earth for him.

"I think that we need to rally around Mr. Leonard and support him," Holcomb replied.

"I agree. Mr. Leonard told us to be truthful with the detective."

"Look, both of us know that he was unhappy in his marriage. What if the detective asks about that?"

"Whoa, stop there. We don't know that for certain," Hasse interrupted. "If you remember, the three of us talked about it. The sudden change in Mr. Leonard about a month ago, it was like he had made a decision and appeared less anxious. We all speculated that he had made a decision to divorce his wife. What else could it have been?"

"Yes, you may be right. But suspicion is one thing, facts are another. As you are well aware, Mr. Leonard is a very quiet man who doesn't share his feelings. If he was having marital difficulties, that was solely his business. All marriages have their ups and downs," Holcomb said.

Hasse grinned at her.

"Is there something you want to share?" Holcomb asked.

Hasse laughed. "Of course not. I will admit that living with another person is challenging, but we work it out. I think that Mr. Leonard and his wife would have worked it out, if she had lived."

Holcomb sighed. "I suppose so."

"Do you think that Mr. Leonard might be a suspect in his wife's murder?" Hasse suddenly asked.

The question caught Holcomb by surprise. "I can't believe that. We have known him for years. If he is a suspect, it's ridiculous. He is incapable of murder!"

The outburst caught Hasse by surprise. *Were some repressed feelings for Mr. Leonard seeing the light of day?*

There was a knock on the closed door, and Detective Gates entered. She introduced herself and apologized for being late. She sat down in Mr. Leonard's chair across the two women. They each stood up and introduced themselves and shook hands with her across the desk. Sam took out her notebook and laid it on the desk in front of her. She smiled at the ladies as they sat down again. Sam noticed that the two women were wearing cotton dresses. The dress Hasse was wearing had a floral design and looked like she had sown it together from a pattern.

"As you are aware, we are investigating the murders of two people, Stacy Leonard and Norman Stafford," Sam began.

Both of the women's eyes were unblinking and riveted on Sam. She had their attention.

"The purpose of my visit today is to eliminate Mr. Leonard as a suspect in the murders. I will need your cooperation during this interview and to be truthful and factual. Okay, any questions?"

"Is Mr. Leonard really a suspect?" Holcomb asked.

"We are only trying to eliminate him as a suspect," Sam replied.

Holcomb let out a big sigh of relief. Both women shook their heads. No questions.

"Did either of you know Stacy Leonard?"

"Yes, we knew her but not well," Hasse answered. "Mr. Leonard is very protective of his private life, keeping it separate from his work life."

"Would you agree?" Sam asked, looking at Holcomb.

She nodded in agreement.

"So neither of you knew her outside of work? In other words, you didn't socialize with her?"

"No," Holcomb answered.

Sam made a note in her notebook as the women looked on.

"On the Friday of Stacy's death, I understand that Mr. Leonard left work early to attend a bowling tournament in Milwaukee. Is that correct?"

"Yes," Hasse answered. "He goes once a year to those tournaments with his bowling team, and he looks forward to the time away from Monroe. He generally talks about it a week or two before he leaves."

"So was there anything unusual or different about his leaving this year?"

Both women looked at each other.

"No, not really," Holcomb said. "He is a workaholic, and the time way from the job is good for him. Everything was as normal."

"Do you agree?" Sam asked, looking at Hasse.

"Yes. He was excited to go."

"As far as you know, he wasn't anxious or nervous or seemed out of sorts about anything the day he left?"

"Not that I could tell," Hasse replied.

"When did you hear about Stacy's murder?"

"At the store, Saturday afternoon. A customer came in and told us."

"Were you surprised?"

"I think shocked is the more accurate word," Holcomb said. "We just couldn't believe it. The whole town was talking about it, both the murder and the Stacy's affair with Herbert Milz. We were concerned and worried for Mr. Leonard, being that he was in Milwaukee."

"You knew about the affair?" Sam asked in disbelief.

"Town gossip," Hasse said.

"When did you see him next?"

"He came into the store Monday morning and told us that we would have to run the place ourselves until further notice. We could call him if an emergency came up. He gave us his sister's telephone number. We already had his home telephone number on file."

"How did he seem to you?"

"What do you mean?" Holcomb asked.

"His demeanor, his behavior."

"I think he was in shock. His eyes were glazed over. He looked away and not directly at us when speaking. We felt sorry for him. After all, his wife had just been murdered," Hasse said.

Sam hesitated before asking her next question. So far, she had only taken one note.

"To the best of your knowledge, was his marriage to Stacy a happy one?"

A discernible silence fell over the room.

"Why did you ask that?" Holcomb finally asked.

"It's only a routine question during a police inquiry. We want to get to know the victim and the spouse and their relationship as much as possible to better further our investigation. If you feel uncomfortable with the question, we can move on."

Hasse looked at Holcomb, who nodded.

"We had our suspicions that all wasn't right with the marriage," Hasse softly said.

"Explain," Sam replied.

"Look, first of all, just to be clear, we are convinced that Mr. Leonard didn't murder his wife. It isn't in his nature. But we suspected something was happening in the marriage that Mr. Leonard kept to himself."

"Why do you say that?" Sam asked, eyeing her.

"Some time ago, something changed. It was very noticeable to us. He was spending more and more time at the store. He rarely spoke about his wife. In fact, other than bowling, he didn't talk about his personal life at all. From time to time, we would ask about Stacy, bringing her up in general conversation, but he either changed the subject or said she was fine. Of course, we knew that wasn't the case, and we didn't pursue it. That being said, life seemed to be grinding him down."

"Anything to add?" Sam asked Holcomb.

"No, not really. We all felt sorry for him."

"Did you know his first wife?"

"Yes," Holcomb replied. "She was a wonderful person. Being killed in an automobile accident was horrific and so sad. Mr. Leonard dearly loved her, and I don't think he really got over her death."

"Do you know of anyone who would want to harm Stacy Leonard?"

Both women looked at each other and shook their heads.

"We didn't know her very well, other than she was a beloved music teacher at the high school," Hasse said.

"Were you aware that Mr. Leonard was thinking about divorcing his wife?"

The question stunned Holcomb, and she sat bolt straight up in her seat. "No!" she exclaimed. "I didn't know that!"

"Okay, then did either of you know Norman Stafford from New Glarus, the man who was found murdered in the New Glarus Woods State Park?"

"I didn't know him before I read the account of the murder in the newspaper," Hasse said.

Holcomb shook her head. Sam jotted down a couple of notes in her notebook. The women intently watched her.

"To your knowledge, does Mr. Leonard own a handgun?"

"I don't know. We don't have a gun in the store. If he owns one, he has never mentioned it to me," Hasse said.

Sam looked at Holcomb. She shrugged. "If he owns a handgun, I am not aware of it."

"One last question, on the night that Mr. Stafford was killed, do you know where Mr. Leonard might have been?"

Holcomb wrinkled her eyebrows, thinking. "From what I can recall, he left the store as usual and said he was going home."

Sam looked at Hasse.

"I had the afternoon off."

Sam closed her notebook. She looked at both women for a long moment. *Did she believe them?*

"Any questions for me before I leave?"

Holcomb cleared her throat. "Do you think Mr. Leonard murdered his wife and Mr. Stafford?"

"Why, do you think both victims were killed by the same person?"

"Why not? I am not a police detective, but isn't it obvious?"

Sam was impressed by Holcomb's answer. "At this time, we are considering all possibilities. That's what we do as investigating police officers. In the end, the truth will come out, and we will arrest the killer or killers."

The interview was over. Sam and the two women stood up and shook hands. Sam thanked them again for seeing her. On her way out of the pharmacy, she thanked Mr. Leonard for setting up the interviews and the use of his private office. Sam stopped at the front door and froze. A thought suddenly leapt into her head. She turned and waved her hand, beckoning Mr. Leonard who was watching her. He walked toward her with a quizzical look on his face.

"Can you tell me where you were on the night that Norman Stafford was killed?"

Leonard recoiled and turned pale. "Are you accusing me of murder?" he asked in disbelief.

"No, not at all. I am trying to eliminate you as a suspect. Where were you?"

"Let me think. I left work and went straight home."

"Can anyone verify that's what you did? Alibi you?"

"No. Like I said, I went home, heated up some leftovers for supper, read my book, and went to bed."

"Okay," Sam said and abruptly exited the pharmacy. She walked the short distance back to the PD, lost in thought.

Was Paul Leonard the killer? Were his employees lying to her? Did they know something about him that they weren't revealing? The level of paranoia that police officers go through during a murder investigation, not knowing if people are lying to them, is maddening. However, she had one idea that gave her hope—Agnes Keel. She would call Agnes to see what time Paul Leonard got home on the evening that Norman Stafford was murdered. Was his car there all night? Did he leave and come back home? Sam quickened her pace.

At her desk, she looked up the telephone number of Agnes Keel and called her. Agnes answered on the sixth ring.

"Who's there?" she asked.

Sam smiled. "Detective Gates from the Monroe PD. Remember me?"

"Who?"

Sam took the next two minutes explaining who she was. Finally, the tumblers clicked— Agnes remembered her.

"So what do you what to know, dear?"

"I want you to check your log book for Wednesday, May 29, and tell me when Paul Leonard came home from work and if he left again."

"What's that, dear?"

Sam repeated the question two more times. Agnes put the receiver down and retrieved the notebook.

"I have the notebook in my hand. So what day am I looking for?"

Sam remained patient. "Wednesday, May 29."

"Okay, I am looking."

Silence. Sam could hear the ruffling of pages.

"I have it. The page is empty."

"Empty?" Sam exclaimed.

"Why yes. Blank. I remember now. I had stomach cramps and stayed in bed all day. Have you ever had stomach cramps? A damned nuisance, if you ask me."

Sam thanked her for her time and hung up. She leaned back in her chair and shook her head. With all the chaos surrounding the case, the chief hadn't received the search warrants. It had been almost three weeks since Stacy Leonard was killed. It was time to shake the tree and see if anything falls out. The warrants should do it. At least that was Sam's hope.

CHAPTER 18

The search warrants were issued and all carried out at the same time Wednesday afternoon. They were looking for a handgun or any evidence of the ownership of such a gun. Sam led the team at Paul Leonard's house, Captain Miller led the search at the Cadiz Springs cabin, and Chief Johns was at the home of Herbert Milz. All the searches were coordinated to begin at 1:00 p.m. Paul Leonard was at home during the search. He sat on his front porch as a team of police officers went through his house and the grounds. He looked despondent. Herbert Milz unlocked the cabin and let the police officers in. He waited outside in his car. Linda Milz was in a frantic state, surprised by the unannounced visit. Chief Johns handed her the warrant, which she took her time reading. The police officers behind the chief were getting antsy. She handed the warrant back to the chief and told him that her constitutional rights were being violated, and she threatened to sue the chief and the police department for damages and personal pain and suffering. After she let them into the house, she called her lawyer and swore at him. Chief Johns found all this bravado very amusing. Her lawyer showed up fifteen minutes after the search began, read the warrant, and tried to calm Linda down. She told Johns that she was going to the club and to lock up the house after they were finished and not to steal anything. Johns was happy to see the back of her. Later that afternoon, Johns, Sam, and Captain Miller met at the PD to debrief the searches. Johns sat at his desk, looking disappointed and perplexed. Sam and Miller waited for him to begin.

"I don't think the searches were a total waste of time. Even though we didn't find the gun, we put the suspects on notice that we were keeping them in the frame."

Sam and Miller nodded.

"So how did Paul Leonard and Hebert Milz look to you as the searches progressed?" Johns asked.

Miller began. "After Milz unlocked the cabin, he went and sat in his car. He laid his head back on the headrest and closed his eyes. His face was expressionless, unemotional, and looked as if he were in deep thought. He remained that way until the search of the cabin was completed. We looked around the grounds but didn't find anything. I had one thought though: If he were the killer, he could have tossed the gun into the lake."

"Good point. How about you, Sam?"

She shifted her weight in her chair. "The search of the Leonard place revealed nothing new. I felt a little weird walking into the living room. The last time I was there, Stacy Leonard lay dead on the floor. Well, anyway, Leonard sat on the front porch, looking depressed, as we went through the house. He watched as the officers inspected the grounds. He didn't seem nervous or upset. If he was worried that we may find the gun, he didn't show it."

"So neither man showed any concern that we may find the gun?" Johns asked.

"No, I don't think so," Sam replied.

"So in other words, if one of them was the killer, he knew that the gun wasn't there to be found. That knowledge, in and of itself, must have been reassuring."

"Sounds about right to me. How did it go at the Milz residence?" Sam asked.

"After we got through the gatekeeper and her lawyer? We didn't find the gun after a thorough search. That woman really gets under my skin."

Sam laughed. "So where does that leave us?"

"Do you need me for anything else?" Miller interrupted, looking at his watch.

"Thanks for your help, but I think we can handle it from here," Johns replied.

Miller stood up and patted Sam on the shoulder. "Good luck," he said, leaving the chief's office and closing the door behind him.

Johns steepled his fingers and looked at Sam. "You had a very good question—where does that leave us?" Johns said. "Have we learned anything new from our interviews?"

"Not really," Sam responded. "If I were perfectly honest with myself, I would have to admit that I am stuck. My intuition is letting me down. There is something about this case that I can't square. We have two prime suspects, but my gut tells me that neither one of them is the killer. My original thought was to make their lives a living hell, tear their lives apart, until one of them confessed. But now I am not so sure. What am I missing? I have gone over all my case notes several times, and nothing jumps out at me. And now the searches for the missing gun have left us empty-handed. Where do we go from here?" Sam paused.

Johns stared at her. As hard as he tried, he couldn't come up with any answers. Reinterviewing everyone wasn't realistic and probably a waste of time. *If they lied to us the first time, what would change? Sam was right.* Murderers make mistakes, so what are they missing here, trying to solve this case, that elusive piece to the puzzle?

A comfortable silence fell on the room, but a cloud of frustration and defeat hung heavily over their heads. Neither one of them spoke for several minutes.

"Why does Linda Milz get under your skin?" Sam suddenly asked.

Johns looked at her with a vacant stare, as if trying to remember something from his past. Sam knew very little about his early life. Even though they were very close colleagues, his personal life was rarely brought up or discussed. Sam knew that he was born and raised on a farm outside of Monroe and married to Beth and had two teenage sons. He tried very hard to keep his private life and his professional life separate. Sam didn't know why she asked him the question, mostly out of curiosity, a change of subject. Johns leaned back in his chair.

"When I was a very young boy, the Great Depression was in full swing, awful and demoralizing the countryside. I was ten years old at the time. Some farmers were losing their farms, and some were hanging on by sheer willpower and faith. I can remember seeing my father cry when telling my mother that we were in danger of losing our farm. It broke my heart seeing him that way. On the south side of Monroe, a wealthy couple lived in a big house with a big yard. The husband had a job in Madison, having something to do with state government. His work must have been important because he had an apartment there and only came home on the weekends. The care and maintenance of the house was being neglected. His wife hired my father to do the odd jobs and repairs needed to keep the place up. My father was a talented handyman and could fix anything. The extra money he earned from his labors was greatly appreciated since cash money was scarce. The extra money became an expectation, and we became dependent on it . . ." Johns paused. Sam was transfixed on his story.

"My father told my mother that he didn't particularly like the woman he worked for, but they desperately needed the money. He didn't say why he didn't like her, being a man of few words, so it was interesting for me to hear him verbalize his disapproval. One summer morning in July, after the chores were done, he asked me to accompany him to the house in Monroe because he needed help. He told me that I was going to be his third hand repairing a wooden porch, stuff like holding on to the other end of a board. I was thrilled and excited to be with my dad.

"When we arrived, the lady of the house appeared and demanded to know who I was. The tone of her voice and her demeanor scared me to death. I saddled up next to him. My knees felt weak. My father explained to her that he needed help repairing the porch and I was there to help him. Her mouth opened and closed in astonishment. She told him, in the starkest of words, that if I were injured on the job, she would take no responsibility. Then she belittled him because he didn't ask her permission in advance to bring me along to help. She cursed him and told him that she wasn't paying any extra money for the job. My father was embarrassed and humiliated at her outburst. I started to whimper. He held my hand and lightly squeezed it. I couldn't understand why my father just stood there, silently taking the abuse. I felt sorry for him.

She abruptly turned on her heel and went back inside the house with a very red face. We didn't see her again. That night I had nightmares about that horrible woman. My father tried to comfort me by telling me that the lady was under a lot of stress missing her husband and that the terrible Depression was affecting everyone. We should feel sorry for her. Even as a child, I couldn't forgive her and what she did to my father that summer day. I wanted to beat her up or something like that to punish her. I can tell you this: That evil woman and her face was forever burned into my memory."

"Did you ever see her again?" Sam asked.

"No. After the Depression, the house was sold, and she moved to Madison."

"Did your father ever speak of her again?"

"He never spoke about her, and I never brought the incident up. But it still makes me angry when I think about it."

A wry smile crossed Sam's face. "Okay, now I get it, a kind of repressed anger. Linda Milz reminds you of that evil woman you carry around in your head."

Johns smiled. "You are right, of course. The tone of her voice, the condescending arrogance, and the total disregard for other people's feelings sum it up."

"So why did you share that terrible memory with me?" Sam asked.

"Let's take some time to puzzle out Herbert Milz. If I had the resolve, as a child, to fantasize punishing that horrible woman who belittled my father, what psychological effect was the affair and his dysfunctional marriage have on Herbert?"

Sam nodded. "Right. Let's pull that thread and see where it takes us."

"As I see it, before his affair with Stacy Leonard, Herbert was trapped in a horrific marriage to an abusive woman. His only escape to save his sanity was the work at his business and his cabin in Cadiz Springs. His naivety about women was his fate. He had no idea what he was letting himself in for when he married Linda. When the honeymoon was over, and the real Linda emerged, he must have been shocked and devastated by his mistake. His remorse and hatred toward her were building over the years, a life sentence to be sure."

"That's pretty harsh," Sam interjected.

"Nevertheless, that's what I think."

Sam looked at the chief who was slightly wringing his hands. "Continue," she said.

"Over time his repressed anger against his wife increases. God only knows the number of times he fanaticized killing her. Then what happens to him? Stacy suddenly appears and sweeps in to save him from his misery. He is ecstatic. His emotional well-being skyrockets to new heights. He has met someone who loves him, someone who cares for him, someone who fills the emotional void that he so desperately needed. He is smitten and in love. That is a powerful thing, Sam. It transcends all reason, throwing caution to the wind. Are you with me so far?"

"I think so, makes sense to me," Sam replied.

"Herbert feels betrayed by his wife. His affair and love for Stacy is his new reality, a new beginning. Stacy shares with him that she is going to divorce her husband. Can you imagine the thoughts running through Herbert's head? He is probably fanaticizing about leaving Linda and marrying Stacy. He has left reality behind and has entered into another world."

"I think I know where you are heading," Sam interrupted and said, "All is going well for Herbert. His affair has him on cloud nine. He suspects something may be wrong but has convinced himself that Stacy loves him. Then the hammer drops squarely on his fantasy and squashes it like a bug. Stacy makes love to him for the last time and then afterward tells him their affair is over, kaput. No warning, no explanation. She leaves him at the cabin and drives away. He is in a state of extreme physical and emotional pain and anger. His world just came crashing down. He goes back to the office and starts drinking. All the repressed anger against his wife erupts, shaking him to his very core. Stacy now becomes the object of his anger. His wife betrayed him, and now, for a second time, Stacy betrays him. What is he to do? He is blind with rage. Somehow he has access to a gun. He drives to Stacy's house, confronts her, and kills her. He drives back to Monroe and finds his wife passed out on the sofa and puts her to bed. So far, so good?"

Johns nodded. "The years of slowly-building pressure for all that anger had to be released. Herbert couldn't stop himself. His emotions took hold of his psyche, and he killed Stacy."

Sam wrinkled her nose as she thought about the chief's theory. Did it make sense in the light of day? "So how about Norman Stafford?" Sam asked.

"Somehow Herbert learned that Norman was Stacy's other lover and killed him after luring him to the New Glarus Woods State Park. Or just give this a thought: Norman contacted Herbert, knowing that he was the killer. Remember, the second car parked in front of Stacy's house on the night of the murder? It very well could have been Stafford who followed him home. Herbert killed him to keep him quiet."

"But why would Norman contact Herbert? Why not go directly to the police? Was there something in it for him or something else going on? Like blackmail?"

"I agree with you that all the pieces aren't fitting neatly together yet. But they will."

"So where do we go from here?" Sam asked.

"I am convinced Herbert knows more than he is telling us. I think this is a crime of passion, especially in Stacy's case. And as for Norman Stafford, who knows? Premeditated? I will reinterview Herbert's two employees. Also, I will need to talk to Linda Milz again. Could she be hiding anything?"

"How about Paul Leonard?"

"For now, we will concentrate on Herbert Milz."

"What do you want me to do?" Sam asked.

"Take tomorrow off from the case and give it a rethink. If Herbert's alibi doesn't hold up, we can bring him in for more questioning."

"So you think Herbert is our man?"

"For now, he is my prime suspect."

am followed the chief's advice and took Friday off. She and Karin had a wonderful day together. They had lunch in the hospital cafeteria with Drew and spent the early afternoon in Twining Park, playing and relaxing in the sunshine, watching children flying multicolored kites. They walked passed by a young mother who was breastfeeding her baby. Sam was suddenly overwhelmed with the feeling of life, love, and the gift of children. The day was perfect.

After Karin's afternoon nap, Sam drove to the nursing home at three thirty to visit Sharon. She was delighted to see them and had a big smile on her face when Sam and Karin entered her room. She was sitting by the window. Sam placed Karin in her arms, and Sharon gave her a big hug and kissed her cheek. Karin giggled and grinned from ear to ear.

"So what's new around here?" Sam asked.

"Well, actually, I do have some news. One of the aides told me that a Mrs. Agnes Keel will soon be admitted."

Sam flinched and was taken aback by the news. She hadn't heard that from the social worker. Sharon immediately noticed Sam's reaction.

"Do you know her?" she asked.

Sam explained to Sharon that Mrs. Keel had been interviewed as a witness concerning the Stacy Leonard murder. Her brief explanation lit Sharon's fuse. She immediately wanted to know if Mrs. Keel was a suspect. Sam spent the next several minutes explaining that Mrs. Keel was not a suspect and she was helping with the investigation. Sam immediately regretted bringing it up. However, Sharon wouldn't let it rest and pressed Sam on the investigation. She felt the crimson warmth on her cheeks as her exasperation with her mother increased. The last thing she wanted was for Sharon to speculate about Mrs. Keel and badger her with questions after she arrived at the home.

"What else did the aide tell you?" Sam asked.

"Not much. Only that she will reside in the dementia wing."

Sam exhaled and relaxed a little with a sigh of relief. Her fears slowly abated. Mrs. Keel will have a layer of insultation from the prying inquisitive eyes and ears of her mother. Karin seemed to be enjoying the back and forth between her mother and grandmother as she squirmed around on Sharon's lap.

"Anything else of interest in your life?" Sam asked.

"One thing that may interest you, one of our elderly residents recently died in her sleep. She didn't have any family that visited her, and she died alone. The staff brought in flowers and lit a candle on her bedstand. A priest came and said prayers over her while the staff looked on. They took a moment to share stories and shed tears over the corpse. For everyone there, it was a very touching tribute to a woman who was all alone in the world. I cried when I heard about it. The Rettig Funeral Home hearse came and took her away." Sharon paused and looked at Sam with an accusing eye.

Sam immediately understood what Sharon was telling her. "Not to worry, Mom. You won't die alone."

A wry smile crossed Sharon's face. She had made her point. After an hour of small talk and fawning over Karin, Sam departed and went home. She was cooking a spaghetti dinner for Drew. After dinner, she played with Karin and put her to bed. She poured herself a glass of wine and relaxed in the living room. Drew went into the garage to put away some gardening tools and rejoined her for a time. He was tired and went to bed early, leaving Sam alone with her thoughts. Her day with Karin was picture-perfect. Now, in the quiet of her living room, she laid her head back on the sofa and closed her eyes, mulling over the case.

Was the Chief correct in assuming Herbert Milz to be the prime suspect? she mused to herself. What about the other theories that they had hypothesized? Were they now on the back burner? She remembered the old saying that sometimes we build castles in the air and then try to lay a foundation of facts underneath them.

Putting Milz aside for the moment, Sam reviewed the other possible suspects. What about Paul Leonard? He was definitely conflicted in his marriage to Stacy. The inability to communicate with his wife spoke volumes. The marriage was doomed from the get-go. They were both on a journey without a clear destination, a marriage wrought with secrets and lies, starting with those fateful first footsteps down the aisle to the altar. It was one of those marriages in which each of them married the other to fill a void, a vacuum, in their lives. In this instance, one half plus one half did not equal one. Paul married her out of the grief he felt losing his first wife. He desperately wanted her back, thinking that Stacy could fill that hole in his heart and be his surrogate wife. Stacy probably needed financial security, and the marriage would certainly give her that. So when the tide went out after the honeymoon, they both must have realized that they were swimming naked. So if he was going to divorce her, why kill her? Then what about Norman Stafford? Why kill him? Sam didn't buy the notion that Paul Leonard was the killer, but on the other hand, sometimes the improbable doesn't make it impossible. Maybe something happened that he is keeping hidden that led to both murders. She would have to keep an open mind and rely solely on the facts.

Other than those two, who else could be the killer? Sam took another sip of her wine. Who, indeed? The overwhelming circumstantial evidence that she and the chief discussed is that one of their two suspects has to be the killer. But which one? Another thread that hasn't been fully pulled or explained yet is the murder of Norman Stafford. Maybe the truth is hidden in the shadows of his death but lies in a different direction. What if Stafford had a girlfriend who was madly in love with him and he left her for Stacy Leonard? Another crime of passion? This unknown girlfriend finds out about Stacy, goes to her house, and kills her. Norman then confronts her with his suspicions. She lures him to the New Glarus Woods State Park and kills him to keep him quiet. Then this unknown mystery woman is home free. The police haven't interviewed her and doesn't even know that she exists. Is that a possibility? Sam made a mental note to talk to Norman's parents about his former girlfriends. She had the sinking feeling that this was a very long shot but worth looking into.

So who else? Sam opened her eyes and sat straight up in her seat. Donna Crandall— Herbert Milz's receptionist and bookkeeper at the auto business. What did the chief say? He had the impression that Crandall was in love with her boss. A single middle-aged woman who had worked for years helping Milz create and grow a successful business. A woman of intelligence and loyalty to her boss and the business. Could this be an example of unrequited love? If so, it must have broken her heart to see Linda swoop in and badger Herbert into marrying her. The marriage was a sham and broke his spirit. He started drinking and working late to avoid going home. All his pain was in plain view for her to observe day after day. He deserved better. Did she lie about not knowing with whom he was having an affair? After all, Monroe is a small town and thrives on local gossip. If he needed comforting and an affair, why not her? All he probably needed to do was ask. Was she telling the truth about the night of the murder? Sam's imagination was in overdrive. In her mind's eye, she could see what was happening to Herbert Milz. First, his marriage to Linda and then the breakup with Stacy causing him much anguish and pain. Maybe Crandall was the one who snapped. She drove to Stacy's home to confront her and then murdered her. Somehow Norman Stafford found out and threatened her with blackmail or whatever. So she killed him as well. Sam shook her head. She chucked to herself and fell back into the soft cushions of the sofa.

"What the hell am I doing?" she asked herself. "Creating conspiracy theories about mystery women and unrequited love?"

She jumped up and took her empty wine glass to the kitchen and rinsed it out. After getting undressed and putting on a pair of short pajama bottoms and a tee shirt, she snuggled under the sheets next to Drew who was softly snoring. She tossed and turned. She was too tired to go to sleep, and her mind was racing. Her fitful, jerky spasms woke Drew up.

"Okay, so tell me what's on your mind?" he asked in a sleepy dreamy voice, not quite awake.

Sam propped herself up on one elbow, kicking off the sheet. She was wide awake. "Sorry, Drew. I am a mess."

"So tell me about it," he drowsily replied.

"The chief has focused in on one prime suspect for both murders. His logic makes sense, but I am not so sure he is right. There are more questions to the case that remains to be answered, and those thoughts keep niggling me."

"Explain."

"Herbert Milz is the man the chief suspects. A pathetic sort of man in my opinion. Very naive when it to comes to women. Well, anyway, Stacy Leonard, an attractive woman, starts flirting with him, touching him, and making sexual innuendos. It was like an overture, an opening for him to love her. Milz hates his wife, and this unexpected attention was a lifeline thrown to him. The sexual passion missing in his marriage is there for the taking. He falls madly in love with Stacy, and he doesn't have a clue that he is being used or what he is rushing into. The affair overwhelms him. He is besotted, not realizing that Stacy is using him as a means to an end, which is divorcing her husband. When she suddenly and abruptly ends the affair, Milz is heartbroken. The chief thinks that Milz snapped and killed her. And then for some unknown reason, he also kills Norman Stafford. He had the means, the opportunity, and the motive."

"Makes sense to me."

"But does he have the temperament to kill? I can't square his personality with a violent act of murder. Two murders, I might add. I just can't see him as the killer."

"Okay, so who do you think the killer is?"

"That's my dilemma. My gut instinct isn't helping me. I just don't know."

"Maybe you need more facts."

"You are right, of course. I do pride myself on finding all the relevant facts pertaining to a case and piecing them together to solve a murder. But I just don't have enough information. That's my problem.

When I was in the living room, I conjured up two theories that now seem totally ridiculous."

"Why do they seem ridiculous?"

"I feel I am grasping at straws."

"But are you? I have heard you say numerous times that theories, no matter how farfetched, are important to any case. Just follow them wherever they go and dismiss them when they become a dead end."

"Did I say that?"

"Something like that."

"So you are telling me to investigate my wild ideas and theories just to see if they lead to anywhere important?"

"Can't hurt. If you eliminate them, then you can get some sleep . . ." Drew paused. "See, I have solved your problem."

A silence fell between them as Sam stared at the ceiling, pondering what Drew had said. Suddenly, she could hear his soft, slow rhythmic breathing, telling her that Drew had fallen asleep. She patted him on the shoulder, got up, and went into the kitchen for a glass of cold water. She went into the living room. She stood in the darkness, staring out at the lit street. The street was quiet. A crescent moon was drifting lazily across the sky, and the celestial stars were shining brightly, another beautiful starry night in Monroe telling her that the universe was in sync. She turned around and made her way to the sofa. The soft cushions were very inviting. Her mind started to free fall again, starting with her list of suspects to her mother in the nursing home. She then zeroed in on Agnes Keel and all her talk about folk myths, ghosts, death, and the curse of Burr Oak Farm.

Sam wondered if Mrs. Keel looking for ghosts through her binoculars was akin to Sam looking for the mysterious killer. Mrs. Keel believed in ghosts, and Sam believed that the killer was out there somewhere, she just couldn't see him. The similarities were striking. The ambiguities of her riddle were frustrating her, just as the notion of Mrs. Keel wanting to see her late husband's ghost was bizarre. Would Stacy Leonard's ghost suddenly appear and reveal who killed her? If it was only that simple. Sam was happy to learn that Mrs. Keel was going to live at the nursing home. She would have to visit her.

Trying to piece together a motive for the murders, Sam recalled a class she attended at the University of Wisconsin as an undergraduate. It was a psychology class that talked about people needing to be emotionally connected: babies to mothers, children to parents, husbands to wives. When that connection is severed, a relationship is broken off, and people panic. They feel hurt and scared. They pull away. That emotional disconnect causes couples to fight, feeling threatened and frightened, a downward cycle that is destined for separation, divorce, or worse. The emotional disconnect was evident for both Leonard and Milz. Leonard was destined to divorce his wife before Stacy was murdered, and Milz was trapped in a horrific marriage. Leonard seemed to have a plan to extricate himself from a failed marriage, but what about Milz? Was the chief right in making Milz his prime suspect? The emotional toll on Milz after Stacy ended their affair must have been so devastating that reason and rational behavior flew out the window. The old saying that humans are only three parts rational and one part irrational would certainly apply. Extreme emotional distress could change that equation. Left unchecked, could Milz have murdered Stacy in a state of uncontrollable rage? The answer to this question was probably yes. Milz could have murdered Stacy, but what about Norman Stafford? For some reason, he may have been only collateral damage. Maybe Norman knew that Milz killed Stacy and he was blackmailing him. It seemed to Sam that Stacy's murder was one of passion, and Norman's murder was premeditated. In order to avoid being found out for murder, Norman had to be eliminated. All this seemed to make sense. But was Sam putting too much faith into her assessment of Milz's personal character, in that he didn't have it in him to be a killer?

As the minutes dragged on, Sam was no closer to unraveling the case, and her frustration was growing. The *aha* moment wasn't coming to her. She decided the prudent thing to do was to remain patient and pursue her inquires. Perhaps something will surface to move the case along. At least that was her hope. She decided that her next step would be to call Norman Stafford's parents and schedule an appointment.

CHAPTER 20

Chief Johns was determined to follow-up on his theory that Herbert Milz was the killer. He reread Milz's written statement to the police. Was it truthful and accurate? Having no other leads, he needed to pressure him on his version of events and to reinterview his employees, especially Donna Crandall. If she was in love with him, as he suspected, could she be withholding crucial information? He called Crandall first, and she agreed to meet him Monday morning at ten o'clock at the police station. Then he called Milz. He agreed to an interview at eleven o'clock, following the Crandall interview. The chief didn't want them comparing notes between the interviews. If she changed her story, then he could apply more pressure on Milz.

At the appointed time on Monday, June 10, Donna Crandall walked into the police station. She was wearing a summer cotton dress and open-toed sandals. Her shoulder-length hair was parted on one side. Johns greeted her and ushered her into the interview room. He offered her a cup of coffee, which she refused. She seemed very nervous. Her hands were shaking. After they were seated, Johns tried to relax her with small talk about the weather. She glared at Johns like a trapped animal, a no-nonsense woman on her guard. Johns sensed this was going to be a difficult interview. Captain Miller joined them and stood by the closed door, observing the proceedings. Crandall eyed him suspiciously. Johns repositioned himself in his chair and began.

"Thank you for coming in this morning. As you are aware, the investigation of two murders is ongoing and being conducted by the police department. I have asked you to be here today to help us clarify a couple of points."

Crandall stared at him unblinking. She remained silent. Herbert and she had discussed the interviews after the chief called and set up the times. He maintained his innocence, and she believed him. He told her to tell the chief the truth and not to incriminate herself. She was very loyal to her boss and didn't want to see him hurt in anyway.

Johns continued. "I want you to tell me again about the Friday night Stacy Leonard was murdered. You stated that you were at the office, ready to leave, when Herbert Milz returned to the office at 5:30 p.m. and he was visibly upset . . ." Johns paused and looked at the frozen expression on Crandall's face.

"Haven't I already told you all I know?"

"Yes. But I want you to go over the events again, just in case you remember something new."

"Are you accusing me of something?"

"No. I am only trying to get a clear picture of what happened that evening at the office."

"You think that Mr. Milz killed Stacy Leonard, don't you?"

Johns paused and leaned back in his chair. "Look, I am asking the questions here, so don't get defensive. I am sure you want the same thing as I do: to find the killer and to clear Herbert Milz. Am I correct?"

"He didn't do it."

"How do you know?"

"I have known him and worked for him for years. He is not capable of murder," Crandall said with emotion.

"Okay. So, let's eliminate him from our list of suspects. In order to do that, I will need for you to answer my questions."

Crandall looked down at her hands. The fact that she saw Mr. Milz driving recklessly north toward New Glarus on the night of the murder was deeply troubling her. There had to be a reasonable explanation, but she had kept that knowledge to herself, even from Herbert. She knew in her heart he was no killer! She looked at the chief. "Okay. So what do you want to know?"

THE CURSE OF BURR OAK FARM

"Let's go over again what you remember about that night when Milz came back to the office."

Crandall sat up in her chair. "Like I said, he returned to the office when I was about to leave. He rushed past me without a word and went into his office and closed the door. He looked like he was in great distress. I heard the sounds, though his closed door, as he had made himself a drink. I recognized the clink of the whiskey bottle against a glass."

"Was that the first time he drank on the job?"

"No. I had heard the sound before when he was stressing out about his wife. Jim and I had previously talked it. Jim told me that Mr. Milz would drink before going home at night. Very sad."

"What did you do after Mr. Milz went into his office and closed his door?"

"I didn't know what to do. I thought for a moment that I would go into his office but decided against it. I assumed that something must have happened between him and his wife. I didn't want to get involved."

"That was the last time you saw him?"

"Yes. Until Saturday morning at the office when I told him about Stacy Leonard's murder."

"How did he react?"

"The best that I can describe it was that he was in shock."

"What happened next?"

"He left the office and drove away without saying a word."

"When did you learn that Mr. Milz and Stacy Leonard were having an affair?"

Crandall slumped down in her chair. "After he left and drove away, Jim and I talked about it and speculated that Jim was right about him, and Mr. Milz was having an affair. And the woman was probably Stacy Leonard."

"Was that the first time you knew the identity of the woman?"

"Yes. Town gossip later confirmed it."

Johns paused the interview and steepled his fingers. *Was she telling him the truth? Protecting her boss. If she were in love with Milz, could she have killed Stacy?* Johns shook his head. That idea just didn't make any sense.

"Moving on, you stated earlier that you didn't know Norman Stafford. What can you tell me about him now?"

"Only what I read in the newspaper and town gossip."

"Did Mr. Milz know him?"

Crandall gasped. "If he did, he never mentioned it to me."

"Do you know of anyone who would have wanted to harm Stacy Leonard?

The question caught Crandall by surprise. "No," she hastily replied.

"One more question, does either Herbert or his wife own a handgun?"

"Not that I am aware of."

Johns glanced at his watch. An hour had passed, and he didn't learn anything new or interesting. Crandall was steadfast sticking to her story. She didn't reveal anything that he could pressure Milz with. He stood up and thanked her for coming in for the interview. As he escorted her to the front door, they passed Milz sitting in a chair in the waiting area. Crandall smiled at him. He was wearing a blue short-sleeved button-down oxford shirt and a pair of khaki pants. She turned and smiled at him again as she left the station. Captain Miller took a short break, waiting for the next interview to begin. Johns asked Milz if he wanted a cup of coffee or a glass of water. He declined. Johns went to the break room and poured himself a cup of coffee. He gathered up Milz and took him to the interview room. After they were seated, Miller joined them by taking up his position beside the closed door. Milz looked apprehensive. He wasn't looking forward to the interview.

"Thank you for coming in today," Johns began. "I have interviewed Donna Crandall, and I have a few questions for you. Are you sure that I can't get you a cup of coffee or a glass of water?"

Milz shook his head, staring at the chief, who took a sip of his coffee. He was trying to look casual, like two men engaging in a conversation about the weather, to put Milz at ease.

"I have some questions that are niggling me about the two murders that need answering. Are you sure that you are up for our interview today? I can postpone it until a later date if you like."

Milz sat up in his chair. "I am ready to answer any questions that I can," he replied in a soft voice.

"Okay. On the day of the murder, you told us that Stacy Leonard broke up with you at your cabin in Cadiz Springs, ending the affair. You were devastated by the unexpected news. After she left the cabin, you spent some time there and returned to work at 5:30 p.m. When you entered the office, you saw Crandall, who was getting ready to leave for the day. You went directly into your office and closed the door. Then you poured yourself a drink from the whiskey bottle that you kept in your office. You stayed in your office drinking alone until approximately 9:30 p.m. when you went home, found your wife passed out on the sofa, and put her to bed. Jim Hull knocked on your door at 8:00 p.m., announcing through the closed door that he was leaving. So from eight o'clock until nine thirty, you sat alone in your office, drinking and thinking. Am I correct in my summary?"

"Yes," Milz weakly said.

"On Saturday, when you went into work in the morning, Crandall told you about the murder of Stacy Leonard. After hearing that, you abruptly left work without explanation and didn't return again until Monday morning. Is that correct?"

"Yes. I went to my cabin to think. I was in shock. I couldn't believe it. I stayed there until Sunday afternoon."

The chief paused in his questioning. He noticed a slight tremble as Milz clasped his hands. "So from eight o'clock until nine thirty that Friday night, no one can verify that you remained in your office the whole time, no one can verify that you didn't leave earlier and drove to Stacy's home and murdered her and then drove home and found your wife passed out on the sofa?"

Herbert's face tuned pale. "How can you suggest such a thing? I loved her."

"The absence of an alibi would make that assumption very plausible."

Milz was visibly shaken and taken aback. The chief came right out and accused him of murder. His face instantly turned red. He was angry. "I didn't kill her!" he shouted.

Miller jumped at the sudden outburst. Johns gave Herbert a moment to compose himself.

"Okay. If you were me, what other conclusion could I arrive at to eliminate you from my inquiry? The time of death occurred at the same time you have no alibi."

Milz slumped down in his chair. He was deflated and felt exhausted.

Johns stared at him. "You have stated that you didn't know Norman Stafford, the second murder victim. Is that correct?"

Milz sat up in his chair. "Until his murder, I had never heard of him."

"On the night of his murder, Wednesday night, where were you?"

"I was home."

"Can anyone verify that?"

"No."

"Why not?"

"After I got home from the office around 8:30 p.m., my wife wasn't there. I was tired and fell asleep watching television after a couple of drinks. I woke up about 2:00 a.m., turned off the television, and checked to see if my wife was in bed."

"Was she there?"

"No. I looked out the picture window at the driveway and saw her car parked there. I went outside to check and found her passed out on the front seat. The foul scent of vomit greeted me when I opened the driver's side door. I wrestled her out of the car and put her to bed. The next day I took her car to have it detailed and get rid of that awful sour smell."

"What did you think finding her like that?"

Milz could feel the perspiration slowly moving down his armpits. "Look, my wife is an alcoholic, and I have had to do some pretty disgusting things over the years, things like putting her to bed, cleaning up her vomit, and sleeping next to a woman who reeks of alcohol."

"Do you know what sounds suspicious to me?"

"No," Milz replied in an exasperated voice.

"For both murders, Stacy Leonard and Norman Stafford, you don't have a credible alibi. And your wife, who could confirm your alibi, was passed out drunk both times. Is that a coincidence?"

Milz looked like a man who was cornered like a trapped, terrified animal.

"I am telling you the truth. I didn't kill anyone!" he exploded.

Miller jumped again at the outburst. Johns was getting under Herbert's skin.

"Did your wife know Mr. Stafford?"

"Why?"

"Just answer the question."

"If she did, she never mentioned him to me."

"Did the two of you discuss his murder?"

"No. She was preoccupied and still upset with me for destroying her reputation at the club. I think it caused her to drink even more, if that was possible."

"So, if I get this correctly, you and your wife never discussed the two murders, given the fact that you were having an affair with Stacy Leonard? Did she ever accuse you of killing Stacy?"

Milz was perplexed. It was obvious to him that Johns had him pegged as the killer.

"Look, like I said before, I didn't murder anyone. You can ask my wife or anyone else, but the result will be the same. I am innocent of these two murders."

"Have you told me the truth?"

"Yes. I have told you all that I know concerning the two deaths. For God's sake, I loved Stacy, and I would have never killed her! You can think what you like, but I am innocent!"

The break in the case that Johns was looking for wasn't forthcoming. There had to be something more that Milz wasn't telling him. He felt it in his gut. He didn't have enough evidence to charge him. He stared at Milz for a long moment as Milz fidgeted in his chair.

"Okay. That is all for today," Johns said. "If I find out that you have been lying to me, I will charge you with murder. Do you understand?"

Milz nodded. Johns stood up and took Milz to the reception area where he hastily exited the police station. Johns went back to his office. "It just has to be him," he said to himself. "I will keep digging until I can tie him to the murders."

CHAPTER 21

D rew surprised Sam with an invitation to have breakfast at the Corner Café. He had Tuesday morning off, and Sam's appointment with Mr. and Mrs. Stafford, to meet with them at their home in New Glarus, was set for ten o'clock. After they dropped off Karin at Mrs. Sturzenegger's house, they had a delightful breakfast in the standing-room-only café. Several people stopped at their table to greet them as they enjoyed their bacon, eggs, and hash browns. A second cup of coffee finished off their fine meal. Thankfully, no one brought up the murder investigation. One of Drew's patients stopped by their table and thanked him for the excellent therapy she received after a fall. The heartfelt comment made Drew's day. The noise level was high, and the chatter was nonstop, so they mostly talked about Karin and smiled at the other patrons. The café was, indeed, the meeting place for many of the town's local people. After breakfast, Drew kissed Sam goodbye and drove home. Sam went to the PD.

Chief Johns had told her that the Stafford house was an older white two-story frame home with a front porch located in the 600 block of 1st Street, in the residential street just south of the shops and the Tschanz Insurance Agency. Sam told the couple on the telephone that the investigation was ongoing and she needed some background information on Norman. They readily agreed to the meeting. Johns had already debriefed her on his interviews with Donna Crandall and Herbert Milz. His assessment afterward was that Milz was the killer, and he felt that they were getting closer to making an arrest.

Sam departed the police station at nine thirty for the drive to New Glarus. She was after two things: first, to get a better understanding of what made Norman tick and, second, to get the names of any girlfriends who could shine any light on his character and state of mind. Her drive was pleasant, warm, and full of sunshine. She easily found the house and parked on the street in front of it. She immediately surmised that Mrs. Stafford must love gardening because the curb appeal of the house was beautiful, like a living floral arrangement. Creeping phloxes, irises, peonies, bleeding hearts, and clematises accompanied Sam up the steps to the front porch.

Mr. George Stafford answered the door bell. He invited Sam in and ushered her into the living room, introducing her to his wife. Mrs. Lydia Stafford was standing in the living room, patiently waiting for her visitor. She asked Sam if she wanted a cup of coffee. She accepted, and Mrs. Stafford left for the kitchen. Sam seated herself on a burgundy flowered sofa and surveyed the room. Mr. Stafford sat down in a recliner across her.

The living room had tall open windows framed in polished walnut, letting in lots of sunlight. Swiss lace curtains covered the windows and swayed gently in the breeze. A well-used, homey, old-fashioned fireplace dominated the north wall. The cast-iron grates were partially hidden behind a bronze fire screen. The 9-foot ceilings featured ornate crown molding. Framed family pictures were hanging on the walls and stood on the fireplace mantel. A chiming mantel clock made for a pleasant rhythmic ticking sound as the pendulum swung evenly back and forth. Red oak hardwood floors and an open pocket door led to an ornate staircase with carved banisters and wide steps located in the hallway. The room was comfortable and inviting. Sam could have very easily read a book in the serenity of the room.

Mr. Stafford was sitting quietly as he watched Sam. Mrs. Stafford returned with a serving tray. On it were three cups of coffee and a creamer with a matching sugar bowl. She placed the tray down on the coffee table in front of Sam. She asked about cream and sugar. Sam told her that black coffee was fine. Mrs. Stafford handed her a cup. Mr. Stafford took a splash of cream and two sugar cubes in his coffee. Mrs.

Stafford also took her coffee black. After everyone was served, Mrs. Stafford sat across Sam in an overstuffed armchair.

Sam began. "Thank you for seeing me today. I am very sorry for the loss of your son. We are actively investigating his death and will bring the killer to justice."

The couple remained silent as they stared at Sam and were comforted with her reassuring comment that the police would bring the killer to justice.

"First of all, can you tell me about Norman?"

"What do you want to know?" Lydia asked.

"I understand that he was living at home. Why was that?"

"After he graduated from college, he moved back in with us to repay his student loan debt and to save money for a down payment to buy his own house."

"Were the living arrangements working out?"

"Yes. He helped George with the yard work and odd jobs. He wasn't here very much because of his work schedule at the insurance agency and spending time with his friends."

"Over the past few weeks, did he seem stressed out or bothered by anything?"

Lydia looked at George who shook his head. "If anything, he seemed to be in a very good mood about something."

"Did he share that with you?"

"We never asked him about his love life, so we assumed that he was dating someone special. Recently, he asked me for a bouquet of cut flowers from my garden. George and I were convinced that love was in the air for him."

"Did you know any of his girlfriends?'

"Heavens yes. New Glarus is a small town."

"Could his new love interest have been one of them?'

"He was really fond of one girl who he had known since grade school. She and Norman would hang out here during their school years. After high school, she started working at the New Glarus Bakery on 1st Street. She is still there."

"So she would know Norman better than the rest of his friends?"

"I would think so."

"Was she the girl that he got the cut flowers for?"

"I don't know. You would have to ask her. She gets off work at noon."

"What's her name?"

"Ella Aebi."

"Was Norman on good terms with his former girlfriends?"

"I would think so," Lydia answered.

. There was a pause in the conversation. Sam thought the couple were remarkably composed so soon after losing a son.

"Other than a new love interest, did Norman talk about anything else, his job for instance?"

"He only talked about buying a house," George interrupted.

Both women looked at him. Up until now, he had been very quiet, listening to the interview.

"Buying a house?" Sam asked.

"George is right," Lydia remarked. "Suddenly, out of the blue, he started talking about purchasing a house again. We were under the impression that he still had a few years to go before he had enough money for a down payment."

"Did you question him about it?"

"No. From time to time, he would bring up the subject. I think it was for our benefit, to let us know that his future plans were still intact and that he wouldn't be living with us forever and a day."

Sam smiled. "So those were the only two things that you can think of that seemed to put him in a happy place?"

"Now that you put it that way, I suppose so, a new love interest and buying a house."

"How would you describe Norman's personality? Was he easy-going, intense, or just plain satisfied with his lot in life?" Sam asked.

The question caught the couple by surprise. "I think you could say that he was goal-centered," Lydia said. "That would describe him the best. He worked hard to get his degree and was very focused on paying off his student loan and saving for a house. He thought that he was underpaid at his job, but he didn't want to commute to Madison for higher wages. To answer your question, I would describe him as a good son, a hard worker, and knew what he wanted out of life."

"Anything else?"

"One thing comes to mind, Norman was a very private person and had his mail delivered to the post office instead of coming here. In fact, the postmaster called and wanted us to pick up his mail and to close out the box. It was full. We will do that this week."

Sam looked at George, who nodded. She glanced at her watch, 11:15 a.m.

"Anything else that you can add that might help me find his killer?"

They both shrugged. "We have no idea who may have wanted to harm our son," Lydia sadly said.

Sam stood up and thanked the couple for their time and the coffee. She assured them that the police were doing everything possible to solve his murder and asked that if anything comes up in the meantime to help her in the investigation, please call her at the PD in Monroe. They told her that they would. Her next stop was the New Glarus Bakery to see Ella Aebi.

* * *

Sam walked into the bakery and was greeted with the sweet yeasty aroma of freshly-baked bread. Looking at the pastry case, she saw a variety of breads, cinnamon rolls, pies, pastries and muffins. She immediately spotted an apple crumble danish, and her mouth watered. There were two customers in the store, one at the cash register and the other one trying to make up her mind as she surveyed the pastry case. The cashier was a young woman wearing a double-breasted white jacket and a white chef's hat. She was of average height, stout, had blond hair sticking out from beneath her hat, blue eyes, and a ready smile. She and the woman at the register were engaged in a friendly conversation. The other customer joined them and placed her order. After paying, both women departed the store, then Sam approached her.

"Hello. My name is Samantha Gates from the Monroe PD. Are you Ella Aebi?"

Ella smiled at her. "That's me. What can I do for you?"

"First, you can get me a couple of your apple danish. Are they good?"

"Absolutely, I made them this morning."

Sam watched as she carefully put the danish into a white paper bag and rang up the total. Sam paid for the treat. She couldn't wait to tuck in.

"Thank you," Sam said. "I am in New Glarus today as a part of our investigation into the murder of Norman Stafford. I understand that you knew him."

Ella gasped. The question was totally unexpected. Her right hand flew to her mouth as her eyes widened. "Yes, I have known him my whole life."

"What time do you get off work? I would like to speak you about Mr. Stafford."

Ella glanced at the clock on the wall. "My shift ends in twenty minutes. There is a park bench outside the store on the corner. I can meet you there."

"Perfect," Sam replied. She left the bakery and easily found the shaded bench. She opened the bag and tasted the danish treat. It was delicious.

Ella shortly arrived and sat next to her. She had changed into a lightweight summer cotton dress and sandals. "How is the danish?"

"Heavenly," Sam replied, licking her lips and closing the white bag.

A welcome cool breeze blew through her hair. Except for an occasional passerby, they were alone to talk. Ella was staring at Sam.

"Like I said, I am investigating the murder of Norman Stafford. In order for me to do my job, I need to get to know as much about him as possible. I have talked to his parents, and they gave me your name. Are you willing to talk about your friend?"

"What do you want to know?" she replied in a sad voice.

"How did the news of his death affect you?"

"I cried all day. I just couldn't believe it, and I called in sick for work."

"So it must have come as quite a shock?"

"Totally. I still can't believe it. Who would want to harm him?"

"As far as you know, did he have any enemies or recent disagreements with anyone?"

Ella paused for a moment. "No."

"Where you lovers?" Sam asked.

Ella blushed and turned a shade of red. "No," she weakly said. "We have known each other our whole lives. I had hoped that our friendship would evolve into something more, but that didn't happen."

Sam gave her a moment. "How would you describe his state of mind in the weeks leading up to his death?" Sam asked.

"A week or so before his death, he told me that he was looking for a house to buy. It was his dream to own a house. I didn't believe him, though, because his parents had told me that he was saving up for the down payment on a mortgage, but that was still several years into the future."

"Why do you suppose he told you that?"

"I don't know. Something must have changed. Otherwise, why would he begin a house search?"

"Good question. Was he coming into money?"

"Not that he shared with me."

"His parents thought that he had a new girlfriend. Can you shed any light on that?"

Ella lowered her head and looked at her hands. "Norman was a difficult man to love," she began. "He was always trying to upgrade his lot in life. He dated local girls he thought either had money or had a good-paying job to help support him in a marriage. Small town gossip pegged his real intentions, and the girls played him. I tried to tell Norman that, but he refused to listen. His dream house and having plenty of money and status was the prime motivator behind his behavior, in my opinion. I gave up thinking I had any chance of a future with him a long time ago, but I continued to be his friend."

"Were you hoping that something would change and you guys would become something more than friends?"

"Yes, you are right. It was a fantasy of mine. But to answer your question, if he had a new girlfriend he was excited about, I can only assume that she had plenty of money . . ." Ella paused to catch her breath.

Sam felt sorry for her. Unrequited love can be a burden to carry. "Do you think Norman was honest? By that, I mean, did he ever get into trouble by stealing or conning someone out of something?"

The question caught Ella by surprise. She paused a moment to think about it. "Only once. He told me about an incident in college that he was rather proud of. He had a part-time job cleaning up college professors' offices at night, emptying waste paper baskets, sweeping floors, stuff like that. In the office of a biology professor, he found the answer sheet to a final exam. He copied down the answers and sold them to any student who was willing to pay. The unusually high grades on a tough final exam caused a scandal. The professor was outraged, knowing that a breach had occurred, but he couldn't prove it. By then, the semester was over, and the students had all gone home for the summer. Norman was questioned, of course, but he denied any knowledge of the incident. He told me he pocketed over a hundred dollars. I tried to prick his conscience about the morality of it. He laughed and blamed the professor for carelessly leaving the answer sheet on his desk after he left the office for the day."

"Did you find his story in keeping with his character?"

"I hate to admit it, but I can't say I was all that surprised."

A moment of silence passed between them. The woman Norman was secretly dating remained a mystery, but Sam felt it had to be Stacy Leonard. And how about Norman suddenly talking about buying a house? Where was the down payment coming from? Stacy? Blackmail? She needed to discuss all this with the chief. Sam thanked Ella for meeting with her and told her again that the danish was delicious.

CHAPTER 22

onna Crandall had not slept a wink Monday night after her second interview with Chief Johns. She had been having difficulty concentrating at work and was making silly mistakes. Her boss Herbert Milz was also a mess. He was convinced that he was the prime suspect in the murders and it was only a matter of time before he was arrested. He was spending more time away from the office at his cabin in Cadiz Springs. His drinking was getting worse. Donna was now feeling emotionally closer to her boss than at any other time since joining the sales office as they discussed the interviews and possible scenarios behind closed doors in his office. This had created a certain intimacy between them.

Donna thought it was ironic that the death of Stacy Leonard had forged this bond between Herbert and herself. Herbert steadfastly denied any involvement in the death of Stacy Leonard or Norman Stafford. Donna totally believed him, but seeing him erratically driving north toward New Glarus on the night of Stacy's murder gave her pause. She couldn't bring herself to tell Herbert that she saw him.

Donna was beside herself and felt that she was going crazy. She knew she needed to talk with her sister to help sort out her feelings. So on Tuesday, Donna called Joyce and invited herself to supper that evening, knowing that Joyce's husband, Donald Schulz, a Green County sheriff deputy, would be at work until his second shift ended.

When she arrived for supper, Donna had two gin and tonics, which surprised Joyce. They chatted over a tuna casserole meal before Donna confided to her that she was in a state and needed to unburden herself. After supper, Donna asked for another G & T. Knowing her sister, Joyce knew that Donna had something weighing heavily on her mind. The more alcohol she consumed, the more relaxed and emboldened she felt. The genie in the bottle was doing his work. Donna confided how anxious she was after her two interviews with the police and couldn't sleep at night. Suddenly, Donna broke down and uncontrollably wept. Joyce comforted her and demanded to know what was wrong.

"I think the man I love might be a murderer," she sobbed.

Joyce was stunned. She already knew that her sister was secretly in love with Herbert. Letting go of Donna's shoulders, she stared at her. "Okay, explain," she said, looking at Donna directly into her eyes.

Donna stopped crying and wiped away the tears with the back of her hand. "On the Friday night that Stacy Leonard was murdered, I saw Herbert speeding toward New Glarus after I left your house to go home."

"So what is the problem?"

"Herbert told the police that he went straight home from the office on the night of Stacy's death. That was the same day Stacy broke off their affair. Herbert came back to the office in an awful state. When I left work a short time later, he was in his office drinking. Then later that evening, after leaving your house around nine o'clock, I saw him speeding out of town toward New Glarus. He lied to the police about going straight home. I lied to the police to cover for him. I wanted to believe him, or think I did, that he didn't kill Stacy. But how do I really know? Are my feelings all jumbled up and blinding me from the truth?" Donna paused.

"So what do you think?" Joyce asked.

Donna ignored her question. "I lied to the police," Donna said, repeating herself. "I told them I didn't see Herbert after he left the office Friday evening until Saturday morning. Does that make me an accomplice? Am I going to jail? I don't know what to do. In my heart, I want to believe and protect Herbert. On the other hand, should I tell the police the truth?"

After blurting all this out, Donna buried her face in her hands. The tears flowed between her clasped fingers. Joyce grabbed a box of

Kleenex and handed it to her. She was astounded by the news. Was it true? Was Herbert the killer? Her husband had been tight-lipped about the investigation. Did he know? What was she going to tell her sister?

"Look, Donna. I don't know what to say. If you feel in your heart that Herbert is the killer, you should go straight to the police. But if he is innocent, should you tell the police anyway? To clear your conscience. You need to think about it."

"Do I tell Herbert what I saw that night?"

"That's up to you. I suggest you go home and think about it."

"Will you tell your husband what I witnessed and lied about it?"

"Quite frankly, I don't know. We have never kept secrets from each other. I may ask his advice. Okay?"

Donna didn't say anything. She just nodded. She had to get this heavy burden off her mind to give her some peace. She felt better and hugged Joyce, thanking her for listening. She dried her eyes and got up to leave.

"Are you able to get yourself home, Donna?" Joyce asked. "I could take you."

"No. I'm okay. I can manage. Thanks."

And with that, Donna drove herself home just before nine o'clock.

* * *

Joyce mixed herself a G & T and sat in her living room alone, gulping it down. She had a horrified look on her face as she looked at the clock on the fireplace mantel. Her husband's shift was over at 10:00 p.m., and he should be home around 10:30 p.m. What was she going to tell him? Would her sister go to jail for lying to the police? She mixed herself another drink.

Donald walked into the house shortly after 10:00 p.m. He could immediately see something was wrong. Joyce tightly hugged him. She smelled of booze.

"Okay, so what's the trouble? Did you wreck the car, burn your supper, or is your mother coming to stay with us for a month?"

Joyce laughed at his humor. She instantly felt better. Donald would know what to do. They sat on the sofa, and she told him the whole story.

189

He remained silent, listening as she spoke. After she finished, Joyce fell back into the soft cushions, exhausted.

Donald remained quiet. He was thinking. "First of all, I don't think Donna is in any trouble with the law if she goes to Chief Johns and tells him what she knows. I am not in the loop pertaining to the investigation, but I think Donna has vital information that could help. Just because she saw Herbert's car heading toward New Glarus on the night of the murder doesn't necessarily make him a murderer. Too many unanswered questions. I am confident that the police will sort it all out. I suggest that you call Donna and tell her to contact Chief Johns."

Joyce felt relieved and leaned over and kissed her husband on the cheek. She jumped up and immediately called Donna, knowing she would still be awake. Donna listened carefully to what Joyce said and told her sister that she would call Chief Johns first thing in the morning.

Wednesday morning, Chief Johns was at his desk, drinking his third cup of coffee. He had trouble sleeping last night. The case was wearing him down. Beth was worried for him and asked if she could be of any help, claiming that she was losing her beauty sleep because of his tossing and turning. Johns rarely discussed an active murder case with his wife, but he was at his wits' end. He thought about his wife's offer. Perhaps, in verbally talking to Beth about the investigation, something would happen, an *aha* moment. But it didn't work. He spent an hour methodically taking Beth through the facts. She offered up some suggestions, which he and Sam had already discussed. He had gotten out of bed and spent the rest of the night on the living room sofa, in his pajamas, wide awake.

The chief was sitting at his desk, staring into space when the telephone rang. Shirley told him that Donna Crandall was on the line. He listened to her with great interest and excitement as Donna told him what she observed on the night of Stacy Leonard's murder. Johns pumped his fist into midair. Yes! This was the break he was looking for. He told Donna to immediately come to the police station and submit a written statement. He jumped up from his desk and found Sam at her desk. He told her what had just happened. He was excited.

After Donna wrote and signed her formal statement, Johns called Herbert at Milz Auto Sales. Johns requested that Herbert come to the station at 11:00 a.m. for a follow-up interview. He and Sam would conduct the interview. Herbert sounded reluctant but agreed to the interview. At exactly 11:00 a.m., Herbert entered the PD, where Johns was waiting for him and took him directly to the interview room. Sam shortly joined them, closing the door behind her. She and Johns sat across Herbert who was nervously wringing his hands. He was sweating. Johns immediately launched into the interview without the normal beginning niceties to put the interviewee at ease.

"Tell me again what you did after you left work on the night of Stacy Leonard's murder," Johns asked in a low monotone voice. He was staring directly at Hebert, knowing that he had his quarry cornered in a lie. Sam stared at Herbert, making small beads of sweat appear on his forehead.

Herbert recounted his consistent story about going directly home from work and finding his wife passed out and putting her to bed. After he was finished, Johns put his elbows on the table and looked Herbert directly in the eye.

"You are lying!" he exclaimed.

Herbert jumped. He felt the sweat pouring down his armpits. He didn't say anything. He just stared at the chief with a look of horror on his face.

"We have a witness who saw you driving erratically north out of Monroe toward New Glarus on the night of the murder around nine o'clock. Is that witness lying to us?" Johns demanded.

Herbert slumped down in his chair. His face was ashen. "No," he weakly said.

Johns settled back into his chair. "So you have been lying to us?"

"Yes."

A long moment passed. Johns was letting Herbert squirm. He looked very distressed.

"Can I get you a glass of water?" Sam offered.

"Yes, please."

Sam jumped up and fetched Herbert a cool glass of water. After handing it to him, he gulped the whole glass down.

"So tell us what happened that night," Johns said. "And this time tell us the truth."

Herbert looked down at his hands, not wanting to look directly at Johns. He began speaking very slowly.

"Like I said, after Stacy ended our affair in Cadiz Springs, I was very distraught. I went to work and started drinking. I couldn't believe what had just happened. I was crushed emotionally beyond words. The more I drank, the more I felt I was losing my mind. My broken heart was too painful to bear. Throwing all caution to the wind, I decided to drive to Stacy's house and confront her. She told me that her husband was in Milwaukee, so I knew she would be home alone. The angry beast in my soul had been unleashed . . ." Herbert paused.

Johns and Sam stared at him.

"Did you go to New Glarus with the intention to kill her? Seek revenge for what she did to you?" Johns asked.

"No, no, no! It wasn't like that! I loved her. I couldn't kill her. I only wanted to talk to her."

"So what happened next?"

"I got into my car and started driving to Stacy's house. I had too much to drink and was having trouble staying in my lane. Once I got onto Highway 69 heading north, I was weaving. One oncoming car flashed its headlights at me while I was hugging the center line. I moved to the right, and my tires touched the shoulder of the road, throwing gravel. I sobered up enough to the realization that I could kill myself or someone else if I didn't get off the road. When I got to Monticello, I turned around and drove straight home. I found my wife passed out on the living room sofa, like I said. I put her and myself to bed. I didn't learn about Stacy's death until the next day at work when Donna told me."

Johns and Sam glanced at each other.

"Are you telling us the truth?"

"Honest to God. I did not kill Stacy!"

"Why should we believe you? You lied to us once, and now you want us to believe that you are telling us the truth?"

"I only lied to you as not to incriminate myself. There were no witnesses."

"You are mistaken. There is one who will testify that you were lying to the police."

Herbert was a deflated, defeated man; a man who was now in the soup by his own stupid actions and lying to the police.

"Do you know what I think happened?" Johns asked.

Herbert glanced up at him.

"I think that you were so distraught being played for a fool that you drove to New Glarus and confronted Stacy. You were drunk, so you weren't thinking clearly. You and Stacy had words. In a fit of anger, you shot her two times. Then you raced back to Monroe, put your wife to bed, and waited to see what would happen next. When Donna Crandall told you about the murder, you acted surprised and somehow convinced yourself that you didn't kill her."

Herbert didn't interrupt.

"Then I think that somehow Norman Stafford found you out, and you murdered him as well to keep him quiet. So why kill him? Was he blackmailing you?"

Herbert sat bolt upright in his chair. "You have it all wrong! I loved Stacy, and I didn't kill her. I didn't even know Norman Stafford. That is the truth," Herbert said, exhaling in a weak controlled voice.

"The only piece of evidence we need is the gun, and once we find it, I will charge you with murder!" Johns blurted out.

Herbert looked as if he was going to faint.

"If I were you, I would retain a criminal lawyer. And if Stafford was blackmailing you, we will find that out as well."

A long moment passed without anything being said. Sam was quiet, giving the chief all the time he needed for the interview.

"You have to look at your fate in this investigation," Johns slowly began. "We will shortly have enough circumstantial evidence to arrest you and charge you with two murders. You had the means, the opportunity, and the motive. And most importantly, you don't have an alibi for either murder. All we need to do is find the gun for a conviction. I think we can convince a jury that you are guilty, and you will spend the rest of your life in prison. However, if you plead guilty and we reduce the charges to manslaughter, you could be eligible for parole in twenty to twenty-five years. Think about it, Herbert. Ask a lawyer. I am sure he would agree to the charge of manslaughter as your best option.

"Are you telling me that I should plead guilty for two murders that I didn't commit?"

"I am only thinking about what's best for you."

"Go to hell!" Herbert screamed. "I loved Stacy, and I didn't kill her!"

Johns looked at Sam who was staring at Herbert. The interview was over. Johns didn't arrest him but told Herbert not to leave the area without notifying him. Sam ushered Herbert to the front door and returned to the chief's office.

"So what do you think?" Sam asked. "Are you still convinced he is the killer?"

"Yes. We need to search the Cadiz Springs cabin again for the gun, also the lake. I wouldn't be surprised if he threw the gun into Lake Beckman."

Sam wrinkled her nose.

Johns eyed her suspiciously. "So you aren't convinced he is the killer? What's bugging you?"

"I just can't see him being the killer. I may be wrong, but I have this feeling that we are missing something, a small detail that we have overlooked. Okay, so he lied about going straight home and driving to Monticello on the night of the murder. Suspects lie all the time, but that doesn't mean that they are all killers. The death of Norman Stafford has me stumped. Why him? Why kill him?"

"Okay. Okay. I get your point. In the meantime, I will follow up searching Cadiz Springs for the gun. You can pursue your line of inquiry into Norman Stafford. All I need is the gun for a conviction. If I were a betting man, I would push all my poker chips toward Cadiz Springs."

Sam smiled at him. "Are you bluffing? Poker chips?"

Johns grinned at her.

CHAPTER 23

Lydia Stafford was waiting for her husband to return from the post office. The postmaster had called again and pleaded with them to close out the Norman's box and retrieve the overflowing mail. In all the frantic activity following Norman's death and his funeral, his mail was the last thing they were concerned about. After Detective Gates visited them, they had spent a lot of time digesting the interview. Ella Aebi called and told them about her meeting with Gates. She was at a total loss as to who could have killed Norman. Lydia shared with her that they too were at a loss. She and George couldn't think of a single person who would want to harm Norman. Lydia thanked her for the call. "Why couldn't Norman have dated and married Ella?" Lydia lamented.

Norman's death was a real mystery. There must have been something going on in his life that he kept hidden, a secret that had fatal consequences. But what was it? In the days leading up to his murder, he wasn't depressed or anxious about anything as far as they could tell. In fact, it was the opposite. He seemed happy and carefree. They, of course, thought he had a new girlfriend and was smitten, a girlfriend he wasn't ready to reveal to them. All these thoughts had them perplexed.

George was taking his time getting the mail, so Lydia poured herself a cup of coffee and sat on the living room sofa. The only sound was the ticking of the antique pendulum clock on the fireplace mantel. She looked at Norman's smiling face in a framed picture sitting next to the clock. His death seemed surreal. She could still see him sitting in the overstuffed chair across her, telling them about his hopes and dreams. The notion and excitement of owning his own home was his dream. The pride of homeownership was an obsession with him. His only complaint was that saving up the money for the down payment was taking far too long and was infuriating. He considered finding a second part-time job. George offered to loan him money, but Norman refused. He was going to do it on his own. He told them that his down payment goal was $10,000 for his dream house. More than the required 10 percent for a $50,000 house. Sad and painful remembrances occupied her thoughts as she stared at his picture. It was only a matter of time before his shadow would permanently fade from the living room.

Lydia heard the back door open. George's voice rang out, "I'm home." She jumped up and greeted him. In his hand was a brown paper bag stuffed with mail. Lydia told him she would get him a cup of coffee and they could sort the mail in the living room. George went into the living room and put the bag of mail on the coffee table in front of the sofa. Lydia shortly joined him and handed him a steaming cup of coffee. They sat together on the sofa.

"Where do we begin?" George asked.

"Well, let's separate out the junk mail first and put it into a throwaway pile. Then we can sort through any unpaid bills and any other important stuff. How did it go at the post office?"

"Bernie Kemp retrieved the mail and gave me a form to sign, terminating the box rental. Norman had paid a year in advance, so Bernie wanted to know, given the circumstances, if I wanted a refund."

"What did you tell him?"

"I refused the refund. It was only a small amount of money."

"Is that what took you so long?"

"No. I ran into Pastor Ellefson, who wanted to chat. He was picking up the mail for the church. He asked about you and how we were doing."

"What did you tell him?"

"I told him we were devastated by Norman's death but coping the best we can. I also told him about Detective Gates coming to see us. He told me again how sorry he was for our loss and to come to see him if we wanted to talk. He was only a phone call away. He is a very nice man . . ." George paused and took a sip of his coffee.

"What do you think? Should we schedule an appointment?" Lydia asked.

"I don't know. What do you think?"

Lydia leaned back into the soft cushion of the sofa. "I think we should. I don't think I am over the shock of our son's death, and we will probably need some help coping with his loss as time goes by."

"I agree. Sometimes, when I hear a sound in the night, I still have a glimmer of hope it was Norman coming home after a late night out. His passing seems like some tragic Broadway stage play that we are living through in real time."

A tear trickled down Lydia's cheek. She dearly missed her son. A moment of silence passed between them. She flicked away the tear away with her index finger. "Let's get on with it," she abruptly said.

For the next fifteen minutes, they sorted and pitched the mail. They were surprised at the amount of junk mail that had accumulated. After they were finished, only a short pile of mail remained, five pieces. The only bill was for a car payment. Living with his parents had its advantages. The other four pieces of mail were from the bank and the insurance agency. They opened the bank mail first and found one statement for his checking account and the other was a statement for his savings account.

"I feel funny opening these statements from the bank," George said. "Norman never shared his financials with us."

"Well, we never asked," Lydia reminded him. "We never told him about our finances either. Now that he is gone, it doesn't make any difference, does it?"

"I suppose you are right," George said, shaking his head. George unfolded the checking account statement first and read through it. "According to this, Norman has a checking account balance of $376.18, not a fortune, but no surprise."

"So how about his savings account? His house down payment account?"

George opened the statement, looked at the balance, and his jaw dropped.

"What's the matter?" Lydia asked.

He handed her the statement. It took her a moment for her to process what she was looking at.

"Oh my god!" she exclaimed. She reread the statement and handed it back to George who read it over again.

"Can this be right—$8,200?" George carefully laid the statement down on the coffee table.

"Where did he get that amount of money?" Lydia asked.

George slowly came to his senses. He picked up the statement again and read through it more carefully. He pointed to one entry. "Look here. Four days before his death, he deposited $5,000 into the account. What does that mean? Where did he get the money?"

Lydia's mind lit up like a roman candle during a Fourth of July celebration. Her head was exploding. "George! Remember, when Detective Gates was here, she wanted to know if anything unusual was happening in Norman's life. We told her he seemed happy and upbeat about something. Could this be it?"

"But where in the world did he get the money? A single deposit of $5,000!"

Lydia felt faint, and her face paled. She looked down at her hands. "That is a very good question. Was Norman mixed up in something nefarious that led to his death?"

George felt an ache in the pit of his stomach. "We need to call Detective Gates!" he exclaimed.

Lydia jumped up and called the Monroe PD. Her call was passed through to Detective Gates.

"Hello, Mrs. Stafford," Sam cheerfully answered. "What can I do for you today?"

"You told us to call you if we found anything unusual pertaining to our son. Just now, we found something that has us really worried and concerned."

Sam sat straight up in her chair. "What did you find?"

"George went to the post office and retrieved Norman's mail. In the mail, we found two bank statements. His savings account statement showed a $5,000 deposit four days before his death. What does that mean?"

Sam gasped. She knew exactly what that meant—blackmail money. "Can you bring the statement to me at the PD, or should I drive to New Glarus?"

"George and I can bring it to you. We should be there in about twenty minutes."

Sam thanked her and rushed into Chief Johns's office. She excitably told him the news. His face tightened, and his eyebrows furrowed as Sam relayed the news from Lydia Stafford.

"Do you know what this means?" Sam asked.

"Yes, blackmail," Johns quickly answered.

"Yes. Another piece of the puzzle has fallen into place." Sam's mind was racing. "The car parked on the side of the road the night Stacy Leonard was murdered had to belong to Norman Stafford. He saw the car and the driver as it sped down the driveway after the murder. He followed it. In his mind, he must have seen a huge opportunity and took advantage of it. If your theory is correct, he was blackmailing, who, Herbert Milz! Suppose that after Herbert paid him $5,000, Norman got greedy and wanted more money. Herbert was trapped. He probably reasoned that the blackmail would never stop. He agreed to another payment and told Norman where to meet him, at the New Glarus Woods State Park. Unfortunately for Norman, his greed led to his death."

They both remained silent, mulling over Sam's scenario. Shirley knocked on the chief's door and announced that Mrs. Stafford was in the lobby. Sam jumped up to see her. After thanking her and George for driving to Monroe, she went back to the chief's office. She looked at the $5,000 deposit and handed the statement to Johns. He took his time confirming the entry and picked up the telephone to call the Bank of New Glarus. He spoke to one of the vice presidents who fetched the teller who received the deposit. She remembered the transaction and confirmed that Norman deposited the money, telling her that he sold some land and it was a cash deal. It was a bit unusual, being that it was such a large amount of money, but Norman assured her that all was well. Johns thanked her and hung up.

"We are getting close!" Johns exclaimed.

"Do you want me to check with the First National Bank to see if a $5,000 cash withdrawal on either Herbert's personal account or his business account occurred a week before Norman's murder?"

"Yes. Even if we don't find the smoking gun, the money should be the final nail in Herbert's coffin. He would have a hard time explaining that away."

"I have a thought," Sam said.

Johns looked at her with an "oh shit" expression on his face. "Okay, what is it?"

"We have been so focused on Herbert Milz that Paul Leonard has been all but forgotten. Just to cover our bases, I think I will also ask to see a copy of his financial transactions for the same period. I am not saying that we will find anything, but just to be sure . . ."

Johns steepled his fingers. He knew that Sam was right. She had questioned Herbert's guilt from the get-go, so if Leonard was totally cleared, that may change her mind. "Good idea. I am totally on board. Good luck."

Johns picked up the telephone and called the courthouse and asked Judge Dietmeire for the search warrants. The warrants would be waiting for Sam to pick up in an hour.

"I am on my way to the courthouse," Sam said, jumping out of her chair, leaving the chief's office.

Once outside the PD, Lydia Stafford was waiting for her. "I couldn't go home," she said. "What can you tell me about the money and Norman's involvement? The suspense is killing us."

Sam could see the anguish in her face. George was staring at her from his car window. "I wish I could give you some information. This is an active murder investigation, and thanks to your help, we feel we are closer to making an arrest. That's all I can tell you at this time."

Lydia wouldn't let it go. "What about the money in Norman's savings account? Can you tell us how it got there?"

"I am sorry, but I can't at this time. I will tell you this: We have a theory concerning your son's death, and we are pursuing it. It wouldn't be fair to you or to us to make that theory public knowledge. Consider this: If we are wrong, innocent people could be harmed. You wouldn't want that to happen to anyone, would you?"

Lydia looked deflated. "I suppose not."

"I understand your frustration of not knowing who killed your son. Chief Johns and I are working very hard to bring his killer to justice. You and your husband will have to remain patient and trust us to do that. Can you do that and let us do our jobs?"

Lydia nodded. She turned and walked away to her husband who was waiting for her in their car in the police station's parking lot. Sam quickened her step as she rushed to the courthouse. She could feel the adrenaline pumping through her veins.

CHAPTER 24

am was surprised at the speed that the warrants were issued and signed off by the judge. After leaving the courthouse, she quickly walked across 10th Street to the First National Bank. She showed the warrants to a vice president who consulted with the bank president. Sam was ushered into the president's office. Peter Anderson greeted her and asked her to take a seat in front of his desk. Sam handed him the warrants.

"I can see by these warrants that you wish to examine the financial records of two of our clients. I can verify that both Mr. Leonard and Mr. Milz have accounts with us, one personal and a second for their businesses. Am I correct in assuming that you want to see the accounts for each man named in the warrant?"

Sam nodded. "That is correct. The police are conducting a criminal investigation and verifying the financial activity in their accounts will help in that investigation. That's the reason for the two warrants."

Anderson was shocked by the request. He personally knew both men and considered them upstanding citizens with excellent business acumen. A feeling of disbelief fell over him, but he needed to comply with the request. "I will introduce you to the bank's head bookkeeper. She will be able to assist you."

He and Sam left his office and walked the short distance to the bookkeeper's office. She stood up from her desk when they entered the room. He introduced Sam to Violet Stamm and explained the situation. She was a tall woman dressed in a fashionable tailored blue business suit. Her hair was tied up neatly in a bun, and she wore thick black framed glasses. Anderson told her to cooperate with Sam's directives. He turned and left them alone, closing the door behind him. Sam sat down across her.

"So what can I do for you?" she asked in a matter-of-fact voice.

"The police are conducting an investigation into two murders. The names of Herbert Milz and Paul Leonard have come up during our inquires. In order to clear their good names, we need some financial information. Hopefully, you can provide that for us."

"What do you want to see?"

"I would like to see the financial activity in their accounts over the past six months, both personal and business."

Stamm gasped. They were good clients of the bank. Sam could see the surprise on her face. After a moment, Stamm left her office. She returned a short time later with the ledger books. She handed them to Sam and sat down on the chair behind her desk. She stared at Sam. Sam shifted her position in the chair opposite her and opened Leonard's business account ledger first. It was laid out in easy-to-read detail, showing monthly deposits and checks written against the business account with the corresponding balances. She took her time looking for a $5,000 withdrawal. Stamm was staring at her as Sam poured over the ledger, focusing all her attention on the account's withdrawals. Neither woman spoke. Satisfied, Sam handed the business ledger book to Stamm. She didn't find what she was looking for. But in reality, she didn't expect to see the withdrawal. Then she opened his personal checking account ledger book. Nothing unusual or revealing was found there.

She then turned her attention Herbert Milz's. Her hands were slightly shaking with excitement and anticipation as she opened the ledgers for his accounts. Her index finger slowly moved over the business entries and withdrawals. She started in January and ended last Friday with the last posted entry. She couldn't believe it. The $5,000 withdrawal wasn't there. She laid the ledger down on her lap and stared into space. She then picked up the personal checking account ledger and pursued slowly through it in great detail. Nothing. A dead end. She shook her head in disbelief. She stared into space. A moment later, she picked up the ledgers again and double-checked them. Did she miss something? Anything? After she was finished, she handed the books to Stamm.

"Is there anything wrong?" Stamm asked.

Sam ignored her question. "What the hell?" she asked herself. The final nail in the coffin that the chief was looking for didn't exist; it had vanished. The chief, who was anxiously waiting for her return, would be crushed. Sam stood up and thanked Stamm for her cooperation, left the bank, and hurried back to the PD. She rushed into the chief's office and sat down.

"Well?" Johns urgently asked. His anticipation was great.

Sam squirmed in her chair for a moment, remaining silent. The chief experienced an *oh-shit* moment.

"It wasn't there," she said in a low voice.

Johns wrinkled his eyebrows. "What wasn't there?"

"The $5,000 withdrawal we were looking for from either man."

A deafening silence fell over the room. A dark cloud descended, matching the mood in the room.

"Are you sure?" Johns asked in an astonished but deflated voice.

"I double-checked the ledgers. No $5,000 withdrawal in the past six months."

Johns leaned back in his chair. The disappointment was clearly visible and written across his face. "Jesus" is all he could say. "Where does that leave us?"

"Do you think either man had the $5,000 in cash in their homes or at their businesses?" Sam weakly offered.

"I don't know, but why would they? That's a hell of a lot of money to leave lying around."

Sam didn't respond. She couldn't see it either. It didn't make any sense. The chief's demeanor was one of deep disappointment. Sam felt sorry for him.

"Could I have been wrong about my theory of Milz?" he sadly asked. "I was so sure that Herbert was our killer. He had to be. But now, what am I to think?"

"We still have the missing gun to fall back on," Sam offered.

"What if we can't find it? Then what?"

Sam was at a loss for words. "I don't know. We will have to go back to square one and reexamine the case. The killer is still out there, and we just need to find him."

Johns sat staring at the ceiling for a long moment, shaking his head. "We will conduct the search at Cadiz Springs as planned. If we can't find the gun, then we will have to go back to the beginning, like you said, and reexamine all the facts as we know them. Perhaps I will bring in Captain Miller. Maybe he will have a perspective on the case that we have overlooked. In the meantime, go home and get some rest. We will meet again after the Cadiz Springs search, unless something comes up."

Sam left the chief's office, told Shirley that she would be at home if she was needed. Driving home, she had mixed feelings. Was Herbert really the killer? She still had her reservations and wasn't totally convinced. At the same time, she felt empathy for the chief. He so badly wanted this case to be closed with a conviction. She doubted the gun would be found at Cadiz Springs. After she got home, she decided to call Janet, her long-time friend from Madison. Talking to her always cheered her up, and she needed some positive energy. It had been ages since she last talked to her, and she wanted to catch up. Afterward, she would fetch Karin from Mrs. Sturzenegger.

Sam poured herself a glass of iced tea and sat on her living room sofa. Instead of calling Janet, she couldn't get today's disappointment out of her head. The abrupt mood change in the chief was affecting her. She had to guard against getting too down about the case. She needed to reassess the facts in the privacy of her own thoughts. Going over the facts again, taking small steps, seemed like a good start. Was anything overlooked and missed, something so obvious that was hiding in plain sight? She went to her writing table and retrieved a pen and a pad of paper. She then lay down on the sofa and closed her eyes. In her mind, she went back to the very beginning: seeing Stacy Leonard's prone cold body lying on the floor in the living room of her house, two bullet wounds in her chest and blood-stained carpet. Seeing a dead body was something she never got used to, a human life brought to a violent end. It still sent shivers down her spine.

So who were the suspects? Police protocol always looks at family members first. Paul Leonard, her husband, had the means, the motive, and the opportunity. He had no alibi for the night of the murder. Also, the facts point to the theory that Norman Stafford was at the scene of the murder that night, sitting in his car on the shoulder of the road, and followed the killer in his car. Why was Stafford there in the first place? In theory, he was having an affair with Stacy and was probably surprised when he spotted an unknown car parked in front of her house, knowing that her husband was in Milwaukee. His curiosity, maybe jealousy, made him follow the car; after which, he returned to Stacy's house and found her dead. Did he see and recognize the driver of the car? Could it be Paul Leonard?

What did he do next? According to his parents, he was in a good mood before his death. Could it be that his dream of buying his perfect house was coming true? All he had to do was blackmail the killer for the down payment. He must have known who the killer was because the extortion worked. He received $5,000 in cash, but he wanted more for his down payment. It was easy money. So he went back to the killer a second time and demanded more money, and that led to his death.

Then we have a second suspect, Herbert Milz, who also had the means, the motive, and the opportunity. He had no alibi for the time of the murder, and he lied to the police. The same theory could be applied to him. After he killed Stacy, Stafford followed him home. Stafford then returned to Stacy's house, found her dead, and blackmailed him. He got the $5,000 but got greedy and demanded more money. Herbert killed him to protect himself from further blackmail and as a witness against him. Following this line of logic, Herbert must have the gun, being that Stacy and Stafford were killed with the same handgun.

Sam was sure that it was the right sequence of events, but who was the killer? Which man? Looking at it a different way, if it wasn't Leonard or Milz, then who? Sam opened her eyes and sat up. She felt the frustration growing in her body. She finished her iced tea and stared out the window. *Who are we missing? Someone who may have wanted Stacy dead?* The $5,000 payment was a mystery. Who could afford to give Stafford that amount of cash, a small fortune to the average working man, if it wasn't Leonard or Milz?

Sam picked up her pad of paper and wrote the names Stacy Leonard and Norman Stafford in the center. Then she drew a double circle around them. She started writing the names of people close to the case on the outside of the circle: Paul Leonard, Herbert Milz, Donna Crandall, Linda Milz, Ella Aebi, Joy Holcomb. She stared at each of the names. Who would benefit the most from the murders? Once again, she was stymied. The only two names that made any sense to her were Paul Leonard and Herbert Milz. So what was she missing, a minute detail that would unlock the mystery?

She decided to call Janet and to take her mind off the case. She reached for the telephone. Then suddenly, an *aha* moment popped into her head. An insight that lit and fired up her neurons. *What if I have this case turned around, backward?* Her mind was suddenly at full throttle. What if Norman Stafford killed Stacy and was paid the $5,000 for his trouble? Then to keep him quiet, he was murdered. Sam jumped up and paced rapidly around the living room. She was excited. Can it be true? After she settled down, she went to the refrigerator for a refill on her iced tea. Instead of the sofa, she opted for a high-backed overstuffed armchair to sit and think. Does that theory make any sense? She needed time to shake the other theories of the murder out of her head and to make room for this new one. She wrinkled her eyebrows and set her jaw. So who paid him? Where did the money come from?

So Stafford goes to the house to kill Stacy but sees a strange car parked in front of it. He doesn't know who it is but sees it speeding down the driveway and turning west toward State Highway 69. He is curious and follows the car. He returns to the house a short time later, kills Stacy, and drives home. He deposits the $5,000 in his savings account after Stacy's death. So far, so good. Who would he know on my list of people that would know him? The name leaped off the page—Paul Leonard. No one else they asked knew Stafford. The two would have known each other because of the life insurance policy. So instead of a messy expensive divorce, Leonard contacts Stafford, and they plan the murder and split the insurance money, a murderous plot that Norman agrees to. Because the insurance claim hadn't been paid yet, Leonard somehow comes up with the $5,000 and gives it to Stafford. Sam slumped down in her chair and closed her eyes.

Her mind was reliving the night of the murder. At the bowling tournament, Paul Leonard became so ill that he couldn't bowl. Was it really food poisoning, or was it a guilty conscience knowing that his wife was going to be murdered that night? Then what about Stafford? His parents said he was in a good mood leading up to his death. Was he a man of no conscience and would do anything for money? Even murder? The similarities between the two were fascinating to think about.

So what about the gun? Sam wrinkled her nose as she thought through that question. Let's say that Leonard paid Stafford to kill Stacy and gave him the handgun. After the murder, Stafford returned it to him. Then that same gun was used to kill Stafford, and afterward, Leonard disposed of the gun. Does that make any sense? What about the love triangle? Stacy breaking off her relationship with Herbert for who, Norman Stafford? Maybe that was part of the plot to throw suspicion on Herbert. Stafford conned Stacy into having a relationship with him. Sam's mind was now in overdrive.

Let's assume that Herbert Milz was still lying to the police. He didn't turn around in Monticello but drove to New Glarus and had angry words with Stacy. They had a row, and he left her, alive, in a rage, and drove back to Monroe. Stafford probably didn't know him and followed him to see who he was and where he lived. Herbert's emotional response to the sudden breakup had sent him over the edge. He wasn't thinking clearly. He was a mess. That night was probably a blur to him because of his intoxication. No wonder the chief was so insistent that he was the killer.

Sam stood up and walked to the picture window. She took a deep breath as the light vehicular traffic passed in front of her house. Her first reaction was to call the chief with her new theory of the murders. But a little voice inside her head told her not to make the call. She had been down this path before, making assumptions and speculating without the factual evidence needed to back up her theory, in a sense getting trapped inside a theory and not thinking through it to its possible conclusion. So what was she going to do? She decided to contact Paul Leonard and ask him about the gun and if he kept large amounts of cash on hand. He would probably lie to her, so she had to rely on his body language and demeanor when she challenged him. Also, she needed to ask his employees the same question. She hoped that the pressure she applied would break something loose, something that would validate her new theory. She would tell her theory to Drew tonight after supper to see if it still made sense. Perhaps Drew would have an interesting insight, comment, or take on it. She totally forgot about calling Janet and rushed out the front door to pick up Karin.

CHAPTER 25

Donna Crandall sat at her desk at Milz Auto Sales, staring at the wall. It was 9:30 a.m. Monday, June 17, and she had just gotten off the telephone with Linda Milz, who was furious. She demanded to know where Herbert was. He hadn't been home in days. Donna told her that Herbert had stopped coming into the office and was probably staying at his cabin at Cadiz Springs. Linda demanded that Donna drive to Cadiz Springs and tell that worthless shit husband of hers to get his ass home. People at the club were asking questions, and it was so beyond embarrassing. She ended her loud angry tirade by slamming the telephone down in Donna's ear. Donna hung up the telephone receiver, giving it the defiant finger. "Take that, you bitch!"

Donna was really worried about Herbert. She and Jim were running the business during his absence. All the events surrounding Stacy's death had totally depressed Herbert. Jim mentioned that Herbert may become suicidal if some kind of intervention didn't occur. The very thought of suicide horrified Donna. She desperately wanted to go to Herbert to see if he was okay. A couple of times, she convinced herself to make the drive to Cadiz Springs but chickened out at the last minute. Now Linda had given her the excuse she needed. She found Jim and told him about the call with Mrs. Milz. He agreed that Donna should leave work immediately and drive to Cadiz Springs. He was equally concerned about Herbert. Donna jumped into her car and headed west along State Highway 11 for the cabin. She parked next to Herbert's car and knocked on the front door. She barely recognized Herbert when he answered it. He was wearing wrinkled unkept clothes, his hair hadn't been combed in days, his complexion was blotchy, and his face was covered with a scruffy wiry beard. He was barefoot, and his eyes were bloodshot. He looked unwell and surprised to see her. After her initial shock at his appearance passed, she invited herself in. "We are worried about you," Donna said.

Herbert looked at her through his blurry eyes. "Would you like to sit down?"

Donna glanced around the messy room. She removed some papers from one of the living room chairs facing the picture window and sat down. Herbert cleared the chair next to hers and joined her. They sat in silence. Donna was in a state of disbelief. Sitting next to her was the man she loved looking like hell. She immediately wished she had come sooner. "How are you doing?" she asked.

"I am fine," he replied in a raspy voice.

Something inside Donna snapped. She suddenly felt embolden. Herbert wasn't fine! She no longer felt like an employee who needed to respect her boss. She leaned toward him in her chair and looked him in the eye. "Look, Herbert, you are not well. Just look at yourself!"

Herbert's eyes widened.

"Do you have a working shower here?"

Herbert nodded.

"Good. I want you to go into the bathroom and take a hot shower. Afterward, I want you to shave and change into some fresh clothes. Brush your teeth. Do you have clean underwear and clothes?"

"Yes," Herbert replied. "In the bedroom."

"Then get going. I will do the dirty dishes and tidy up the cabin while you are making yourself decent. Understood?"

Herbert stood up like an obedient child and went directly into the bathroom located next to the bedroom. Donna heard the shower running and turned her attention to the small kitchen and living room. She didn't know the water situation in the small cabin, so she waited for Herbert to finish his shower before doing the dishes. The cabin smelled stale, so she opened two windows and the front screened door.

She immediately felt a cool breeze on her face. She didn't know where stuff went, so she made little neat piles to be sorted later. She found two empty whiskey bottles on the kitchen counter, which she tossed into the trash bin. After Herbert's shower, she washed a stack of dirty dishes. Plenty of hot water ran out of the tap, for which she was grateful. Satisfied with her work, she sat down again, looking out the picture window at Lake Beckman. The view was beautiful and mesmerizing. No wonder Herbert loved this place. She heard the bathroom door open as Herbert made his way into the bedroom. A short time later, he emerged and joined Donna in the living room. He was a transformed man, clean-shaven and his hair was parted on one side. He smelled of scented soap.

"Sit down," Donna instructed. "Don't you feel much better?"

Herbert eased himself into the chair next to Donna. "Thanks for coming to see me. I was going mad."

"Have you eaten anything today?"

"I open up canned food and heat it on the stove," he weakly responded.

"Are you hungry?"

"Not really, but I could sure use a cup of coffee."

"I will make a pot," Donna said, jumping up.

As the percolator did its job brewing the coffee, Donna sat down again next to Herbert. "Both Jim and I are very worried about you. We are keeping the business humming along in your absence, but we miss you."

"Sorry to worry you," Hebert said in a low contrite voice. "This whole business has turned my world upside down. I didn't know what to do."

The smell of freshly-brewed coffee started to permeate the cabin.

"What can I do to help you?" Donna asked. The sincerity in her voice was very welcome.

"I need to talk to someone."

"I am here today because I care about you, and I am a good listener." The sound of her voice was soothing and reassuring.

"I want you to know that I didn't kill Stacy Leonard or Norman Stafford."

"I know that Herbert," Donna said softly.

"I was such a fool thinking that I was in love with a woman who was using me. Oh god! How could I have been so stupid?"

"She charmed and bewitched you. You shouldn't be too hard on yourself. Tens of thousands of men have fallen prey under a woman's spell from time immemorial."

"How do I get over the embarrassment of it? People will look at me and think that I am a silly, naive man who acted like the village idiot."

"I wouldn't worry about those people. You need to learn from the experience, no matter how painful it was, pick up the pieces, and move on. It wasn't your fault."

Herbert was silent for a moment, thinking about what Donna was saying. She stood up and fetched two coffees. Herbert preferred his coffee black with two lumps of sugar. Donna knew that. She served Herbert his mug of the steaming black liquid and got one for herself. Herbert took a sip and smiled. "Thanks, I needed that," he said. "I am feeling much better having you here."

Donna smiled. She was thrilled and excited about her frank and intimate conversation with Herbert. She felt emotionally close to him. Her heart was racing. Herbert was in a more conversational frame of mind.

"One thing has been bothering me. How did the police know that I lied to them about going straight home from work the night Stacy was killed? They said they had a witness, but they didn't say who it was."

Donna felt a pit in her stomach. Should she tell Herbert the truth? "It was me," she meekly said.

"You?"

"When you came back to the office on the day Stacy was killed, you were really upset. I could hear, through your closed door, that you started drinking. I went home and then to my sister's house for a short visit. On my way home, I saw you driving erratically north toward New Glarus. At first, I didn't tell the police because I didn't want to get you

214

into any trouble. I lied to them . . ." Donna paused and waited for a response.

"So you told them later?"

"Yes. I couldn't believe that you killed Stacy, and there had to be another explanation when I saw you driving north that night. After talking it over with my sister, I decided to tell the police."

Herbert reached over and grabbed her hand, squeezing it gently. His touch sent a shiver down her spine. "You did the right thing. You told the truth, and I respect you for that."

Herbert holding her hand like that sent soothing waves of electrical impulses throughout her entire body. She could feel his heart beating through the gentle clasp of his hand. "But because of me, the police have made you their prime suspect," she lamented.

"Look, you are a wonderful and an honest woman that I have known for years. I didn't kill anyone, and at the end of this long nightmare, I will be exonerated. I am sure of it. So don't worry about it. You did the right thing by telling them the truth."

Donna felt relieved. The heavy burden of guilt bearing down on her shoulders was lifted by a kind gentleman. Herbert continued holding her hand. Donna didn't want him to let go.

"Your wife telephoned me this morning."

Herbert immediately released her hand. "What did she want?" he asked.

"She wanted to know if you were at work, and she told me that you hadn't been home for days. She said that I could find you at Cadiz Springs and to send you home."

"Is that all she said?"

"No. She was angry and said your absence was creating uncomfortable questions for her from country club members."

Herbert started to laugh and then laughed hysterically and uncontrollably. Donna stared at him in amazement. He was obviously enjoying the moment.

"Was she drunk or sober when she called you? Did she slur her words?"

"I don't know. But I can tell you this: She was very upset and slammed the telephone down in my ear."

"Good!"

"Good?"

"Yes. I am finally getting through to that bitch!" he gleefully shouted.

Donna's mouth flew open. The hatred that Herbert felt for his wife came through loud and clear.

Herbert noticed her reaction. "Sorry about that. But it felt good saying it."

"Is it true? You haven't been home for days?"

Herbert stood up and looked out the picture window with his back to Donna and began to speak. "Three or four days ago, I can't remember exactly when, Linda lost her mind. She got up early and joined me for breakfast. She was obviously hungover and looked awful. She didn't have time to put on her war paint. Well, anyway, in an evil temper, she unloaded and delivered the most vile and disgusting attack on my character. She was totally out of control. She was screaming and yelling while pacing around the kitchen floor. I had never seen her like that before. She had her moments in the past, but she totally lost it. She blamed me for everything gone wrong in her life and our marriage. She said the biggest mistake she ever made was to marry me. On that one point, I totally agreed."

Donna smiled.

"Then she went into this nonsense about her reputation being ruined at the country club. The members were gossiping behind her back, and she only had one true friend left she could trust. She carried on and on for what seemed like an eternity. She finally stopped and leaned against the kitchen sink with her back to me, exhausted."

"Did you defend yourself?" Donna interrupted.

"What would be the point? She lives and thrives in a self-centered narcissistic bubble. Sad to say, but our marriage is one of convenience for her, not for me. I made a huge mistake marrying her, and I have been suffering ever since."

"So what made you decide to come here?"

"I suddenly realized during her diatribe that I was at my breaking point. My troubling police interviews and Chief Johns accusing me of being a killer, the stress of it all, was getting to me. And now, with Linda screaming in my ear, I panicked. I suddenly had an overwhelming urge to kill her to shut her up. The feeling scared me. I sat mute, not saying anything. She turned around and glared at me, demanding that I say something. I remained silent. She cursed me and charged out of the kitchen. I knew at that moment that I was coming to the cabin to sort things out in my head. I was a mental mess, and I needed time away from her. Two or three bottles of whiskey later, I was still a confused mess, that is, until you came today."

Donna's heart skipped a beat. Did she have a chance with Herbert? One thing was for sure, she would stay by his side until the bitter end.

"What now?" Donna asked.

"I will go back to work to put some normality back into my life. I love the business, and I miss it."

"Will you go back home?"

Herbert hesitated. "No. I will continue stay here at night and let the old witch stew in her own juices."

"Should I call her back with your decision?"

"No. I don't want you to get any more involved in my marital problems than you already are. It wouldn't be fair to you. I'll call her. You go back to work, and I will shortly join you."

"Okay. It will be good to have you back."

Herbert suddenly and unexpectedly walked to Donna, stopping in front of her, and gave her a big hug. "Thank you," he whispered softly in her ear as they embraced.

Donna felt her body go limp in his arms. Her heart rate exploded—pure bliss!

CHAPTER 26

After telling Drew about her new theory of the case and Paul Leonard, he encouraged her to follow up and pursue the lead. His only comment was that she seemed to be in a battle or conflict of different theories with the chief. Sam corrected him. Differing theories didn't mean she was at odds with the chief. During a murder investigation, all points of view, thoughts, and ideas had to be respected. The truth was often hidden in the investigative maze. The fog has to lift to clearly see the outcome. Drew agreed with her analysis. He could hear the excitement in Sam's voice as she debated whether or not to involve the chief. After all, it was just another theory. Besides, the chief was orchestrating another search for the gun at Cadiz Springs, and that would be occupying his time. For now, she would do the legwork and report her findings to him at a later date.

After arriving at work, she called the pharmacy and was told that Leonard had taken the day off and was at home. She called him there and told him she needed to interview him, as well as his employees, again. He wasn't thrilled about the request but agreed. He told her that she could talk to the employees after lunch and he would meet with her at his home later that afternoon.

The meeting with the employees didn't reveal anything new. They seemed nervous being interviewed a second time. If Leonard was in contact with Norman Stafford, they weren't aware of it, not to mention the fact that they never heard his name until it appeared in the newspaper. They rarely did any business, prescriptions or otherwise, with the residents in New Glarus. Also, they were surprised at the suggestion of $5,000 in cash at the ready. The group was very skeptical that Leonard could have that much in cash either at the pharmacy or at his home. He was very tight-lipped about finances and was very thorough when accounting for every cent at the business. Even a minor discrepancy would cause him fits. He was stickler for detail and insisted on a detailed paper trail for income tax purposes. When asked about his demeanor after the death of his wife, all they could say was that he had become withdrawn and distracted. One employee did mention that she overheard Leonard on the telephone discussing the insurance policy on his wife but didn't have any other details. None of the employees knew if Leonard owned a handgun or not.

Sam paid particular attention to Joy Holcomb. She seemed despondent during the questioning. *Was she holding anything back?*

Satisfied the employees were telling the truth, Sam told them that the investigation was ongoing and not to share with anyone the details of today's interview. They readily agreed.

Returning to the PD, Sam was discouraged. She didn't learn anything new to support her theory that Leonard paid Stafford to kill Stacy and afterward, he kills Stafford. She needed to lean hard on Leonard and pressure him for answers.

At 3:30 p.m., Sam parked her car in front of Leonard's house. Squinting in the bright sunshine, she looked up to the ridge at the house where Agnes Keel lived before going to Parkview Nursing Home. Sam was pleased that Agnes was safe now. She climbed the steps to the front porch, and Leonard opened the door before she knocked and greeted her. He invited her into the living room. The blood-stained carpet had been replaced. She sat down on the sofa, and Leonard sat across from her in a high-backed armchair. He was silent and nervously waiting for Sam to begin. No small talk. She took her time, observing his discomfort.

"Thank you for seeing me. I spoke to your employees after lunch, and I am here to clarify some details concerning the death of your wife and Norman Stafford."

Leonard slightly shifted his weight in his chair. "What do you want to know?" Leonard asked in a defiant tone of voice.

"The death of Norman Stafford is very puzzling. Tell me again how you knew him."

"Like I have already said, I didn't know him at all, except for the time I signed the insurance policy in his presence. Other than that, I had completely forgotten about him, that is, until his death."

"Did you know that your wife was seeing him at the same time she was having an affair with Herbert Milz?"

Leonard's face reddened. He was clearly angry and upset. "I only found out about the affair with Milz after her death. As for Stafford, I didn't have a clue."

"Are you sure?"

"Yes. Don't you believe me?"

Sam didn't respond.

"Look, my wife and I weren't on speaking terms for quite some time. We both knew the marriage was over. I can't believe that she was stupid enough to be screwing two guys at the same time. But then again, how well did I really know her?"

"But you knew about Herbert Milz and your wife?"

"I suspected someone, not specifically Milz."

Another long pause followed. Sam was trying to get under his skin.

"And you said that neither you nor Stacy own a handgun?"

"That is correct."

"Do you still stand by your statement of not owning a handgun? If you are lying, we will arrest you."

A pale pallor fell over Leonard's face. He felt stressed. "I am not lying!" he exclaimed, raising his voice. "Why do you keep asking me these questions?"

Sam ignored him. "Do you have large amounts of money in cash at the store or in your home?"

"What?"

"I want to know if you ever had $5,000 in cash at the ready?"

Leonard sunk back into his armchair. He narrowed his eyes and stared at Sam. "No! And just what are you accusing me of?"

"Lying to the police!" Sam shouted at him.

Leonard jumped. "I am not lying to the police. I have already told you all I know," Leonard said, clenching his fists.

"I want you to relax and listen carefully to what I think happened."

Leonard stared at her with wide-open eyes. Sam had his full attention.

"When you realized that your marriage was over, the idea of financial ruin played heavily on your mind. A life's work of financial security was being threatened. Somehow—and we will find out how—you contacted Norman Stafford and hatched a scheme to murder your wife. I don't know why you picked Stafford, but he turned out to be a good fit for your purposes. Sharing the insurance money with him was all the incentive he needed. You had an iron-clad alibi being in Milwaukee at the time of the murder. You gave him the gun, and after the murder, he returned it to you so you could properly dispose of it. Also, you paid him $5,000 cash after the murder before you collected on the insurance claim. How am I doing so far? Sound familiar?"

Leonard didn't respond. His unblinking eyes stared at Sam. He was grinding his teeth.

"So moving on, something went terribly wrong. Stafford wasn't happy with the $5,000 and wanted more money. He threatened you. What could you do? If you gave him more money, he would just come back and blackmail you for the rest of your life. You lured him to New Glarus Woods State Park with the promise of another financial payment. Then you shot him with the same gun he murdered your wife with. Two problems solved. Only then did you dispose of the gun. The police have been chasing their tails thinking that the same person killed twice, but that isn't necessarily so, is it, Mr. Leonard?"

"Have you lost your mind?" Leonard shrieked. "Are you trying to get me to confess to a murder when I am completely innocent? If you think you have any shred of evidence to back up your wild theory, I would like to see it! I didn't conspire with Stafford to kill my wife. And I didn't kill Stafford! I am dumbstruck that this bizarre fairy tale of yours is all you can come up with investigating the murder of my wife!"

Sam could readily see that Leonard was frustrated and angry. If he was lying, his absolute insistence that he was innocent of murder was at least consistent. The breakthrough she was hoping for didn't materialize. Was she wrong in hypothesizing her new theory? Leonard's defensiveness and demeanor were convincing. A long moment passed between them.

"Anything else, Detective? Are you going to arrest me?" he asked in a sarcastic tone of voice.

"No. I am not going to arrest you. However, we consider you a person of interest, and you will remain so until we solve these murders. If you are planning to leave the area, notify us at the PD." Sam stood up, thanked Leonard for seeing her, and made her way out of the house, leaving Leonard sitting in his chair, watching her leave.

As she drove back to the Monroe PD, she figured that the search of the Cadiz Springs cabin and surrounding area should have been completed. She and the chief needed to debrief. When Sam entered his office, the chief looked dejected. She sat down across him.

"No gun?" she asked.

"No gun."

"Was Herbert Milz at the cabin when you searched it?"

"No. When I called him at the office, he told me the key was under a flower pot on the front porch and to search the place to our heart's content. He also told me that he was staying there at night instead of going home. He said that he had another row with his wife and she was really upset when we went through his financials at the bank. It was none of our business."

"Did he want to see the search warrant?"

"No. He said we wouldn't find the gun anyway because it wasn't there, and he reiterated the fact that he hadn't killed anyone."

There was a pause in the conversation.

"I had a new theory of the murders, and I pulled on that thread before telling you," Sam said.

Johns eyed her suspiciously. "Okay, out with it."

For the next ten minutes, Sam told the chief her new theory of the murders and the interviews with Paul Leonard at his home and his employees at the pharmacy. After she was finished, the chief steepled his fingers.

"That was interesting, to say the least. Leonard must have been horrified being face-to-face with you and hearing your theory that he must be the killer."

"I think I shocked his system. Well, anyway, he stood by his story that he was innocent of any conspiratorial murders. I did wind him up pretty good, but he didn't crack."

"Okay, so where are we in the investigation?" Johns asked.

"I think it is more of what we don't have, for instance, the gun or a straight line between either Leonard or Milz to Stafford. It just isn't adding up. I am sure we are missing something that is right in front of us."

"Let's go back to the $5,000 for a moment. Who would have access to that amount of money in cash? Paul Leonard and his employees have ruled him out, if they were telling the truth. You didn't find anything in Herbert's accounts at the bank for such a large withdrawal of money. Who else comes to mind?"

"Well, the only other person is Linda Milz. Any thoughts about her?" Sam asked.

"Linda Milz?"

"I know it is a long shot, but she certainly has the money. She is a character, that's for sure. But you do think she is capable of murder?" Sam mused.

"Now that's an interesting thought. During the investigation, we have pretty much ignored her as a possible person of interest. The bartender at the country club and her husband have alibied her for the nights of both murders. Other than being a narcissistic drunken witch, what do we really know about her?"

"Did Herbert have anything of interest to say about his wife?"

"Like I said, I only talked to him over the telephone. He said that Linda was really upset when you went through his financial accounts at the bank. She threatened to sue the PD for harassment and an illegal search of his private financial information."

Sam laughed. "Okay. Let's assume for a minute that you are Linda Milz."

Johns groaned. "Do I really need to be her?"

"Bear with me. You are a big fish in a small pond, being that you are wealthy and a country club member. Your wealth gives you a certain status and an air of importance in the community. Your husband starts having an affair with a schoolteacher, the wife of a pharmacist, a person of lower status. You are infuriated and embarrassed. Your peers at the country club talk behind your back. You can't stand it. The embarrassment is severely dinging your ego, and you need to put a stop to the affair. So instead of confronting your husband, you go and see the woman who is making your life miserable, Stacy Leonard. For whatever reason, you take a gun along with you. For what purpose, to scare her? Who knows? Something goes terribly wrong, and you shoot her, maybe by accident. You panic and race home before your husband arrives and pretend to pass out drunk on the sofa. Does that make any sense?"

Johns was engaged. "So according to this new theory, Herbert is telling us the truth about turning around in Monticello and driving home without going all the way to Stacy's house?"

"Wouldn't it be ironic if he passed his wife speeding in the opposite direction?" Sam asked.

"The bartender did say that Linda was totally wasted that night, but was she?" Johns wondered out loud.

"Remember what he said about getting big tips for his discretion?" Sam offered.

"So where does that leave us with Norman Stafford?"

"Good question. We need to assume that he was parked on the side of the road when Linda speeds down the driveway and back to Monroe after killing Stacy. He must have followed her and learned where she lived and her identity. He drove back to Stacy's house and found her dead. He contacted Linda and blackmailed her for the $5,000. Later he demanded more money, and she killed him as well. Does any of this make sense?"

"Do you think?" Johns responded, lost in thought.

"I hate to admit this, but as much sense as putting Paul Leonard in the frame and accusing him of murder. All theories! No facts! Without data, I am just another person with an opinion," Sam mused.

"I will give you this: You can sure spin a good yarn!"

Sam chuckled. "Am I that obvious?"

"Totally."

"There is only one way to find out. We will need another warrant."

"For Linda Milz's bank account?"

"Yes. I know we are grasping at straws, but this may prove to be interesting. What else do we have?"

"Judge Dietmeire is going to love this," Johns said. "When the case is closed and solved, I will need to buy him a beer or two at Baumgartners for his patience with us."

CHAPTER 27

Millicent "Millie" Chesebro was worried about her best friend Linda Milz. They had known each other since grade school. Millie was an uninteresting, awkward, plain-looking woman with big breasts. In middle school and high school, Linda was attractive and always had boys buzzing around her like a swarm of bees. Millie stayed close to Linda and dated some of her cast-offs. She was smart and played on Linda's insecurities and quickly became her enabler and confidante. Millie's husband, Thomas Chesebro, owned a dry-cleaning business in the 1100 block of 16th Avenue, south of the courthouse square. He was a very successful businessman and a workaholic. When he was single, Linda introduced him to Millie. Being a socially inept man when it came to dating women, Linda had to talk him into marrying Millie. The marriage gave her immediate financial security and a big home on Lake Drive across Lake Francis as well as a country club membership. For all that, Millie won the lottery and was indebted to Linda for life. Linda became a frequent visitor to her home, playing cards and drinking into the wee hours of the morning.

On Thursday afternoon, Linda was late to their weekly scheduled bridge tournament at the country club, making everyone wait for twenty minutes. No problem, though, by then, the drinks were flowing and the conversation was loud. Linda was emotionally upset and totally distracted when she arrived. No apology or explanation given as she took her seat and her usual drink arrived from the bar. Play started. Normally a very good bridge player, she was making silly mistakes.

She was ordering and gulping down more than her usual number of drinks. She and Millie were partners, and they lost every game. Even the ladies playing against them sensed something was terribly wrong. Linda wasn't herself. When asked if everything was okay, she shrugged and said, "Everything is fine."

Millie didn't believe her for one minute. When the tournament was over and the prize money handed out, the women adjourned to the bar. Millie took Linda aside. Instead of going to the bar, they remained upstairs in the restaurant area and ordered more drinks. Millie looked Linda straight in the eye. "What the hell is wrong with you? And don't you dare lie to me."

Linda fidgeted in her chair. The drinks shortly arrived. She took a big gulp. "The police are investigating the two murders, and they think Herbert is the killer."

Millie gasped.

"By the way, they have interviewed the both of us."

"I didn't know that," Millie said.

"So I don't tell you everything. Well, anyway, they got a warrant and went through all of Herbert's financial records at the bank."

"What were they looking for?"

Linda shrugged. "Beats me. But it really upset Herbert. They reinterviewed him, and Chief Johns actually accused him of murder. How absurd is that? Herbert is a total mess. He has really screwed up my life!"

"How so?"

"First of all, he betrayed me and had an affair with a married schoolteacher. Why did he do that? After all I have done for him, I still can't believe it! Then he is accused of killing her. Herbert is a jelly fish with no backbone. He couldn't harm a fly, much less kill one. Chief Johns is an idiot for even thinking such a thing. Have you ever met him? A man with no imagination and not knowing his place. He interviewed me like I was a low-life criminal! Who does he think he is? Some sanctimonious monk? The truth is that the police enjoy a bit of voyeurism, looking into other people's lives. The nerve of the man."

Millie was shocked. No one ever got under Linda's skin, but it seems the chief of police succeeded. "Is that all?" Millie asked.

Linda picked up her glass and finished her drink, smacking her lips. "No. It seems that the gun used to kill Stacy is the one bit of evidence needed to arrest Herbert. They have searched my house and Herbert's cabin in Cadiz Springs. They didn't find the gun in either place. No surprise there! So now they got a warrant and searched the cabin again."

"Did Herbert tell you that?"

"Are you kidding? The bastard has moved out and is staying at the cabin. I haven't seen him or talked to him in several days."

"I told his airhead secretary to go fetch him and send him home, but she miserably failed in her task."

"So he is still working at the business during the day and he is spending his nights away from you at the cabin?'

"That's about the size of it."

"Why haven't you shared any of this with me before now?"

"It's a personal matter that I want it to remain private. The only reason I am telling you now is that I am going crazy. I can't sleep at night, so I got some sleeping pills from my primary doctor at the clinic. What do you think I should do?"

"Are you asking me for my advice?"

"No. I don't take advice. I only want your opinion."

"In your mind, are you convinced that Herbert is innocent of murder?"

"Absolutely."

"Then you should stand behind him, no matter what happens. Remember that you are a respected member of the club and people will be looking to see how you react to this unfortunate situation. Standing tall with Herbert will make you look strong and determined. On the other side of this, you will prevail with your reputation intact."

"What about Herbert staying at his cabin?"

"I wouldn't worry about that. Like you said, he is under a lot of stress. He needs time to sort all this out and come to the realization that he made a big mistake. Cheating on you with a schoolteacher? What was he thinking? In your heart of hearts, you will forgive him, and the members will applaud you for your charity."

Linda smiled. She liked the sound of that.

"Anything else bothering you?" Millie asked.

Linda leaned back in her chair and closed her eyes. She was thinking. "You are right, Millie. The police don't have anything on Herbert, and they are grasping at straws. They need probable cause to make an arrest, and they haven't done that. I think that they are bluffing and hoping that Herbert will do or say something stupid."

"Do you have any idea why the police went through his financial accounts?" Millie asked.

"I haven't a clue. He is a straight arrow in his business dealings and has his own checking account."

"You have separate checking accounts?"

"Of course. I control all the money, so I have a separate account to remind him of that. If he needs any extra money, he can always beg me for it."

"Has he ever done that?"

"No. His business generates enough income for his needs. I don't even pay him a monthly maintenance allowance. In fact, I really don't know how he spends his money. We never talk about it. I pay the monthly bills for the house, the annual taxes, and my country club expenses."

After saying that, Linda seemed to lighten up and be in a better mood. Sharing her problems with Millie made her feel better.

"Say, why don't you come to my house for a light supper? I am not much of a cook, but I can rustle up something. I want to thank you for listening to me."

"I can call Thomas and tell him that he is on his own for supper tonight."

"Can he handle it?"

Millie laughed. "I sure hope so."

They stood up and went to the bar.

"The drinks are on me," Linda said, signing the bar tab.

After they arrived at Linda's house, she scanned the refrigerator. She found some leftover pasta and reheated it. She then made herself and Millie another drink, brandy old-fashions. Millie wandered into the living room and looked at some framed family pictures of Linda's parents before they died.

"I remember your mother. She was such a kind woman."

"I miss her," Linda said, joining her.

A random thought popped into Millie's head. "Your mother was the only woman I knew who carried a gun in her purse. Why was that?"

Linda hesitated before answering. "It was my father's idea. It had something to do with his wealth and the fear that my mother would be robbed."

Millie's eyebrows narrowed. She was thinking and trying to bring up a memory. "Didn't she take you to the shooting range north of town when you were a teenager?"

"How in the world did you remember that?"

"I don't know. Just a fleeting thought. Whatever happened to that gun? I remember it as being quite small."

"I haven't a clue. In fact, I haven't thought about it in years. Probably lost forever. I can smell the pasta. Let's eat."

After supper, the rest of the evening was spent in the living room laughing and reminiscing about their high school loves and adventures. Millie was feeling the effects of the alcohol and told Linda it was time for her to go home. As they stood up, the telephone rang. Linda answered it on the third ring. She intently listened to the caller, not saying a word. The muscles in her face tensed up. When she hung up, she collapsed on the sofa. She was in state of shock. Her face drained to a deathly white pale pallor. Her lips tightened, revealing a weak shadow of a ghoulish smile. Millie was immediately concerned.

"Bad news?" she asked.

Linda looked past Millie at the wall behind her. In a monotone voice, she began to speak, not so much to Millie, but to herself.

"That was a friend of mine who works at the bank. She told me that the police came in this afternoon and had a warrant to review my financial records. They were looking for a $5,000 withdrawal made in the past couple of weeks."

"Why would they do that?"

"I don't know. Just more harassment." Linda looked as if she was going to faint.

"I am not leaving you here alone in the house tonight. You look awful. I will call Thomas and tell him that you are unwell."

"No, no, don't do that. I will be okay."

"What's wrong? That telephone call couldn't have been all that distressing."

Linda seemed to compose herself. "I don't know what came over me. The stress of Herbert and the police poking around in our private affairs is finally catching up to me," Linda said in soft voice.

"Are you sure I can't stay? It wouldn't be a bother for me."

"I will be all right. Thanks for the offer."

"Well, if you are sure."

"I am. Please go home. We both need our rest."

"Okay then, if you insist. I will stop by tomorrow and check on you."

CHAPTER 28

am marched the search warrant for Linda Milz's bank records over to the bank in the hopes that this wasn't going to be another dead end. The bookkeeper was surprised to see her again. When Sam found the withdrawal of $5,000 from Linda Milz's checking account dated four days after Stacy Leonard's murder, she was ecstatic. She enthusiastically pumped her fist into the air. The adrenaline was pumping madly through her veins. The bookkeeper had a shocked quizzical look on her face at Sam's reaction to her discovery.

"Did you find what you were looking for?" she asked.

"Yes!" Sam couldn't wait to get back to the PD and tell Chief Johns.

* * *

When she arrived, Shirley took her aside. "The chief received an emergency call from his wife. Beth called about thirty minutes ago and complained of a sudden attack of nausea, vomiting, and chills. He rushed home and took her to the hospital. He called me from the emergency room. The diagnosis was a ruptured appendix. She was being prepped and taken into surgery."

Sam couldn't believe what she was hearing. Her news about Linda Milz and the $5,000 discovery suddenly faded from her mind. Immediately, her heart went out to Beth and the chief. "Is the chief still at the hospital?" she asked in a concerned voice.

"As far as I know."

"I am on the way!" Sam exclaimed.

She left the PD and hastily walked to her car and drove the short distance to the hospital parking lot reserved for emergency room visitors. Upon entering the emergency room, she found the chief sitting in the waiting room. He looked worried and pale. Looking down, he was holding his head in his hands. Sam immediately thought he was praying. She sat down in the chair next to him. He glanced over to her.

"How is Beth doing?" Sam asked.

"She is being prepped for emergency surgery. They called in a doctor who was scheduled off today to perform the operation. I am so worried and sick. My stomach is churning."

"Was this attack sudden?"

Johns looked back down at his hands. "This morning, before I left for work, Beth told me she wasn't feeling well. She had a pain in her stomach. She was looking a little pekid. I asked her if she should go see a doctor, but you know Beth, she declined. She needed to see a death angel before going to a doctor."

Sam smiled. That was an apt description of Beth. "She must have felt her condition worsening after you left for work."

"Yes. She knew this murder case had me all consumed and didn't want to worry me with a little indigestion problem. I should have paid more attention to her this morning."

It was clear to Sam that the chief was blaming himself. He and Beth were very close, and God forbid, if anything bad should happen to her, it would destroy him. They sat in silence. Sam decided that the news about Linda Milz could wait. The important thing now was for the chief to be at his wife's side.

"I don't know what I would do if Beth doesn't survive this attack," Johns said in a soft voice.

Sam reached over and held his hand. "You shouldn't think that. The doctors here are very good, and I have every confidence that Beth will pull through the surgery and live to a ripe old age. It may even change her opinions about doctors."

Johns grinned. "I hope you are right."

A long moment of silence passed between them as Sam and Johns watched people and nurses milling around the front desk. Some of the people seated themselves in the waiting area. A nurse walked up to Johns and introduced herself. "Your wife will be going into surgery in fifteen minutes. Please come with me. You can be with her before she is wheeled into the operating theater."

"How is she doing?"

"She is sedated, but she will know that you are with her."

Johns stood up and followed the nurse through the waiting room area and disappeared into the long corridors of the hospital.

When they left, Sam went to the Physical Therapy Department, looking for Drew. The woman at the desk outside his office told Sam that he was with a patient and should be finished in a few minutes. Sam decided to wait for him and sat in the waiting room outside his office. The overwhelming compassion she felt for the chief and his wife was palpable. She prayed to God that Beth would be okay. When Drew appeared, he saw Sam and gave her a big grin. "Ah, an unscheduled appointment. I always give good-looking ladies preferential treatment."

"Something has happened," Sam said.

Drew immediately knew something was wrong. "What's happened?"

"Can we talk?"

"Let's go to the cafeteria. My next patient appointment isn't for an hour."

Drew told the woman at the desk that he would be in the cafeteria if he was needed and to page him. He and Sam grabbed a cup of coffee and found a table along the west wall, away from prying ears. After they were seated, Drew looked at Sam. "So tell me what's happened."

Over the next few minutes, Sam filled Drew in on the events concerning Beth's emergency appendectomy and the chief being with her. Drew could hear the anguish in her voice. Over the years, she and Johns had developed a bond of respect and friendship that transcended that of supervisor and employee. They were colleagues of equal rank. She felt the chief's pain. After sitting in silence for a moment, Drew asked how her day was going. The question snapped her out of her melancholy.

"I have cracked the case," she said in a sober matter-of-fact voice. Her earlier enthusiasm had faded over her concern for the chief and Beth.

Drew was taken aback. Her answered shocked him. "You have?" he said in disbelief.

"Yes."

"You know who murdered the two victims?"

"Yes," Sam replied in a hushed voice.

"Have you told the chief?"

"No. I only found out today. Once Beth is out of danger, I will tell him, probably tomorrow morning."

"Will the killer escape capture with a delay in arresting him?"

Sam shook her head. "Not a chance."

"Well, are you going to tell me the name of the killer?"

Sam noticed the cafeteria filling up with people.

"Not here. I will fill you in tonight at home," she whispered, looking at her watch. "I need to get back to the ER."

Drew stood up and kissed Sam on the cheek. "I am so proud of you. See you tonight."

After Drew left, Sam went back to the ER waiting room. The chief was sitting by himself in the corner.

"How did it go?" she asked.

"I held her hand and told her that I loved her."

A tear escaped his swollen red eye and slowly moved down his cheek. He brushed it away with the back of his hand.

Sam felt her heart in her throat. She choked up. "Did she know that you were there?"

"I think so. She gently squeezed my hand."

"Is she in surgery now?"

"Yes. I was told to wait here and the doctor would come and see me after the operation."

"I will stay with you," Sam said.

"That isn't necessary. I will be all right."

"I insist."

They sat in silence watching other people mill around in the waiting room while waiting for the doctor's report. Suddenly, Beth's parents arrived. Johns jumped up and greeted them with hugs. He introduced Sam to the couple. Seeing that she was no longer needed, Sam said her goodbyes as the trio engaged in a very intense conversation concerning Beth's health. Sam told the chief to call her at home when the operation was over. He hugged her and thanked her for being there for him.

* * *

When Sam arrived home, Drew was all smiles and bursting with curiosity. Karin was playing on the living room carpet with some of her toys. Two glasses of wine were sitting on the coffee table. He handed Sam a glass after she hugged Karin. They sat down on the sofa.

"So tell me. I am dying to know."

Sam took a sip. The wine tasted good and refreshing. "First of all, the chief will call me later tonight with a report on Beth's condition and the surgery. This whole incident has unnerved me." Sam could see the excitement in Drew's face. "I can see that you are coming apart at the seams since I left you at the hospital, so I will fill you in on the case."

She had Drew's undivided attention.

"The killer is Linda Milz," Sam began.

Drew's jaw dropped. "The wife of Herbert Milz?"

"Yes."

"How in the world did you figure that out? Until recently, you were at such a loss."

"The key to solving this case was the money trail, and I just couldn't see it. There it was, hiding in plain sight. When Norman Stafford's parents told us about the $5,000 cash deposit into his savings account, after the murder of Stacy Leonard, we knew that it was no coincidence. The mistake we made was focusing too much on our two prime suspects.

This afternoon I found the $5,000 withdrawal from Linda's account, and the final piece of the puzzle fell into place."

Drew still had a quizzical look on his face.

Sam continued. "So how about Herbert Milz and Paul Leonard, you may ask. After all, Linda Milz seemed to have an iron-clad alibi for both murders, so we pretty much ignored her."

"Okay, but why her? I mean why would she kill two people?"

"I will talk it through with the chief tomorrow, but here is what I think—"

"The chief doesn't know she is the killer?"

"Not yet. He has more important things on his mind at the moment."

Drew leaned back in his seat hanging on her every word.

"According to the chief, Linda Milz is an arrogant self-centered snob. Add in a good measure of alcoholism and what do we have? A woman capable of murder? She married a weak man she can control, dominate, and abuse. I personally think she was incapable of loving anyone. Well, anyway, Herbert feels trapped, so in desperation, he falls in love with a woman who flirts with him and is using him for her own purposes. Of course, he is besotted with her and doesn't realize the ruse and convinces himself that she is in love with him. Totally delusional on his part and a recipe for disaster . . ." Sam paused and took a sip of her wine. Drew was staring at her, unblinking.

She continued. "Linda somehow finds out that Herbert is having the affair. She is humiliated beyond reason. Her slave husband has betrayed her. So what should she do to save face? I think she went to Stacy's house to confront her. She has a gun with her to probably scare Stacy off. But something went terribly wrong, and she shot Stacy two times . . ." Sam paused for a moment reflecting on her theory of what happened. She was satisfied in the belief that the case was solved.

Drew remained quiet staring at his wife, not interrupting her.

Sam continued. "According to Agnes Keel, there was a car parked on the shoulder of the road with its head lights switched off, in front of Stacy's house, on the night of the murder. We have surmised that the car belonged to Norman Stafford. He saw Linda's car speeding down the gravel driveway and saw the driver probably not knowing who she was.

He then followed the car to Monroe. He must have been surprised to see it parked in front of a posh house on the golf course. He probably went back to Stacy's house and found her dead body on the living room floor. He was saving money to buy a house and by quickly adding two plus two together, instantly hatched a blackmail scheme. And it worked. He contacted Linda who paid him $5,000 cash for his silence. He probably thought that it was easy money. But he still needed more money for the down payment for a house and went back to Linda a second time. She agreed to pay his demand and meet him at the New Glarus Woods State Park. Little did he know that his greed was going to get him killed."

Drew wrinkled his eyebrows. "If the first murder was, say an accident, are you saying that the murder of Norman Stafford was premeditated?"

"Exactly. She had killed once, so the second time was much easier. And apparently, she thought she had gotten away with murder."

"Are you saying that she was willing to throw her husband under the bus to save herself?"

"Of course. He committed a major sin. He betrayed her. Old Testament stuff. A life sentence in prison would be his punishment for his betrayal that caused her embarrassment and anguish."

"Whoa. That's a little harsh."

"I think it goes straight to her character."

"Then what did she do with the gun?"

"Good question. After we bring her in for questioning, we will find out."

"Do you think she will confess to the murders?"

"Probably not and will lawyer up. But she will also fully understand and realize that she is in a jam. How is she going to explain the $5,000 that went from her bank account to Norman Stafford's bank account after the murder of Stacy Leonard?"

CHAPTER 29

It was Friday morning, and Sam was sitting at her desk at the PD. The chief had called her at eight o'clock last night, telling her that Beth had successfully come out of the surgery and was resting comfortably. She was expected to stay in the hospital for three to five days and rest at home after that for three to four weeks. The doctor predicted a full recovery. Johns was really relieved that everything turned out okay and thanked Sam again for being with him in the waiting room. The inflection of his voice was one of tremendous relief and his prayers being answered. Her presence meant a lot to him. He also told Sam that he would report to work at eleven o'clock Friday morning after visiting Beth in the hospital. Sam didn't share her news about Linda Milz, instead waiting to tell him after he came to work.

Sam spent the morning piecing together the events of both murders and how everything tied together now that Linda Milz was the presumptive killer. It all made sense to her, and a clear picture of the tragic events had emerged. She hadn't personally interviewed Linda, so the impressions of her came from the chief's description of her. Sam was looking forward to interviewing Linda. Mulling over the investigation, she shook her head because she had it so wrong accusing Paul Leonard of murder. It was just part of the process of getting to the truth, but she still felt guilty putting him through the trauma of it all. Her plan was to debrief the chief on her findings, and together, they would collect Linda Milz for an interview and then arrest her. He would be excited to get this case closed.

At 10:45 a.m., Chief Johns entered the PD and thanked everyone for their prayers and gave them an update on Beth's condition. A welcome relief was felt by everyone at the good news. Sam and the chief went into his office and closed the door. Sam brought him up to speed about the $5,000 withdrawal from Linda's bank account and how it tied in with Norman Stafford. The chief remained quiet as Sam laid out all the facts. He was calm and relaxed, listening to Sam. The stress of the case was quickly receding. The euphoria of a difficult case being solved was greatly satisfying. After Sam finished her analysis, the chief complimented her on cracking the case. They agreed to pick up Linda at her home and bring her into the station to be interviewed and charged. After the decision was made, the telephone suddenly rang. Johns picked it up after the second ring. Shirley was on the line, telling him that a Millie Chesebro was on the line.

"Chief Johns," he said, answering the call. He held the receiver out so Sam could listen in on the conversation.

"My name is Millie Chesebro, and I am a good friend of Linda Milz."

The chief's eyes widened, and Sam moved closer to the telephone. "What can I do for you?"

"I am worried about Linda."

"What's happened?"

"She has disappeared."

The chief's jaw tightened. "Please explain."

"Well, last night, I was at her house. She was acting very strange. By that, I mean not her normal self. Well, anyway, she received a telephone call from a friend at the bank who told her that the police went through her financial records looking for a $5,000 withdrawal. Linda nearly fainted upon hearing the news. She looked unwell. I offered to stay with her, but she told me to go home. I was up half the night worrying about her. I went to her house this morning to check on her, and her car was gone. Fearing the worst, I called the hospital to see if she had been admitted and then her husband at the auto sales business. They hadn't seen or heard from her. I am very worried."

"What kind of state was she in after you left her last night?"

"Well, I would say emotionally distraught, I suppose."

"And you have no idea where she might be?"

"We had been drinking pretty heavily. If she drove off somewhere after I left her, she could have crashed her car and be lying in a ditch somewhere."

"I will check with the Green County sheriff's department," Johns offered.

"Please call me at my house if you find out anything. I am really worried about her." Millie gave the chief her home telephone number and rang off.

Sam and Johns stared at each other.

"What the hell," Johns said. "Where could she be?"

Johns called the sheriff's department. No accidents reported. He then called Hebert Milz.

"Hello," Herbert said.

"This is Chief Johns. We are looking for your wife. Apparently, she has gone missing. Do you have any idea where she might be?"

"It's a funny thing you called. I spoke to Millie Chesebro earlier today, asking me the same question."

"I just got off the telephone with her myself. Do you have any idea where Linda might have gone?"

There was a momentary silence on the line. Herbert was thinking. Sam whispered to Johns if Linda could be at the cabin in Cadiz Springs.

"Could she be at your cabin at Cadiz Springs?"

"She hasn't been there in ages. I suppose she could, but I doubt it. I have been staying there at night. She wasn't there when I left for work this morning."

"Would she have a key to the cabin?"

"She knows the spare key is under a flower pot on the porch."

"Can you think of anywhere else she might be?"

"No."

Johns hung up the telephone.

"Let's go to Cadiz Springs, I'll drive."

CHAPTER 30

Linda Milz couldn't sleep after Millie left and went home. She tossed and turned and finally went to sleep, only to be awaken by a nightmare. She got out of bed, put on her bath robe, and sat on the sofa in her living room in the dark. She stared out the picture window into the darkness of the night. A feeling of dread filled her body. She knew exactly what the $5,000 was all about. It was only a matter of time before she was charged and arrested for murder. The thought of going to prison annoyed her—a life sentence for two murders. Her fate was sealed, and she couldn't do anything about it. She felt a hopeless feeling of dread. Stacy was an accident, but Norman, he deserved it! The loud ticking of her mantel clock was unsettling. *Tick, tock, tick, tock.* Her time was running out. What was she to do? The answer to that question, the solution to her problem, came with a sudden clarity of mind. The realization brought on a great calmness. She had a plan.

At 8:30 a.m., she left the house for the cabin in Cadiz Springs. She knew that Hebert wouldn't be there because he was an early riser and always the first one to arrive at work. In her car, lying on the passenger side seat was an unopened bottle of very expensive whiskey and her sleeping pills. Just as she surmised, Herbert's car wasn't at the cabin when she parked in the driveway. Moving the flower pot on the porch to one side, she easily found the spare key and entered the cabin.

"So this is where Herbert and his hussy screwed each other like a couple of minks."

She placed the whiskey bottle and the pills on the coffee table in front of the sofa. She found a clean glass in the kitchen. She was looking for a pad of paper and a pen. She found a tablet of paper with "Milz Auto Sales" on the top and a black ballpoint pen. She sat down on the sofa and opened the whiskey bottle, poured herself a drink, and took a sip. Looking out the picture window at Lake Beckman, she noticed how beautiful the lake was in the morning sun. She picked up the pad of paper and began to write.

CHAPTER 31

When Sam and Johns arrived at the cabin, they spotted Linda's Buick Riviera parked in the driveway. Upon entering, they saw her dead body curled up in the fetal position on the sofa. Her eyes were open, staring into empty space.

"Oh my god!" Sam shouted.

Chief Johns felt for a pulse. "She is dead," he said, closing her eyelids.

The empty whiskey glass and the empty bottle of sleeping pills on the coffee table was all the explanation they needed. Sam picked up the writing tablet lying on the coffee table and began to read. She stopped. "You need to hear this," she said to Johns.

They sat down in the two armchairs across Linda's lifeless body. Sam slowly and deliberately read the suicide note out loud to the chief.

To whom it may concern:

I am writing this note to state the true facts of what happened. Chief Johns is an idiot, so I am writing this to set the record straight. He doesn't have any sense as a police officer, and he couldn't pull a roasted peanut out of his ass using both hands! It all started when I got back from Florida. Herbert was acting strangely. He was in a good mood. I immediately had my suspicions something wasn't right. This wasn't at all like him. My dear friend Millie told me that she heard thirdhand that he was having an affair with a schoolteacher named Stacy Leonard. At first, I couldn't believe it. Herbert having an affair? Ridiculous! I dismissed it as idle gossip. As time passed, I became increasingly worried. Herbert's behavior was my clue. I soon realized that my reputation at the club was being threatened, and I was probably the butt of jokes behind my back. That was intolerable, and I couldn't sleep at night. I didn't directly confront him because if I was wrong, it would have humiliated me and made me look weak. I couldn't allow that.

The suspicion and the rage I felt started to simmer. I was drinking heavily. I was getting stressed out. I decided a direct action was needed to be taken and confront this Stacy woman and warn her off. My mother kept a handgun in her purse when I was a child. She even took me to the firing range and let me shoot it. My father bought it for her. I remembered where it was stored, and sure enough, the bullets were there as well. On that fateful night, I followed Herbert from his workplace to Cadiz Springs in my car. I immediately knew where he was going. I had been to the cabin once after we married. A dump, if you ask me. I parked about 50 yards away and waited. Mostly out of sight. A second car arrived. A blue Chevrolet Nova. A woman jumped out and entered the cabin. My heart almost leaped out of my chest as it was beating so hard. I could feel the heat on my face, thinking about what was happening inside the cabin. After a while, the woman rushed out of the cabin, got into her car, and sped away. I followed her to her home on Exeter Crossing Road near New Glarus. I went back to the club and started drinking. The more I drank, the madder I got. I slipped away, unseen through a side door, and drove to Stacy's house. The gun was sitting in the passenger seat. I intended to scare her with it. I parked in front of the house, grabbed the gun, and went inside. Stacy was surprised to see me, like she was expecting someone else. We had words, and I told her to stay away from Herbert. She started laughing in my face. I told her to stop, but she got hysterical and starting calling me awful names. She wouldn't stop laughing, so I pulled the gun out of my pocket. She took a look at it and laughed harder. The next thing I remember was hearing two shots and Stacy falling to the floor. I immediately knew she was dead. I picked up the two spent cartridges, turned off the living room lights and porch light, wiped down the front door handle, and left. I arrived home and slumped into the living room sofa. I heard Herbert coming into the house, so I faked being asleep, passing out drunk. He put me to bed.

I am going to take a break now. My hand is cramping up, and I need another drink . . .

I'm back. I reread what I had written, so I will continue without any revisions.

Two days later I received a telephone call from a man identifying himself as Norman Stafford. He said he saw me racing down the driveway of Stacy's house on the night of her murder and wanted $5,000 to keep his silence. The bastard was blackmailing me. A lowlife like him! How rude! I didn't have a choice. I didn't intend to kill Stacy, but the consequences of doing so scared me to death. I took the cash out of my bank account and agreed to meet him at the New Glarus Woods State Park in the parking lot. He was a smug arrogant man, and he thanked me for the money. I cursed him and left, thinking I was in the clear. A week later, he called again and wanted more money. The nerve of the man! I agreed to give him more money, and we would meet at the same place for the exchange. I *immediately knew I was going to kill him. He was nothing more than a parasite that needed to be squashed. We agreed to meet at 11:00 p.m. I came back from the club at 10:30 p.m. and checked in on Herbert who was soundly sleeping and snoring like a freight train. Sometimes sleeping in twin beds has its advantages. After I arrived at the New Glarus Woods parking lot, I walked up to Stafford's open car window, and he grinned at me and held out his hand. I shot him in the head to wipe that hideous grin off his face. I picked up the spent cartridge and calmly drove back to Monroe and slept in my car, giving the impression that I had passed out drunk. To add some excitement to my plan, I stuck my finger down my throat and vomited in my car, knowing that Hebert would clean it up the next day. He is such a wuss. He didn't even know that I had left the house that night. The next day I went to visit Millie and threw the gun into Lake Francis.*

I found it quite amusing that the police were chasing shadows. Trying to pin these murders on Herbert was absurd. I enjoyed watching him squirm under the pressure of being a suspect. I thought I was in the clear until I realized that I had made a mistake. When Herbert told me that the police went through his bank accounts, I became alarmed. Somehow they must have discovered the $5,000 payment to Stafford. But nothing happened. Thank God we have separate banking accounts. Once again, I felt like I was in the clear and could sleep through the night. But last night, after the call about the police searching my bank accounts, I knew I would be found out. It was only a matter of time.

It was early this morning, when it was still dark outside, that I made my decision. I would simply kill myself. The idea of a life sentence in a small prison cell under the supervision of some uneducated boring prison guard was unacceptable. A person who would enjoy looking down her nose at a posh lady. The very thought of it was maddening and nauseating. I would not give her the satisfaction. Well, that's about it. I have said what needs to be said. I fully understand that my fate was in my own hands, so I have no regrets. I will simply take all the sleeping pills in the bottle and wash them down with some very expensive whiskey. Signed Linda Milz, Country Club Member.

Chief Johns had remained silent, listening to every word. He didn't interrupt her. After she finished, he just shook his head.

"I think she was totally delusional in her world of self-indulgence," Sam said, reflecting on the note.

"She was a troubled woman, that's for sure."

"My only regret is that it took so long to identify her as the killer. Look at the unnecessary distress we imposed on Herbert Milz and Paul Leonard," Sam said.

Johns was silent for a moment. He was staring at Linda's cold, breathless body on the sofa. "I wouldn't be too hard on yourself. Police work is never easy and often messy," he replied.

Sam glanced at the ceiling, squinting. "Do you remember Agnes Keel's log book on the day of the murder?"

"What about it?"

"She had written an abbreviated entry, BR, instead of Buick Riviera. And I missed it."

"I forgive you, Detective Gates. No one is perfect."

Sam smiled. "In the final analysis, I fell into the trap of pursing my own unproven theories and ignoring what was in front of me. This investigation proves once again that only the facts matter. The key to this case was always the money, and I overlooked it and didn't suss it out, a classic example of do as I say but not as I do."

Johns laughed. "Are you talking about me? I did the same damn thing thinking that Herbert was the killer and talked myself into that theory."

"So where do we go from here?" Sam asked.

"I will call Dr. Ken to come and verify that Linda is officially dead and then transport the body to the morgue. I need to call Herbert and tell him that his wife is dead."

As Johns was making the calls, Sam went outside and looked at the beauty of the lake. The case was closed. She felt a great weight lifted from her shoulders. She longed to give Karin a big hug and tell her that she dearly loved her little girl.

EPILOGUE

inda Milz was buried with a short private graveside service at the Greenlawn Cemetery next to her parents. It was a bright sunny day that contrasted with the somber service. Herbert organized the burial service with Pastor Carl from the First Christian Church. Only one distant relative from Linda's side of the family bothered to attend. Millie Chesebro and her husband represented the country club members. After the "Lord's Prayer" was said, the small group dispersed without a word. The only tears that were shed came from Millie.

The employees at the pharmacy supported Paul Leonard during his time of grief and getting his life back together. He continued to live at the farmplace but told some friends that it was time to sell and move into Monroe. The curse of the farm was playing on his mind and was taking a toll on him. A parade of slow-moving cars continued to drive past the house, keeping the myth of the curse alive. The farmplace was guarded by superstition and ghosts!

Herbert found unexpected joy and happiness as his relationship with Donna Crandall blossomed. He sold the house on the golf course and bought an understated modest home in the 22nd block of 9th Street. He let his membership at the country club lapse. He was looking forward to a bright and loving future.

Beth Johns fully recovered from her surgery, much to the delight of her husband. They took a short extended weekend vacation to the Wisconsin Dells to celebrate without the kids.

Sam and Drew talked through the missteps of the investigation. Sam had a hard time letting go of the fact that she felt inadequate and guilty not solving the case sooner. She took Karin to the nursing home to see Agnes Keel. The dementia was getting worse, but she enjoyed holding Karin in her arms, giving her hugs.

CPSIA information can be obtained
at www.ICGtesting.com
Printed in the USA
LVHW091359210521
688136LV00005B/93

9 781664 167407